# Sanctuary

# BEVERLY & DAVID LEWIS

## Sanctuary

BETHANYHOUSE
PUBLISHERS

MINNEAPOLIS, MINNESOTA

*Sanctuary*
Copyright © 2001
Beverly & David Lewis

Cover illustration and design by Dan Thornberg

This story is a work of fiction. All characters and events are the product of the authors' imagination. Any resemblance to any person, living or dead, is coincidental.

Published by Bethany House Publishers
A Ministry of Bethany Fellowship International
11400 Hampshire Avenue South
Bloomington, Minnesota 55438
www.bethanyhouse.com

Printed in the United States of America by
Bethany Press International, Bloomington, Minnesota 55438

ISBN 0–7642–2510–3 (Trade Paper)
ISBN 0–7642–2511–1 (Hardcover)
ISBN 0–7642–2513–8 (Large Print)
ISBN 0–7642–2512–X (Audio)

# *Dedication*

To
Clyde and Susan,
our dear friends in
Connecticut.

## *By Beverly Lewis*

### THE HERITAGE OF LANCASTER COUNTY

*The Shunning*
*The Confession*
*The Reckoning*

❖ ❖ ❖

*The Postcard*
*The Crossroad*

❖ ❖ ❖

*The Redemption of Sarah Cain*
*Sanctuary**
*The Sunroom*

*with David Lewis

## *About the Authors*

BEVERLY and DAVID LEWIS grew up in Lancaster, Pennsylvania, and Aberdeen, South Dakota, respectively. They met and married in Colorado, where they make their home in the foothills of the Rocky Mountains, enjoying their three grown children and one grandchild.

# *Part One*

*God is our refuge and strength,
a very present help in trouble.*

Psalm 46:1

◆ ◆ ◆ ◆ ◆

# Chapter One

SHE HAD HOPED THIS DAY would never come.

Trembling, Melissa James returned the phone to its cradle and hurried to the stairs. She grasped the railing, nearly stumbling as she made her way to the second-floor bedroom. Her heart caught in her throat as she considered the next move. Her only option.

*You can do this*, she told herself, stifling a sob. *You must. . . .*

Quickly, she located an overnight case. The piece of luggage had been packed years before—in the event of such an emergency—wedged between other travel paraphernalia, high on the top shelf of their closet.

Melissa's mind reeled with the memory—the flat, yet familiar voice on the phone just now. The restrained urgency in his words. Her breath quickened, heart faltering.

Tossing a few items of makeup and hair accessories into the overnight case, she grabbed her stationery and pen. Frantic as she was, she would never be able to forgive herself if she did not take time to write a quick note. *That* much, at least, she owed her husband.

Weeping softly, Melissa penned the saddest words she'd ever written. How does a young bride bid farewell to the man she has loved for three perfect years? The man who had altered the course of her life for better. He'd softened the blow of her past, brought purpose to her future. Ryan James, whom she loved above all others.

She stared at the note, caught between life and love, wishing . . . longing for a resolve far different from the one she must choose. Signing the note, she placed it on his oak dresser, propped up against the brass lamp. Ryan was sure to find it there.

Snatching up her overnight case and purse, she rushed into the hallway. Her head whirled with unanswered questions: *What to do? Where to go?*

On the stairway landing, tall windows overlooked the backyard and the cove beyond. Melissa caught sight of the rose garden—*their* glorious garden, now in full bloom—bordered by the stone walkway and blue hydrangea bushes. Each delicate rose petal and leaf was bathed in sunbeams, their beauty mocking her, adding to her sorrow.

Downstairs, she peered tentatively through a tiny window in the entryway. Hand on the doorknob, her breath caught in her throat. *Don't panic!* she told herself.

No time to waste . . . still, she couldn't leave. Heart pounding, Melissa turned, facing the living room one last time. Was it essential to keep Ryan in the dark about her desperate need to flee? Shouldn't she run to his office, tell him the truth, and urge him to go with her?

Squaring her shoulders, Melissa walked to the back of the house. She paused to take in the enclosed sun porch, deliberately memorizing each detail—the fragrance of roses, the pillowed love seat, the hanging ferns in two opposite corners, and the various knick-knacks, souvenirs of their stateside travels. She recalled the intimate, loving words shared, the soothing backdrop of ocean waves lapping against the wide shoreline. This sun-drenched room where Ryan often held her in his strong arms, tenderly stroking her hair as they stared at the wide expanse of sea and sky. Where the dreamy music of Debussy lulled them into a world of serenity and joy—that place where evil cannot harm those who love.

The lump in her throat threatened to choke her. What precious memories! Too many to rehearse, in light of her present peril. Yet she lingered, refusing the urgency that threatened to overwhelm her. She allowed her gaze to wander to the gray-weathered dock, where impatient sea gulls perched on posts, waiting for handouts. To the sailboat, *Mellie*, christened with her own nickname, wrestling with low waves. To the cove and out to Block Island Sound, Fishers Island, and the wide blue of the Atlantic Ocean beyond.

Stricken, she turned toward the living room, where rays of light shimmered on Daisy's satiny coat, their sleeping golden retriever. "Good-bye, sweet girl," she whispered. "I'm going to miss you."

Opposite the sofa, a red-brick fireplace with rustic wooden mantel boasted numerous framed memories. Hand trembling, Melissa reached for a recent photo, recalling Ryan's pose in front of the historic Stonington Lighthouse. He was a slender, yet muscular man, twenty-seven years old, with sun-bleached brown hair and cinnamon eyes. Distinguished cheekbones shaped his tanned face, forming his warm and compassionate expression. Anyone, upon first meeting him, was drawn to his disarming manner. Just as she had been.

*Good-bye, my darling. . . .*

Shuddering anew, she pondered his response to her note. How grieved his dear, handsome face, his tender eyes. Undoubtedly, he would be shocked.

Resisting the impulse to take the photo with her, she returned it to the mantel, glimpsing the wall prints of Monet's *Water Lilies* nearby. Then her eye caught yet another piece of art. Seemingly out of place in a room dominated by French design, the picture depicted Christ holding a lamb. Printed below the image, the tender phrase: *"Come to me all ye who labor, and I will give ye rest. . . ."*

Melissa had never attended church as a young girl, yet she had felt compelled to purchase the print in New London last year. The picture had offered a strange respite from the underlying dread that defined her life, even these recent wonderful years with Ryan.

If only someone were able to push her backward in time to that childhood place of innocence where good, kind people ruled. Folk like dear Mr. and Mrs. Browning—her nurturing neighbors—and Grandpa and Nana Clark, her beloved maternal grandparents. Snap a finger, and there'd she be.

*Time to go!* She caught herself, the urgency returning. Melissa made her way back to the kitchen and peered cautiously through the window. After a time, she determined that it was safe to emerge. She opened the back door and dashed across the breezeway to the garage.

Inside, she locked the outer door and quickly slipped into her white Toyota Camry. Her hand shook as she reached for the remote, attached to the sun visor. She pressed the button, and the garage door rumbled open. For a split second she wondered what she might do if she were suddenly approached, made a prisoner in her own car.

Dismissing the terrifying prospect, she started the engine and backed the car into the driveway, glancing over at the splendid home, second thoughts haunting her.

It was then that she noticed Daisy shuffling onto the breezeway, mournful eyes watching her—almost pleading. Poor thing must've heard her leaving and followed her out through the doggie door. She resisted the urge to rush to Daisy's side, reassuring her that everything was all right. "I'm so . . . sorry," she murmured.

Melissa adjusted the mirror, then looked over her shoulder out of both habit and necessity. All clear . . . so far. Without delay, she pulled into the narrow street, past the gray-weathered waterfront homes and spacious front yards of her neighbors. Dozens of familiar landmarks—private piers and yachts, and Latimer Reef Light in the distance—all

16

linked to her brief fairy-tale life.

*Too good to be true,* she thought as she sped down the street.

All she had ever dreamed of—the fulfillment of her lifelong hopes and wishes—grew more distant with each passing mile, then vanished into the moist sea air.

## Chapter Two

FIVE MINUTES TO CLOSING.

Ryan leaned back in his leather chair, hands laced behind his head, watching the markets close. No less than six computer screens lined the table along the right wall of his office, monitoring live information on stocks, bonds, options, and futures. He had a stake in all kinds of speculative vehicles, but he was *not* a jack-of-all-trades-master-of-none. As an investment manager for New England Asset Management, specializing in stock options and financial futures, Ryan's aggressive portfolio had more than doubled his clients' money during the past year.

He transmitted his orders for the market open tomorrow, then shut down the system. Drained of emotion, he rubbed his bleary eyes. He was not so much spent from watching monitors all day as he was weary of life, of the endless pursuit of the American Dream. Were it not for Melissa, his wife, living might have seemed nearly pointless. She was the one and only reason he wanted to get up in the morning, the reason to struggle through each day, the incentive to return home at night. Making money—loads of it—had become, for him, immensely overrated. Having someone like Melissa in his life was the true reward for his labors.

His spirits brightened when he considered the evening stretching out before them. Tonight he planned to surprise Mellie with lavender Damask roses, heavy with the fragrant aroma of spicy fruit. His wife appreciated the fine art of communicating with flower colors and arrangements. She, an avid reader of such English novelists as Jane Austen and the Brontë sisters, had enjoyed introducing him to the obscure customs of Victorian courtship.

He had debated between yellow and coral, ultimately deciding on the color that represented their marriage: lavender, which meant "love at first sight," Mellie had explained. And how true for them. The first time he'd laid eyes on her, he was finished.

Typically on Friday evenings they dined

at Noah's in Stonington Borough. After a rich dessert, they often walked past the old lighthouse to Stonington Point, overlooking the harbor. Holding hands, they would revel in the sunset from their spot on Dubois Beach, sometimes prolonging the moment by sitting awhile on the massive boulders jutting out into the breakers.

But tonight, for a nice change, Ryan would take her to the Fisherman Restaurant, in the nearby village of Groton Long Point. Following dinner, when they were satiated with superb seafood cuisine, he planned to present a small white box with the words *Northern Light Gems* engraved in gold lettering. He could scarcely wait to see the look on her face. He would place the pearls around her neck, then happily kiss away the tears. The smallest expressions of love always seemed to take her by surprise.

He smiled at the thought and gazed at the silver-framed 4×6 desk photo of Mellie. He never tired of this picture of his young wife. Only twenty-four at the time, she was wearing a light blue T-shirt and tan shorts, her golden brown hair flowing unfettered about her shoulders, complementing her creamy-smooth complexion. He'd snapped the photo on their first anniversary a little over two years ago.

To celebrate that first milestone, they'd returned late in the day to the Watch Hill, where they had exchanged wedding vows. The sunset mingled purple with pink, and she had been mesmerized by the ocean's reflection of the scene. In the midst of her wonderment, she glanced back at him to share the moment. And Ryan had caught her pose, just as she smiled, capturing the perfect blend of her personality: her eager embrace of nature and her gentle spirit with a little twinkle in her eye.

Closing the necklace case, he slipped it into his coat pocket, taking care to lock his executive desk in the middle of a spacious office. The office, located on the second floor of a large converted Victorian house, stood a mere block from the Mystic River Bridge on Route 1.

In the reception area, Margaret Dyson, a plump fifty-five-year-old woman with gray-peppered brown hair, rapidly clicked the keys of her computer. Bernie Stanton, the boss, was sheltered in the confines of his own office on the other side of the lobby. A grim man who barked military-style instructions at the beginning of the day, Bernie often beat a hasty retreat to his own lavishly decorated domain. Only occasionally did he emerge to welcome clients, usually those of renowned affluence.

Marge tolerated Bernie's sour behavior because, as she succinctly put it, "He pays well. If it wasn't for your fresh and friendly face, Ryan, I'd be looking for a cheerful boss."

Ryan, on the other hand, didn't mind Bernie's temperament. He clearly remembered a time, not so long ago, when Bernie was known to smile, long before pressures of work had consumed him, destroying Bernie's marriage of thirty-five years in the process. More significantly, Bernie appreciated Ryan's investment savvy, delegating most of the important investment decisions to him.

"That's it for me," Ryan announced to Marge, closing the door to his office. "Any plans for the weekend?"

"My grandson Brandon's visiting from New Haven," she replied without looking up. "We're headed for the seaport . . . again." She grimaced.

"Why don't you talk him into going to the beach instead?"

"What, and lose most-favored-grandma status? No thanks." Marge smiled and turned to Ryan, a knowing look on her face. "Hey, it's tonight, eh?"

"Got it right here." Ryan tapped the

necklace case in his pocket.

"Expensive enough, I'll bet?"

"Would've paid more."

"My, my. Aren't we still in love." Marge winked. "By the way, isn't your college friend coming out this weekend?"

"Denny flies in tomorrow. Providence airport."

Marge nodded, obviously remembering his friend. "Still talks a lot about church?"

"Denny's a good man, just a little overboard about religion."

"Sees a goblin in every closet?" Marge chuckled.

"More like a devil in every heart."

"One of those extreme types."

"Yeah. Hellfire and brimstone and all that."

"You could use a little church yourself," Marge said, making an impish face.

Ryan forced a smile. "Don't start."

"By the way," she replied, changing the subject, "now that you're in the habit of buying jewelry, let me remind you—Secretary's Day is coming up."

"You mean the usual paperweight won't do?" Ryan gave a smirk.

Marge laughed heartily at that, and they continued their banter. Ryan was anything but stingy, and Marge knew it. Last year, to celebrate Secretary's Day, Ryan had convinced Bernie to send Marge, her daughter, and grandson to the Bahamas for a five-day reprieve. Overwhelmed with gratitude, Marge had sent daily postcards to the office until she returned bearing souvenirs and gifts. Tanned and refreshed, she had taken one look at the pile of work on her desk and frowned mischievously. "Miss me?"

"Does a fish miss the sea?" Ryan had replied.

He smiled at the memory and reached for the doorknob. "Don't get any ideas about another vacation. We almost fell apart here without you."

Marge nodded. "Takes a man of character to admit how much he needs his secretary."

"An honest man," he said softly, waving good-bye. He was glad to hear Marge chuckle, basking, no doubt, in the pride of indispensability.

◆ ◆ ◆ ◆ ◆

Ryan parallel parked in front of Mystic Florist. There he picked up Melissa's rose bouquet, hurried back to the car, hoping to miss the traffic jam at the drawbridge, and headed east on Route 1. But his timing was off. The light changed to red and he heard the loud whistle as the Mystic River drawbridge began to rise. He was sure to be stuck in traffic for a good ten minutes, at least. Tapping the steering wheel, he thought ahead to Denny's scheduled arrival tomorrow.

Dennis Franklin was an unusual specimen. A bachelor, Denny had played college football and *nearly* made the pros. Had it not been for a minor knee problem, his best friend might have wound up playing for the Denver Broncos. Instead, Denny had worked for a while in security before landing a teaching job in a Denver high school. Quite a comedown for some guys, but not for Denny.

His thing was religion now. He attended church three times a week, even conducted street meetings on the weekend in Denver ghettos. A big man—six feet five—Denny commanded respect wherever and whenever he opened his mouth.

Melissa liked Denny. During his last visit, she'd peppered him with questions. Naturally, the preacher-man was happy to oblige. Though Ryan had never admitted it, Melissa's obvious interest in religion made him uncomfortable. Much to his relief, she'd dropped the discussion once Denny left for home, and things soon returned to normal.

Waiting for the boat traffic to pass and the drawbridge to be lowered, Ryan thought about the weekend ahead. In the past, he'd enjoyed discussing philosophy and religion with Denny. But lately, Denny's incessantly exuberant, sometimes obnoxious, attitude had finally gotten to him. Not in a bad way. In fact, Denny's arguments had become . . . more intriguing. Perhaps it was time to settle whether or not Christianity had merit. To let Denny make his case, then dismiss it once and for all.

The drawbridge settled into place, and cars began to move slowly across in both directions. Ryan drove less than a mile to Lord's Point—their home—in silence. Built along the beach, the house was a cedar-shingled two-story cape. Thanks to Melissa, the yard boasted a smorgasbord of flowers—pansies lining the walkway, marigolds against the house. Fuchsia baskets hung from the eaves. A paradise of color.

Ryan parked his SUV beside the small one-car garage, reached over to the passenger side, and seized the bouquet for Mellie. Daisy, her usual eager self, met him at the kitchen door. "Hey, girl!" He stooped to pet the oscillating dog with his free hand.

Daisy barked her welcome, panting as she followed Ryan to the kitchen.

Placing the flowers on the counter, Ryan reached for the large vase in the cupboard and set about arranging the bouquet. When he finished, he stepped back to admire his handiwork.

Satisfied, he called to Melissa. "Sweetheart, I'm home." He poured water into Daisy's bowl and scooped dog food into her dish, waiting for Melissa to emerge from one room or another. Daisy scrambled over, nudged Ryan aside, and began gulping the food with loud chomping sounds, the sides of her golden body contracting with each voracious swallow.

"Easy girl. There's more where that came from."

Ryan headed for the sun porch where Melissa often curled up with a book or her diary. On occasion, she set up her easel, creating lifelike paintings of flowers and ocean scenery, as well. The room, graced by plump-cushioned wicker chairs, was dominated by a wall of windows facing the ocean. Melissa, however, was nowhere to be seen.

Ryan checked the downstairs basement. The pool table, centered in the room, was surrounded by Melissa's framed floral paintings. Despite his frequent encouragement, she refused to hang them upstairs on the main level, claiming she wasn't ready for "prime-time" exposure.

Calling to her again, he strolled to the

laundry room, expecting to hear his lovely wife humming to herself as she folded clothes. Instead, the room was deserted, the laundry appliances silent, empty.

Back upstairs, he wandered through the house to the backyard, where Melissa often tended her garden. The smell of salt and seaweed mingled with the wail of a distant sea gull. Across the yard to the south, George, their retired neighbor, puffed on a cigar and raked his own small portion of the sandy beach, obviously frustrated with the recent storm deposit of fresh seaweed. George nodded casually, then went back to work.

Ryan did not find Melissa sitting on the dock, her feet dangling off the edge, feeding the resident swans that often showed up for dinner. Nor was she napping in their tiny sailboat, docked to the pier, as he'd once discovered her on a lazy afternoon—having fallen asleep to gentle, shifting waves.

Ryan trudged up the slope to the garage, Daisy trailing close behind. Opening the door, he poked his nose inside. The space for Melissa's car was vacant.

"Why didn't you tell me, eh, Golden Nose?"

Daisy looked up as if to say, *You didn't ask.*

Ryan chuckled. Melissa was probably out

running an errand somewhere. That was all. There was something strange about her being gone at this hour, though. On a Friday especially. He knew how she despised rush hour, liked to be home *before* he arrived for their weekend together.

He climbed the deck stairway leading into the house and went to the master bedroom. He showered in preparation for the evening, sure she would be back when he emerged.

As he dressed and fumbled with his shirt collar and tie, his gaze fell on the dresser. A note was propped against the lamp. Reaching for it, he scarcely recognized the scribble as Melissa's. Certainly, this was not her usual flowing script.

He held the note, read the hurried message.

The growing dread turned to panic.

## Chapter Three

SHE'D GOTTEN A JUMP on late-afternoon traffic. Interstate 95—the fast lane—was exceptionally wide open, yet she rejected the urge to speed. Not one to push her limits, not while driving, Melissa kept her focus on the roadway and her rearview mirror.

She did *not* relish the thought of encountering the hubbub and congestion of New York's rush hour, though she and Ryan often took this route to one Broadway show or another, to the theater district. Always on the weekend when traffic seemed destined to crawl.

Unable to peruse the road atlas at the moment, she contemplated from memory an alternate route through the city. In the past, when considering her options should she ever need to escape, she had never fully settled on where she would go. Any number of places might offer a safe haven until someone recognized her, caught up with her . . . again. She hated to think of running. After her brief sojourn in Connecticut, she was, once again, a fugitive among strangers.

She turned her thoughts to Ryan, her dear husband and best friend. What was he doing now? Reading her scrawled note, wondering just what sort of woman he'd married? How she missed him. The emptiness, the isolation, was nearly unbearable. With each mile, the hollow feeling swelled, seeping into even the most insignificant crevices of her soul.

She glanced in her mirror. Nothing out of

the ordinary. Only cars, dozens of them. None whose drivers looked familiar.

*Breathe easy*, she told herself. She had to calm down. Just how long she might be gone from husband and home, she did not know. She had planned ahead, though, withdrawing enough money—now hidden away on her person—to coast for several months or more. Ryan wouldn't have minded. Her husband was a highly resourceful businessman, seemed to have a knack for turning everything he touched into gold. *The Midas touch*, their friends often joked.

From the earliest days of their marriage, she and Ryan had never wanted for anything. Just days before their wedding, he'd told her that she could work . . . "but only if you care to. We can easily make it with one income, if you prefer to stay home." So to work or not to work had been entirely her choice.

She had grinned back at him, their discussion turning to the all-important decision of who was to cook and clean house if she did choose to find a job. At the time, she wondered if he was hinting, hoping for a baby right away. But the topic of children hadn't come up. In fact, there was never any dialogue about their future offspring. Actually, though, she was glad they'd had this rather unspoken pact. Now, at twenty-six as she ran for her life, the thought of having a toddler in tow was anything but pleasant.

Adjusting the mirror, she studied the car directly behind her, straining to see the vehicle behind *that* car, as well. She recalled, as a girl she'd often wondered about her father's obsession with his rearview mirror. The notion that he was a fidgety driver seemed to hang in her memory. How old *was* she the first time she mentioned something to him? Seven . . . maybe a little younger?

Anyway, Daddy had been deep in thought as he drove her to school. Hers was a small private school on the outskirts of town, Palmer Lake, Colorado. The Montessori school, where she studied music, art, and creative play, was an elite institution. The place was staffed with good, solid instructors—"the best educators money can buy," Daddy often said. But he never boasted about having money. Not to anyone. Melissa never suspected in those days that she and her widowed father were well-off.

Changing lanes, she remembered a particular drive to the school. "What's wrong with the mirror, Daddy?" she'd asked. Usually a warm and gentle man, he had seemed fairly perturbed by her question and surprised her with staid silence. He continued to peer into the mirror, touching it many times,

31

especially at the red lights along the way. She had not pressed it further.

*Some things are best left alone,* she now decided, making a turnoff the road in front of a police station to consult her road map. If someone, by chance, *were* tracking her, the pursuit would have to cease at least for now. A wise move, and she congratulated herself for it. She had not given careful thought to stopping for food, drink, and other necessities. After all, police stations were few and far between when you needed them.

## • *Chapter Four* •

RYAN SAT ON THE EDGE OF THE BED, dumbfounded. Staring at the note, he tried to make sense of Melissa's message.

> *Dearest Ryan,*
> *I have no choice but to leave now. I can't explain why. Please trust me . . . don't look for me. And try not to worry.*
> *I love you,*
> *Melissa*

Ryan raked his hand through his hair and reread the note, desperately seeking the comprehension that evaded him. *What on earth*

32

*was happening? What was she thinking?*

His mind raced back to this morning when he'd kissed her good-bye. Nothing in Melissa's sleepy smile nor her tender kiss had indicated that she was troubled or . . . *what? That she was contemplating leaving me?*

Ryan shook his head, as if trying to shift his brain into high gear. Had something occurred between then and now? He rose and stumbled to the closet, searching for signs, clues. As expected, Melissa's wardrobe dominated the closet—dresses, slacks, blouses, skirts, jeans, and sweaters. Shoes galore. Nothing seemed out of place.

Then he noticed the top shelf, where various seasonal handbags and two fanny packs were neatly stowed. An empty space indicated an overnight case was missing. So she'd taken *something* along.

He descended the stairs to the living room and began to pace the floor, massaging his already tense shoulder muscles. He read the note again, attempting to read between the lines.

*I have no choice but to leave now. . . .*

*Now?* Did that mean she might return? And if so, when?

*I can't explain. . . .*

If she had to leave, why not explain? Why

leave him desperate and wondering miserably?

Quickly, Ryan ticked off the typical reasons why a woman left a man. He was positive there was no other man in her life. She was not fleeing an abusive marriage. . . .

So had she lost her ability to think clearly? Was *that* it? He'd read of cases where people suddenly—sometimes overnight—lost their capacity to reason, to think. In a panic, they ran away, only to be found later, wandering the streets in a strange fugue, whispering of phantom strangers. But Melissa had exhibited no sign of a nervous breakdown, stress, or encroaching mental illness.

Suddenly, he recalled their weekend plans with Denny. Now totally out of the question. Denny just couldn't come, not with Melissa gone—running from some real or imagined terror.

Thoughts wavering, Ryan picked up the phone and dialed.

Denny tossed several pairs of jeans into the duffel bag, headed to his closet, and removed four T-shirts. Nearly all the shirts had Christian phrases or Scripture verses printed on them. He packed his clothing, wondering how to prepare for New England's fickle weather. Summers were normally hot in

Connecticut, even toward the end of August, but more recently, Ryan had said, they had been plagued with days of unrelenting cloudy, cool weather. *"Unusual for paradise,"* Ryan had joked.

Denny threw in a sweatshirt and a couple pairs of shorts, just in case. Hopefully, sultry beach weather awaited him. He could use a few days of sunny relaxation.

Along with his Bible, Denny was taking a copy of C. S. Lewis's *Mere Christianity.* Last time Melissa had involved him in a deep discussion of the claims of Christ. He had been pleased to find her far more receptive than he would have guessed. But the newly purchased book wasn't for her. She wasn't interested in—didn't require—either logical or philosophical reasoning as to faith. Ryan, however, lived in the skeptical world of *prove it to me.* But the bigger question remained: Would Ryan even read the book? Doubtful.

Denny packed it anyway, in case the subject came up. He grinned. With him, the subject of Jesus *always* seemed to come up. It was unavoidable, impossible to remain silent about something that mattered so much to him. Even with strangers he met on the streets, Denny usually brought up the matter of Christ—delicately. Well, as delicately as possible for a man his size.

There were times when he regretted not getting into professional football. Not because he still craved fame or money, but because of the missed opportunity as a sports pro to influence souls for the kingdom.

Presently, he spent after-school hours and weekends with troubled teens, many who literally lived on the street. There was no greater joy than to roll up his sleeves, get down and get dirty—and make a difference in the life of a needy boy or girl. Helping with food and shelter. Offering a listening ear. Truly caring about their problems.

But lately he felt exhausted, needed time to reflect, to recharge. This chance to fly to the East Coast and hang out with Ryan and his wife had come at a most opportune time. Besides, this getaway would give him time to think through some of his own issues, especially his relationship with Evelyn and the possibility of marriage.

Denny dialed his bedroom phone and reached Evelyn Reed on the second ring.

"Are you packed yet, handsome?" she asked after she heard his greeting.

Hearing her voice was like coming home. She worked nearly around the clock at Denver's Children's Hospital as a nurse, the ideal career for her, a woman with a nurturing and gentle soul.

It didn't hurt his feelings that Evelyn liked to refer to him as *handsome*, even though he knew he wasn't *that* good-looking. For one thing, he was slick bald. The fact that she *thought* he was attractive was all a red-blooded American male like Denny needed to know.

"I'm having second thoughts," he replied grimly.

"About going?"

"About leaving you behind."

"I'll be fine, you big lug. It's only for a few days, right?"

"Suppose so."

She was silent for a moment, then—"I'll be praying for you, Denny. And for your friends Ryan and Melissa, too, that everything goes well."

They chatted a bit longer before he said a reluctant good-bye, hung up, and finished packing. He hadn't left town yet, and already he missed her.

The phone rang again.

Denny pounced on the receiver. Probably Evelyn calling back. "Hey, hon . . ."

"Uh . . . Denny, it's Ryan."

"What's up? Change your mind about my visit?" Denny joked, aware of the hesitancy in Ryan's voice.

"Well . . . actually, yeah."

Denny frowned. "Hey, I was just kidding."

"I'm not. Listen, this isn't going to be a good weekend, after all."

"That's cool." Then, sensing an ominous heaviness in his friend's voice, quickly added, "Everything okay there?"

Ryan sighed audibly. "Not exactly."

"What's wrong, man?"

Denny was stunned to learn about Melissa's disappearance. "Did you guys have a fight or something?"

"No, listen . . . uh, I need to get going. Sorry, we'll talk later."

"I'll call back tonight, okay? You've got me worried."

Ryan hung up abruptly, leaving Denny puzzled. Ryan and Melissa were the "perfect couple." What could have gone wrong?

Denny pushed the suitcase to the other side of his bed. Promptly, he lowered himself to the floor, kneeling like a schoolboy, and began to pray.

◆ ◆ ◆ ◆ ◆

Ryan disconnected with Denny and considered his next course of action. He tried to put himself in his wife's shoes. *Where would I go if I were Mellie?* he wondered.

He considered getting into the car and

driving around to look for her, just to be doing *something*. But he thought better of it. He needed to be near the phone—in case she called.

Daisy padded to Ryan's chair, rested her chin on his knee, and whined softly. Ryan rubbed her golden fur and her floppy ears for a minute, then picked up the phone, dialing Melissa's best girlfriend, Alice Graham. *Ali.*

She answered on the third ring, and Ryan explained the situation as matter-of-factly as he could. Ali's reaction was utter shock, disbelief. "This is nuts. She left a note?"

Ryan read the note to her, which brought a little gasp. "I can't believe this," she whispered.

"The two of you were together for lunch today, right?" he pressed.

"Yeah . . ." She paused. "Oh no . . ."

"What?"

"I don't know . . . it didn't make sense to me at the time, but now—"

"What happened?"

"At the restaurant. We hadn't even finished eating, and . . . she just suddenly wanted to get going. Said she wasn't feeling well, so she got up and left, just like that. Left me sitting there alone. She seemed a little pale. I called later to check up, but she wasn't home."

"What time was that?" Ryan asked, his heart slamming the walls of his chest.

Ali seemed to hesitate. "I guess around two o'clock or so."

Ryan blocked out the rest of the conversation. Melissa . . . *sick?* Why hadn't she told him? What *had* happened today?

## Chapter Five

THE HIGHWAY HAD BECOME A LONG and monotonous box—a rectangular shape, as though the pavement stretching out before her were the base; the blue of the sky, the top; the lush, green barrier of trees and underbrush, the sides.

Melissa scanned the radio, searching for something soothing. She chose an oldies station with frequent news updates featuring snarled traffic up and down I-95 along the eastern seaboard. Such gridlocks were apt to put her in a dire position—stalled. She simply could not afford the risk of entrapment.

So she listened intently for reports of serious snags on the major roads leading into the Big Apple. Populated areas were best, she'd decided. After all, a driver could lose herself in the mayhem of rush hour. And in an emergency, attention could easily be diverted elsewhere. Calculating a host of worrisome thoughts, she weaved in and out of traffic as afternoon hurtled toward evening.

*Any day but Friday*, Melissa thought. Yet, it wasn't as if she'd *planned* to leave on the worst traveling day of the week. Being mid-August posed another problem—last-minute family vacations. The northbound lanes were crammed, bumper to bumper, with cars, vans, and buses headed for the shore.

She thought of the beach at Napatree, near Watch Hill, Rhode Island, where she'd first met Ryan more than three lovely years ago. Had it already been that long?

Glancing at her watch, she took note of the date: August seventeenth. In more than one way, the final full month of summer was extraordinary. Her father would have celebrated his forty-eighth birthday this month, had he lived.

She gripped the steering wheel. She hadn't thought of her dad's birthday in years. And why, on the day of her mad dash away from the evil that tormented her life?

Trying to refocus her attention on driving, she shifted her weight slightly, eyeing the cruise control button. Should she set it in this congestion? Wouldn't it just be a matter of time before she'd have to brake, throwing the setting off? Why bother?

Leaning her head back slightly, Melissa forced herself to relax a bit. Traffic in her lane had slowed to a crawl. *To think I met Ryan in the month of Daddy's birth,* she mused. And yet, in the selfsame month she was leaving everything that was ever good and true.

A never-ending screen of trees and wild ferns on either side of the road appeared to close in on her. Inching her car forward, she noticed the ceiling-sky beginning to fade from its sapphire hue as the sun prepared for its slow dive over distant hills to the west. At times, the pavement itself seemed to disappear as additional vehicles vied for space.

More than once, she was tempted to use her cell phone to call Ryan. Oh, to hear his voice—the notion both thrilled and terrified her. She dared not succumb to temptation. Cell phones were dangerously susceptible to tracing.

By now Ryan would have made a myriad of phone calls to their neighbors, to Ali, and to the florist shop where she was employed. He may have already reported her missing to the police. Calling home was out of the question. The hazard was too great.

She ought to think about settling in somewhere for the night. Somewhere out of the way where she could make her next call from a safe phone. On the other hand, she didn't want to put herself in a more precarious spot—leaving the highway, getting off the road and into a rural area where she could easily become a sitting duck. She'd have to wait until after sundown.

*Daddy always waited for nightfall,* Melissa recalled. Yet she'd never consciously realized this fact as a girl, in spite of the many road trips they'd taken together. She remembered, very clearly, one night when she and her father had set out to visit Grandpa and Nana Clark, her mother's parents. Though she had never known her mother, who passed away when she was two, Melissa loved to visit her only living grandparents. And Daddy never seemed to mind driving the winding, mountainous roads over Loveland Pass, through the long Eisenhower Tunnel, then past Vail and Glenwood Springs, to Grand Junction. They sang campfire songs as they drove. Sometimes, they kept track of out-of-state license plates. And Daddy had his own songs, too. Silly little tunes he made up at will. On occasion they talked of his fondest memories of her mother, though for the most part, he shied away from things too sentimental. Or too painful.

◆ ◆ ◆ ◆ ◆

It was nearly six o'clock when she spotted the exit sign for New Rochelle, New York. She would allow herself a very brief stop at the city nestled on the north shore of Long Island Sound in Southern Westchester County. Just long enough to gas up and purchase a few snacks and something to drink, at "The Queen City of the Sound"—inspiration for Broadway's former smash hit *Ragtime* and home to both Robert Merrill, opera star, and Norman Rockwell, America's popular artist.

Melissa knew the place well. She and Ryan liked to poke around in the shops that lined historic Main Street, where fruits and vegetables could be purchased in the same vicinity as children's toys and athletic apparel.

Glancing in her rearview mirror, she surveyed the car directly behind her. A blue sports car. Hadn't she noticed it earlier? Back near Fairfield, maybe?

Changing lanes, she stepped on the accelerator, but the blue car sped up, nearly on her bumper now. Instantly, her throat closed up. She was being followed, just as she feared!

*Keep your cool!*

Anticipating the exit, she rejected the

urge to use her turn signal. Yet the blue Mustang veered into the far right lane just as she did. She strained to see the driver's face in her rearview mirror. If she could just manage that without causing an accident.

She was about to focus on the man's face when she heard the driver in the next lane blare his horn. A good thing, too, for she nearly plowed into the car in front of her, halfway to the end of the crowded exit ramp.

"Watch where you're going!" the driver hollered, leaning out the window.

"Sorry . . . sorry," she murmured. Her mouth was cotton as she waited, stuck between the Mustang behind her and the car ahead. Seconds seemed to tick by in slow motion. She double-checked the automatic locks in her car. Twice.

Gradually, the backed-up ramp eased a bit. At last she negotiated a sharp right-hand turn, and as she did, the Mustang roared around her, speeding off in a different direction. *False alarm.*

Heart still hammering, she located the nearest gas station and turned in. She leaned back and closed her eyes, willing herself to calm down.

Daddy had said he *needed* the sleeping tablets and that she must always remember to leave them on his nightstand before bedtime. And she had obliged, never forgetting.

Often she had wondered how the tablets made a person feel. At times she had held the tiny round pills in her hands, peering at them, holding them up to the light. Trying to see into them. Did they make your legs and arms tingle before you felt nothing? What parts of your body went numb first? Your feet, legs, arms? What caused such small pills to work? Most of all, why did Daddy need medicine to put him to sleep? She had never asked.

Her father was a compassionate man, more than generous with his hugs. He encouraged her to snuggle up on the sofa with him while they spent part of each evening reading aloud from her cherished picture books or school reading assignments. But tender words came more clumsily. "Mellie, be safe," he'd say each time she left the house for school or Girl Scouts or wherever. Never once did he call after her, "Have a good time," or "Enjoy yourself."

It was always: "Be on your guard. Watch yourself." His consistently serious tone rendered apprehension to her young heart, as did his sober eyes. Not until years later, having been told the full story of her father's fate, did Melissa fully comprehend the significance behind his warnings. Sadly, by that time, the man she'd called Daddy had been deceased for more than a decade.

Melissa purchased her snack items and pumped a full tank of gas, then hurried to the safety of her car. On the road, she kept watch for any vehicle trailing her, for any driver who might look suspicious. Even recognizable.

Juggling her sub sandwich, she managed to drive, though it was a challenge due to the ongoing bottlenecks as she neared the vicinity of each shoreline city or town. The closer she came to the Bronx, the more clogged the traffic. Was everyone in New England driving to the city for the weekend? Never had she seen so many vehicles on a Friday evening.

Thankfully, the day was beginning to cool down. She switched off the air conditioning and turned up the radio. A rambunctious announcer was crowing the high temperature for the day—"eighty-nine degrees." Hotter than usual, true, though coupled with higher than normal humidity, the day was classified "a doozy."

*In more ways than one*, she thought.

Waves of grief threatened her composure as she relived the morning's startling encounter—at a restaurant, no less—followed by the urgent phone call and her desperate escape.

The DJ kept talking about the weather, and she tried to listen, hoping to crowd out the events of the day. "Temps are bound to decrease as summer begins to wind down to fall," the announcer said. "Now, that's *one* thing you can count on."

*One thing to count on . . .*

Not much in life was reliable. Changing weather, hurricanes, high and low temperatures. In the course of things—of life, overall—what did it matter? What did *anything* matter?

Suddenly, she thought of dear Nana Clark, living in the hot, semi-arid region of the country—Colorado's western slope. How long since she'd visited her mother's family? Not since before her father died. She scarcely recalled the actual year, much less the event. Nana and Grandpa hadn't come to the funeral. Too frightened, perhaps. Who could blame them? They'd sent cards and letters, and there were occasional phone calls, too, during the years she'd lived with Mr. and Mrs. Browning. After college she'd disconnected from everyone, her Colorado relatives and friends included. Missing her grandparents and the Brownings, she wished she might have kept in touch somehow.

Flicking off the radio, she exhaled loudly, frustrated and angry with the way life had turned on her. If she were a religious woman, she would ask God for help about now. The way she saw it, praying was for dutiful folk who hadn't completely messed up their lives. People like Ryan's friend, Denny Franklin.

*Oh no!* The realization that Denny was planning to fly in tomorrow hit her. She shook her head, amazed that she'd spaced out his visit. Yet there was no choice in the matter.

Surely Ryan would call off the visit with Denny, wouldn't feel like entertaining his Bible-packing friend. He would be hurt, put in such an awkward position, having to tell Denny his wife had vanished.

The silence in the car trickled out through the cracks, and she was aware of the sounds of tires on the highway, the color and make of the two cars directly behind hers. A gray sedan hung back a bit, the third car in the current lineup.

The eerie dirge of dusk settled in about her. Once the sun was down, things would change for the worse. Darkness always hampered her behind the wheel—not that she suffered from night-blindness. Things just became very different after dark.

Melissa finished her snack and soda,

making an attempt to stay focused, to keep her mind on her driving. A tug-of-war ensued. Wanting, *needing* to concentrate on the road and the types of cars around her, she found that her unruly mind wandered far afield. The struggle was in the way of a dream, a vision of sorts. A fanciful scenario of "what ifs" and tenuous "if onlys." In truth, nothing she could have done would have altered the outcome of this day. Or of her life, really.

Indulging in imaginary games would easily take up a good portion of the trip. If she chose to go beyond Manhattan for the night, that is. New Jersey, Delaware, Maryland . . . where would she stop? When she tired of the driving, as well as her over-scrutiny of the past, present, and future—she might put on one soothing CD after another, humming all the while, just as she often had while traveling by car with her father.

The closer she came to New York's magnificent skyline, etched against the gray of smog and humidity and accompanied by millions of twinkling lights, the more she was tempted to check in at one of the Times Square hotels. Overnight, perhaps. Long enough to make her next phone call and get some much-needed rest.

She glanced at the corridor of trees lining

the highway in the fading light. Was it her imagination? Were the leaves beginning to turn slightly? She fought the urge to stare at their beauty.

For the first time, she was going to miss the autumn glories of New England. Thinking ahead to the annual harvesttime festivities, she caught her breath, recalling Ryan's suggestion that they drive up to Vermont in mid-October. "We'll make a three-day weekend of it . . . over Columbus Day," he'd said just last week, paging through the current Innkeepers' Register. And together they had decided on an elegant village inn at Ormsby Hill in Manchester, former residence of Robert Todd Lincoln's friend and law partner.

They wouldn't be going together . . . or at all now. Another disappointment for Ryan.

She choked back tears, struggling to see the road. How could he forgive her, spoiling their romantic plans this way? Destroying their Camelot?

◆ ◆ ◆ ◆ ◆

Her idea to "get lost" in the teeming masses of Manhattan seemed perfect as she drove south toward the Whitestone Expressway, keeping her eyes peeled for the turnoff to west I-495. Halfway through the Queens Midtown Tunnel, she spotted the gray sedan again. A Buick. Trailing her by a distance of three vehicles, the car was nearly out of the perimeter of her rearview mirror. She was conscious of the lane changes the driver continued to make nearly every time *she* negotiated a turn.

*Don't panic . . .*

Resolving to remain composed, she purposely shifted lanes once the tunnel dumped out to East 36th Street, though she was cautious, mindful of the heavy traffic. The gray car slowed, but seconds later, blinked over and merged into the right lane, on her tail.

Several blocks later, traffic came to a full stop. Unable to accelerate, she was paralyzed in her lane; *all* options were blocked. The gray Buick, only two cars away, was too close for comfort.

At Madison Avenue, the Pierpont Morgan Library—an Italian Renaissance-style palazzo—seemed even more imposing than she remembered, with its pair of identical stone lionesses guarding the grand gated entrance. She shuddered as she stared at them and the monstrous building behind. But in doing so she was able to steal a glance in the vicinity of the silvery car through her outside mirror.

Melissa gasped. She recognized the square face, the man's fierce, raptorial eye.

The familiar white tuft of hair on the left side of his otherwise thick head of dark brown hair—his peculiar trademark—confirmed her worst fear. The same man she had seen earlier today had followed her all the way from Mystic.

She fought to think clearly as she drove. The pulse in her chest and the heat surge to her head made planning difficult. Though she knew her way through Midtown well, making a decision under this kind of pressure—where and how to make the slip, get out of sight, even make a run for it—was beyond her ability at the moment. Penn Station was within five miles, but to get there she'd have to abandon her car and get away on foot, then catch a train out of town. She didn't trust herself on the street, not this far from the train station. The possibility of flagging down a cab occurred to her as the cars began to move again. Out of the question on a Friday night. No, she'd sit tight, hang on to the vehicle she so desperately needed to take her to safety.

*Call the minute you get to a safe place*, the whispered phone warning rang in her ear.

The Buick sedan signaled to change lanes, passing the car behind her. It crept up, now side by side with hers. She dared not glance to her left, dared not look. Not now.

*Mellie, watch yourself,* her father's voice echoed from the grave.

The light turned abruptly red at the next intersection. Tires screeched, horns blared. What would she do if he forced her over?

She opened the glove box, eying the small black container of Mace, a disabling liquid. If necessary, she wouldn't hesitate to use it. But she did not want to allow the man to get *that* close.

Caught in a gridlock of taxis, cars, and limos, she strained to see if the street was marked one-way. The minivan in front of her blocked her view. She thought of turning the wrong way, or even running a red light at some point. Maybe she'd try to get stopped by the police. But no matter what happened to her, no matter how many police she encountered, the gray sedan would keep showing up. The driver would merely circle the block and pick up her trail eventually.

To her right, the gaping mouth of an underground parking garage enticed her, wooed her into its depths. Momentarily, she considered the possible escape route. But no, it was too constrained and concealed. She must stay out of dark places, remain in the open, where people were near. Where the populace could be witnesses . . .

# Chapter Six

LELA DENLINGER looked out the window as she finished her supper. She enjoyed the last few crumbs of apple pie, then drank the remaining sips of her coffee. A bit more lonely than she'd felt in ever so long a time, she stared out across the meadow at the neighbor's barn, a lantern light a-shining for all its worth from an open door at its east end.

Her brother and his wife and their baby had come for a three-day outing from Virginia, leaving just after breakfast this morning. She'd spent the morning redding up after them—washing sheets, dusting, and whatnot. After such a lovely visit with her dear ones, the house seemed almost too quiet.

"What'll you have me do now, Lord?" she whispered in reverence, trusting her heavenly Father's ability to provide for her every need. But, being the sort of woman she was, she liked to offer a helping hand. 'Course, the Creator of the universe didn't need her assistance—any child of God knew that. Still, she wanted to be available, put herself on the altar of sacrifice, if that was what the Lord might indeed have in mind.

Clearing off the kitchen table, she set about carefully washing and drying each dish. As she wiped each of the counter tops and the table clean, she began to sing. "O Master, let me walk with thee, in lowly paths of service free. . . ."

Eager for a bit of cheer to fill the empty house, she put one of her favorite praise and worship CDs into the stereo and sat down with her Bible, devotional book in hand. She liked to read in the early morning, upon first awakening, feeding her heart and mind on God's Word. But today, as gloomy as she felt, she decided she'd have her quiet time twice. Nothing at all wrong with that. Why, her own sister, who was church-Amish and lived down the road apiece, often did the same thing. " 'Tisn't a thing to boast about," Elizabeth would say, just a-smiling and as merry as you please. "Reading what God has to say, no matter what time of day or how often, is a blessed thing, Lela."

And of course she agreed. Far be it for her to argue such a fact. She and Elizabeth were as close as any two sisters could be, though they didn't entirely see eye to eye on church membership, she being Mennonite and Elizabeth embracing the Amish tradition of her husband. Yet both were "homegrown" Pennsylvania Dutch girls, lived so close they could run barefoot back and forth between each other's houses, helped each other do spring and fall cleaning, and most everything else a body needed. The biggest difference between them was that Elizabeth married young, at nineteen, and had herself a fine, growing family already at twenty-seven. Lela was nearly thirty-one, come next week. Never married. 'Course, if the Lord brought someone along who loved her just for who she was, well . . . then, she wouldn't have to think twice 'bout that.

She'd heard the whispers—"maiden lady"—already at church and family gatherings but wouldn't let on that it bothered her. Though, of course, she was becoming just that in the eyes of her community. Still, she held on to a glimmer of hope that someday, in God's perfect timing and will, a godly man might come into her life.

Turning her attention to the devotional book, she found cheer and comfort in the verses found in chapter four of First Peter. "And above all things have fervent charity among yourselves: for charity shall cover the multitude of sins." Reading on, she was un-usually moved by the words: "Use hospitality one to another without grudging. As every man hath received the gift, even so minister the same one to another, as good stewards of the manifold grace of God."

*Hospitality . . .*

Lela had never been one to show the slightest hesitation when it came to opening either her home or heart to family and friends. Even strangers. Habits of generosity were learned early among her people. She, along with her six brothers and sisters, had been taught that the importance of giving comes not from having much or little, but whether one's spirit is at home in community. She recalled Papa loaning his farm equipment to anyone who asked, Mama taking plates of hot food out to the hobos who stopped by. Best she could remember, they always chopped wood in exchange for the meal. Yet Mama liked to go all out, baking her best buttermilk biscuits, hot dumplings, and gravy to satisfy their hefty appetites. 'Course, she and Papa always kept Scripture tracts on hand to pass out, too, along with the food.

Lela's older brothers exhibited generosity in many ways. Often they helped, whether called upon or not, to raise a barn alongside their Amish neighbors. Her sisters were both willing to baby-sit free of charge, least till their own babies came along.

What really bighearted thing had she done lately? Closing her Bible, she felt led to pray about possibly opening her home, maybe renting out her spare room for a little bit of nothing, so eager she was to be a blessing to someone in need.

"Lord, I trust you to handpick the very soul you would send my way," she prayed in the stillness of the house.

◆ ◆ ◆ ◆ ◆

Tired and scared, Melissa searched for a way to make the break. With her heart racing, she had difficulty considering what to do next. The gray car was parallel to hers.

*What do I do now?*

Anything to stop this madness.

The light turned green at last, but she must continue to wait while the cars in front of her inched ahead.

*Move!* She wanted to scream at them. *Just please move!*

At last the intersection gave way, and the cross street was in full view. All clear. She gunned the accelerator, turning a screeching hard right. As she did so, perspiration broke out, dampening her hair on the back of her neck. She heard honking and assumed the Buick was attempting a right-hand turn in the wrong lane, but she kept her attention on the cars ahead of her. No time to look. She must keep moving. Quickly.

At the very next street she made another fast right, onto another one-way street, now heading east. She was going in circles, but she didn't care. She would drive recklessly if necessary. She would escape the man. In order to survive, she *had* to. History was not going to repeat itself. Not this day.

Melissa looked back over her shoulder, saw a glimpse of gray, and realized the stalker had somehow made the turn. Angry and frightened, she wondered why he hadn't leaped out of the car, tried to drag her away when he had the chance. What was stopping him?

*Keep moving*, something in her head prompted her.

*But where to go?* She didn't care to be followed all night. And there was the matter of fuel. When would either of them run low on gas and need to make a stop?

What bizarre maneuverings, either in heaven or on earth, had transpired to put the two of them together in the same restaurant earlier today? What had brought him to the small town of Mystic? Was it just a coincidence? Or had it taken him literally three years to catch up with her again?

She could kick herself, thinking back on

her suggestion to go to S&P Oyster Company, a restaurant overlooking the Mystic River and drawbridge downtown.

Ali had other ideas. She wanted to grab a sandwich and soda at a deli or pop in and out of Bee Bee's Dairy. "That way we can stroll past the boats along the river walk while we eat," Ali had said. But, no, Melissa had insisted they go "somewhere and sit with a view of the water."

Forcing herself to concentrate, Melissa saw that Lexington Avenue was coming up ahead. Suddenly a middle lane opened. Melissa's car shot forward, securing the position. Then she spied a police officer directing traffic at the intersection. His presence did nothing to alleviate her fears. The lights were out, and only a few cars were being allowed through at a time.

*Just great*, she thought, her hopes for making a break dashed. Frustrated, she pulled her hair back away from her face. The officer stood tall and lean in the middle of the busy junction, sporting a navy blue uniform, matching hat, and pristine white gloves. His shoes appeared to have been spit-shined. He was methodical in his approach to directing traffic, motioning only five or six cars through the intersection at a time; turning, moving, arms at a perfect right angle, as though performing a ballet. The man's precise attire and movements fleetingly reminded her of her father and some of his colleagues from the past.

Marking time, she glanced at the gas gauge. She had enough to get her a long, long way from here. If she could just move.

What had possessed her to come this way, through Manhattan on a Friday night? What had she been thinking?

A few more minutes of waiting, and at last it was her turn. She was relieved when the gray sedan was held back, not permitted to go through.

*Now's your chance. Go!*

Keeping her momentum, she floored it and turned right, past numerous skyscrapers, heading south now. Glancing in her rearview mirror, she saw a large service truck blocking the previous intersection.

*Yes!* She laughed out loud. From here, it was a straight shot to East 32nd Street and the Empire State Building. This wide street would lead her to the Lincoln Tunnel eventually. Certainly, it was the long way around, but, hey, this was freedom's way!

High with exhilaration, Melissa had a strong feeling she was home free. Well, not home exactly. Never home . . . maybe never again.

## Chapter Seven

ELIZABETH KING gathered her little ones around her. "We best be thinking 'bout a present for Aunt Lela," she told them after evening prayers. "Her birthday is next week, and you know how much she loves gettin' homemade gifts from each one of you."

Four towheaded youngsters nodded their heads. Mary Jane, age seven, grinned up at her. "I'll be makin' her a perty doily for her hope chest."

Not to dampen her daughter's spirits, Elizabeth wondered how she might focus on the doily and not Mary Jane's comment. "Well, if I were you, I'd make it white."

Her daughter seemed pleased with the suggestion. "Gut idea, Mama. White goes with anything."

The other children talked about making drawings and maybe some birthday cookies. Then, after a bit, they kissed and hugged their parents and headed off to bed.

All but Mary Jane. Being the oldest, sometimes she spent a few extra minutes with Mama before bedtime. "I'm sorry if I said somethin' out of turn," she whispered.

"Meaning what?" Elizabeth asked as they sat near the wood stove in the kitchen.

"Well, you know . . .'bout the hope chest." Mary Jane, eyes blue as the sea, stopped and took a childish deep breath. " 'Sposin' Aunt Lela won't be marryin' anytime soon."

Elizabeth hugged her girl. "We don't know that for sure, now do we?"

Shaking her head slowly, Mary Jane's eyes were wide as ever. "Do ya think God has a husband out there somewheres for her?"

Elizabeth didn't rightly know. 'Twasn't something she and Lela had talked about for the longest time. Far as she knew, her older sister was fairly content in her singleness. She didn't especially seek out social outings or places that widowers would frequent. And honestly, widowers were about the only available men Lela could be thinking of now, considering her age.

"A husband for Aunt Lela?" Elizabeth repeated.

"*Jah*, Mama, that's what I'm askin'." Eager for a response, Mary Jane had the beginnings of a frown.

"I guess that's a task for the Good Lord," was all she said. But knowing her eldest as she did, the girl would be asking again. And again.

Mary Jane was becoming much more aware of things here lately. "You've got yourself a youngster who's mighty perceivin' of folk," Elizabeth's mother had said a few days ago.

That, she knew, was mighty true. Being the oldest of four—so far—Mary Jane wasn't such a handful, really. She was just interested in people. Same as Elizabeth herself.

"Time for bed," she said, shooing her darling toward the stairs. Morning came awful quick around here, especially with the second cutting of alfalfa upon them. Thaddeus would want them all up milking cows, helping in general, come five or so tomorrow.

Before she turned out the gas lamp in the kitchen, she slipped to the dark living room and peered down the road toward Lela's little brick house. She wasn't surprised to see the lights still on downstairs, as her sister often retired hours later than Elizabeth and her family. No need for her to get up with the chickens, after all. Wasn't like she was a farmer's wife.

But the thing that did surprise her was seeing the lights a-blazing in the second-floor bedroom, Lela's spare room. *Whatever is she doing in there?* Elizabeth wondered. Surely Lela had cleaned up after their brother and family left this morning. She kept a very tidy house, her sister did, so it wondered Elizabeth what still needed to be done. Especially at this hour.

"Comin' up to bed?" Thaddeus called to her softly.

"Be right there, dear." She pressed closer to the window and stood gazing down the narrow road, pale in the light of a quarter moon. "Dear Lord, please watch over my sister, Lela. And, if it be thy will, bless her with a nice husband," she whispered into the windowpane.

◆　◆　◆　◆　◆

Only a shard of the moon was visible when Melissa spotted the billboard just after the exit ramp to Keamy, in New Jersey. A wide sign, well lit, touted Lancaster County, Pennsylvania, as the heart of Amish Country—*where time stands still.*

"Exactly what I need," she whispered to herself. "A place locked in time."

She'd heard bits and pieces about the area, mostly about the attractions such as Dutch Wonderland and the Amish Village. Ali and her husband had spent an entire weekend a few years ago shopping the outlet malls, a big draw for tourists. They'd returned home full of talk about horse-drawn buggies and folks walking around in Plain clothing that "would make your head spin," Ali had said.

"Like how?" Ryan had said, laughing, not sure if she were joking or not.

"The men grow beards—no mustaches—and they wear dark trousers with tan suspenders and white shirts . . . and straw hats," Ali explained.

"How do the women dress?" Melissa asked.

"Long, dark, caped dresses and aprons, with little white netting caps called prayer coverings."

Melissa hadn't known what to make of it then, but she'd listened intently. "I've heard of prayer caps," she'd said softly. "Hutterite women wear them, too."

Ali didn't seem to know or care much about other Plain sects, but she was eager to chat about her encounter with the horse-and-buggy people. "You should see how cute the children are!" her friend had said, describing the way the girls wore their hair parted down the middle, "without bangs at all," and braids wrapped around their little heads.

Melissa hadn't been so interested in hearing about "the peculiar-looking people" Ali had talked about, and certainly not all the gawking her friends must've done while in Lancaster. But such a place *did* appeal to her.

She longed for quietude, at least for the night. First, she must acquire a motel, then find a telephone.

For the first time since she'd left Connecticut, she dared to relax a little. A small sense of tranquility lulled her. But only for a time.

Southeast of Trenton, near Holland on Route 276, she glanced in her rearview mirror. There it was again, the undeniable outline of a Buick sedan, coming up close.

Her heart sank. *How did he find me?* Melissa was aghast, overcome with both dread and disappointment. Renewed panic rushed through her veins, charging her body with needed adrenaline.

She'd memorized the highway options earlier, before the sun sank low in the sky, before it was too difficult to reach for the map and study it as she drove. There were two distinct routes available. She could remain on this interstate highway and link up with Route 202 eventually, or follow this super-highway to another multilane artery, onto Route 30, passing through Exton and Gap, wending her way to her final destination.

In way over her head, she felt helpless. She was caught in the grasp of the greatest horror she'd ever known. But she would not give up without a fight.

*Daddy's girl to the bitter end. . . .*

She refused to let herself unravel. "Please, God, help me," she murmured, wondering now, as she drove pell-mell, if God cared at all. "If you're really out there somewhere, help me."

The sound of the Buick bumping her car made her scream. Melissa stomped on the accelerator, flooring it, exceeding the speed limit. This was life or death. Her car roared out ahead, momentarily leaving him in the dust. But she knew the Buick had more power than her car.

Sure enough, seconds later, he was within yards again. Only now they were speeding nearly out of control.

*This is crazy*, she thought. *We're both going to lose it.* She spied the cell phone. She'd been warned not to use it, but she had no choice. She had to get help.

*Wham!* The Buick bumped her again, just as she reached for the phone. The jolt stunned her, lurching her dangerously to the right. She grabbed the wheel with both hands, turned hard to the left, narrowly missing the ditch, but she'd overcorrected and the car began to spin.

Melissa slammed on the brakes, creating a squealing sound, knowing in seconds the

Buick would ram her. But she had no choice. It was either stop or flip over.

Her car careened violently, completing nearly a full circle. Out of the corner of her eye, she saw the Buick swerve into the ditch to avoid a collision. The man fought to control his vehicle, flying past her. He gunned the engine, and the Buick leaped from the ditch in front of her.

The sound of an explosion jolted her to full alert. The gray sedan jerked and leaned stiffly, pitching *back* into the shallow ditch. At a dead stop now, dazed and confused, she stared at the listless car. *What . . . what now?* And then she knew. He'd blown a tire!

Struggling through her tears, she slammed her foot on the accelerator and passed the Buick just as the man opened his door. Instead of an angry face, he leered at her, grinning widely, as if taunting her.

It didn't matter. She was safe . . . for now.

Miles later, still shaking, Melissa made the turnoff to Highway 202. Even if the man changed his tire speedily, he would never find her on this road, never guess where she was headed. To Amish Country—the land that time forgot.

Heading into Lancaster on Route 30, she spotted some restaurants—Miller's Smorgasbord and several others—still open, serving hungry tourists. Motels were plentiful on either side of the highway. Limp and exhausted, Melissa was briefly tempted by a vacancy sign in front of the Steamboat Inn. *Not remote enough,* she thought.

The pressure was beginning to lift. The clench of her jaw had begun to lessen; her shoulders ached but were not nearly as tense as before. She was going to survive. At least, for today.

At the junction of Routes 30 and 222, she followed the road leading north, toward Eden. *Sounds like a pleasant place,* she thought, wondering where all the Plain folk lived. Were they scattered around the county . . . where?

Stopping at a fast-food place, she took a chance and went inside to stretch her tingling legs and to purchase a sandwich and a cup of coffee, inquiring of the clerk about lodging. "Do you know of any inns or B&Bs off the beaten track?"

"Plenty of places to stay around here," the young woman said, smiling. "What exactly are you looking for?"

"Something quiet, away from the noise."

The clerk nodded. "Well, since you're already headed this way, why don't you drive along Hunsecker Road, just up the way apiece. You'll see the sign where to turn. I think you'll find a good many places to stay. Even some private homes with rooms for rent."

"By the week or the day?"

"Whatever you'd like, I suppose. It's coming up on the end of the summer, so you shouldn't have a bit of trouble finding something."

She thanked the woman and hurried back to the car, food in hand.

Wooden boards rumbled as she slowed the car and drove over the Conestoga River via a covered bridge marked "Hunsecker Mill Bridge" on her map. Occasional small openings in the sides of the bridge brought in the slightest bit of light.

Once out in the open, she could see stars winking down at her through the willows and other large trees along the road. She thought again of Ryan's plans for a romantic getaway in Vermont. Columbus Day weekend was the ideal time to travel deep into New England autumn.

Melissa recalled the smell of woodsmoke permeating the crisp, dry air, the crackle of leaves underfoot. They liked to strike out into unpopulated and wooded areas, enjoying a daylong hike into the nearby Green Mountains. One of their favorite things was simply walking in the woods, amidst cinnamon ferns and the colorful undergrowth. There they held hands and talked freely. Always they discovered secluded gardens of milkweed and black-eyed Susans, gurgling streams, low stacked-stone walls, and spicebush swallowtail butterflies. Nature was tangible in such settings, and now, more than ever, she would miss their Vermont experience terribly. But her leaving had altered more than their plans for a romantic weekend. Now *everything* was different.

She might have missed the homemade sign, propped up between the mailbox and the little red flag, if her headlights had not shone directly on the words *Room For Rent*, in big, bold letters.

Pulling cautiously into the driveway, Melissa sat there with the car idling, giving her full attention to a tidy front-gable brick cottage. The land stretched out on either side, dwarfing the house somewhat. When she shut off the ignition, she could hear a host of crickets chirping through the car window. What peace! She longed to sit still, staring up at the expanse of sky and the sliver of a moon.

The front porch light beckoned to her,

and she saw that a lovely grapevine wreath with blazing scarlet sage interspersed with ivy and other greenery made for a quaint greeting. Several lamps were still lit throughout the whole house.

*Is it too late to knock?* she wondered.

Melissa checked the time on the dashboard and saw that it was nearly nine o'clock. She hesitated, thinking how she would feel about company at such a time—*if* she were still at home. But the sign on the mailbox seemed to indicate a vacancy, and now that she looked, there was a sign in the front window, as well.

Getting out of the car, she hurried up the porch steps, realizing she needn't rush anymore. She was fairly safe here on the back byways of Lancaster County. She lifted her hand to ring the bell when the door opened and a woman, not many years older than Melissa, greeted her with a warm smile. "Hello, there," the Plain woman said. "Are you looking for a room?"

"As a matter of fact, I am," Melissa replied, noticing the small netting-type cap, the hair bun beneath, the high neckline, tucked bodice, and long, flowing dress with tiny lavender flowers. The very garb Ali had been so eager to discuss. "I might be staying only one night, if that's all right."

"Oh yes . . . 'Course you can stay as long or as short as you please." The screen door was opened to her and she was welcomed inside. "Please, just make yourself at home."

"Thank you." Melissa felt strange, not knowing the woman's name, but she didn't ask. Instead, she followed the slender brunette up the stairs, where she was shown the spare room and agreed to take it. She was surprised at the price. Thirty dollars per night, including breakfast. The lovely room would be offered at a discount if she decided to stay longer.

"My name is Lela Denlinger," the cheerful woman said.

"I'm Melissa." She gave only her first name, purposely. "I suppose you have a telephone?" she asked, hoping she hadn't stumbled into an Amish household where phones were taboo.

Lela smiled, pointing to the phone in the kitchen. "Oh my, yes, and you're welcome to use it anytime. My home is your home . . . for as long as you choose to stay."

Well, *this* wasn't the sort of reception she'd expected. Relieved, Melissa hurried to the car for her single piece of luggage. "I pack very light," she explained when Lela eyed the overnight case.

"Feel free to help yourself to anything

you find in the refrigerator," Lela offered.

More perks than Melissa ever expected. The more she chatted with Lela, the more she genuinely liked the cottagelike retreat, as well as its owner. She'd stumbled onto a haven, of sorts. A sanctuary at last.

◆ ◆ ◆ ◆ ◆

She waited until the house was quiet, grateful that Lela had left a lamp on in both the living room and the kitchen. At last she had access to a "safe" telephone. Digging into her pants pocket, she found the important number and dialed.

Then to her acute frustration she reached only an answering machine. "Please leave a message at the tone or dial my pager at this number—555-0097," the recorded voice directed.

*Well, I guess it's better than nothing*, Melissa thought. In the dimly lit kitchen, she spoke clearly into the phone, reading off the rather faded number printed on Lela Denlinger's telephone. Hanging up, she sighed, feeling bone tired, weary . . . but at peace, strangely enough.

# Chapter Eight

RYAN AWAKENED SATURDAY to the distant cry of sea gulls. Morning light slipped into the room between the horizontal blinds, signaling the end of an arduous night. His sleep had been fitful, real rest elusive. The clock radio beamed the time: 5:33. Any hope of further slumber evaporated as he glanced at Melissa's side of the bed. How many times had he awakened that night, searching for her, only to experience fresh disappointment each time his brain registered her absence?

Slipping into his robe, he tightened the belt and went downstairs to make coffee. Morning ritual. Daisy followed him into the kitchen, then disappeared through the doggie door while Ryan ground coffee. The hum of the percolator disturbed the stillness, mimicking the sounds of a normal day. Yet today was anything *but* normal.

As he fully awakened, his mind began to race again, as he thought of Melissa out there somewhere, running away, running from . . . *what?*

Daisy lumbered back through her door

and set her expectant gaze on Ryan. Padding to her food dish, she sniffed a little, disdaining the unappetizing crunchy breakfast. She slinked gloomily into the living room and located the spot where a future sunbeam was sure to find her.

Ryan poured his coffee, sipped, grimaced, and poured the entire contents down the drain. He headed upstairs to shower, reliving last night's flurry of activity and phone calls, having finally phoned the police. Around nine o'clock, two policemen had sauntered to the door as if they had all the time in the world. Once inside the house, they poked around and asked the standard formulaic questions. When they saw Melissa's "good-bye letter," their shared glance said it all.

For the next hour the tenor of the discussion changed dramatically. Instead of initiating a rapid search for his wife, they began to treat Ryan as a *suspect*.

Struggling with frustration and worry, Ryan patiently endured their insinuating questions. Finally, one of the policemen stated outright, "There's no sign of foul play, Mr. James. People are free to come and go as they wish. Unless of course . . . you haven't told us everything."

Ryan was glad to see them leave. They

glibly promised to "keep an eye out," then strolled out the front door, presumably to get on with real police business. He was on his own.

Later Denny called back as he had promised and insisted on flying in anyway, to be the proverbial good friend in this "time of trouble." Ryan had felt somewhat relieved, but in the end it didn't matter whether Denny came to visit or not. Only Melissa's safe return could bring him comfort now.

Before getting into the shower, Ryan turned on the water, adjusting the hot and cold, then grabbed the cordless phone receiver and placed it above the shower frame.

Just in case.

◆ ◆ ◆ ◆ ◆

Several times during the night, Melissa had awakened, breaking out in cold perspiration. Each realization of her situation brought a fresh assault of fear. Now, muddled and confused, she pieced together yesterday's events. The unexpected encounter at the restaurant in downtown Mystic, her ultimate desperate flight.

She struggled to sit up in bed, but only briefly. Her head throbbed with the least exertion. *What must Ryan think of me?* she wondered, sinking back against the pillows again. *He must be desperate with worry.* On more than one occasion she had been tempted to call him but had resisted.

It was then that she thought of corresponding with Ryan by e-mail. That should be safe, shouldn't it? The notion gave her hope, though only a flicker. She remembered reading news accounts of on-line virus creators and senders—there must be ways to trace such offenders. If the authorities could locate hackers, then she, too, could be found. Her spirits sank.

In the distance, the sound of horses' hooves tapping the pavement piqued her curiosity. And yet another . . . what was *that* sound? She strained, listening. Such a familiar yet foreign sound—the unmistakable rattle of carriage wheels.

*What on earth?*

She sprang out of bed, taking no time to bother with slippers. Standing in the dormer window, she peered down at the road below and was amazed to see a horse and buggy hurrying along. Where were they headed at this hour?

Melissa glimpsed the driver—a young woman in a dark dress and apron, wearing a little white cap on her head—with a girl at her side, dressed similarly. She guessed they were

Amish, the peace-loving sect Ali and her husband had so enthusiastically discussed after visiting here.

*It's a real-life Jane Austen movie,* she thought, momentarily pleased at the sight. She stood in awe, watching the carriage and horse until they disappeared from view.

Turning from the window, she inspected the room by dawn's light. The bed—surely an antique—was framed by a large brass headboard and footboard. Nearby, the bold scale and fine patina of the cherry bureau reminded her of a dresser owned by Nana Clark. She recalled how thrilled Nana had been to discover such a "find," for her grandmother adored antique furniture.

Sighing, she went and sat in the floral chair in a cozy nook, complete with built-in bookshelves and a gleaming brass floor lamp. The room was even more spacious than her own at home. Tucked way at one end of the room was a second sleeping area, where a single bed nestled behind hand-painted flowery curtains of gentle yellow and lavender. A small wicker table, painted solid yellow, anchored the sitting area.

Leaning back, she felt her muscles relax against the chair. In spite of her anxiety, she knew she'd made a good choice by coming here. After a time she reached for one of the many books behind her and, thumbing through, discovered the author to be a Mennonite minister. So was Lela also a member of the conservative group? Curious to know more about Plain tradition, she read several chapters before returning the book to its shelf.

Then, tiptoeing back to the bed, she sat down, staring at the rag rug beneath her feet. How had she stumbled upon such a whimsical cottage? And what of Lela Denlinger? The woman had been unusually friendly, welcoming Melissa as though an anticipated guest, even family. Was this typical for Plain folk?

The sound of further *clip-clops* enticed her back to the window. Below her, several buggies, spaced as if by an invisible hand, made their way down the road in front of the house. An undeniable calm swept over her as she watched, and for a moment, she felt safe. Safe, for the first time since yesterday morning when Ryan had kissed her good-bye.

*Safe* . . .

All too quickly, she recalled the startling circumstances by which she had come to this idyllic setting. She washed and dressed for the day, wondering when the phone would ring for her.

# *Chapter Nine*

DENNY BOARDED THE 747 bound for Providence, Rhode Island—the second leg of a flight originating in Denver—having changed planes in Atlanta. He was greeted by a smiley brunette flight attendant who offered an array of magazines. Denny patted the pocket Bible in his shirt. "Came prepared," he said, offering a smile.

"I can see that," she replied glibly and continued greeting the incoming line of passengers.

Denny struggled down the narrow aisle, maneuvering his large frame to a row midway through the plane. When he located his seat, he frowned and checked his boarding pass. He was fairly certain his travel agent had booked an aisle seat. A big man, Denny *always* requested aisle seating.

*Bummer,* he thought, sighing. *Maybe God has a reason. . . .*

Walking with the Lord had taught him one thing. Those who endeavored to live in Christ could expect the unexpected. No accidents for a Christian. Even the smallest irritations turned out to reveal God's marvelous intentions.

Denny squeezed into the middle chair between the aisle and window seats. Watching the remaining passengers find their spots, he replayed last night's conversation with Ryan. Denny had called back about ten o'clock and learned that Melissa was still missing.

"I'm coming anyway," Denny had declared. "You need help with this, man." To his surprise, Ryan had agreed, but Denny suspected his buddy was overcome with worry, too drained to protest. So be it. He assured Ryan he'd rent a car and spare him the two-hour round trip. But Ryan had insisted on making the trip personally to meet Denny at the airport.

Closing his eyes momentarily, he thought of Evelyn, missing her. He hoped she'd wait up for his call later that evening.

He was roused from his reflection when a morose-looking, pimple-faced teenager, clad in torn jeans and a soiled T-shirt, moped his way to Denny's row. Mumbling, the kid pointed to the window seat next to Denny. Denny smiled, struggled out of his seat and into the aisle, allowing the boy to pass.

*Hot diggity!* Denny thought. Reclaiming the middle seat next to the boy, he settled in once again, ready to strike up a conversation with the surly one. About that time, an elderly woman tapped him on the shoulder. In her hand she held the ticket to the aisle seat. "Care to switch?" she said, eyeing his giant frame with amusement.

"Thanks, but I'm fine," Denny said, returning a smile. "I'm smaller than I appear in person."

The kid next to him snorted.

"But you need room for your legs, young man," the woman insisted.

"They fit me fine," Denny told her. "They're collapsible."

"Okey-dokey," she said in a singsongy voice and plopped down in the aisle seat. "You're a funny one."

"Thank you, ma'am."

One minor disaster averted. Now on with the adventure. He bided his time, waiting for the right moment. As the plane taxied down the runway and took to the air, the moment arrived. The kid was gripping the armrest, his face a gray-green. Unmistakably, the boy was terrified. *Fear of flying.*

Denny leaned over and whispered, "Don't be afraid, man. God won't let anything happen to us."

The boy's eyes jerked open. "What?"

"We're cool," Denny said casually. "My number's not up yet, and since you happen to be on my plane, your number isn't up yet, either."

"How . . . do *you* know?" the boy muttered.

"Call it a hunch," Denny quipped. "Besides, there's a reason you're sitting next to me."

"Who *are* you?"

He grinned at the kid. "I'm your new best friend."

Frowning, the teen met Denny's gaze, then a slight grin emerged. They bantered back and forth, and in short order Denny worked his disarming wit on the kid. The fear began to dissipate, the shoulders relaxed, and the boy slowly opened up.

The breakthrough came when Denny revealed that he'd scrimmaged with John Elway at training camp. The walls came tumbling down. They talked football for a solid hour before Denny directed the discussion to more serious things.

He learned that the boy's name was Michael and that he'd been in and out of foster homes his entire life. Michael was returning from a visit with his estranged mother in Atlanta who, after two days, could hardly wait to be rid of him. She'd put him on an early flight back to his most recent foster family.

Denny listened as the kid talked. Prayerfully, he sized up the situation, not surprised at all by Michael's armor of rage. But the sword of salvation was stronger. Denny would cut through the rejection and pain with God's awesome love.

When the flight attendants came around with lunch, Michael was ready for some good news for a change. God had already prepared the way.

By the time the plane approached the runway, Denny had indeed made a new friend. Young Michael listened with rapt attention as Denny opened his pocket Bible and presented the Gospel.

"Oh . . . man. This is so . . . well, out there," Michael replied. "I need time to think it through."

"That's cool. Maybe we could hit a youth service somewhere while I'm in Connecticut," Denny replied.

"Church?" Michael frowned.

"Sure, wouldn't hurt to try it. At least once."

Michael considered this, then replied, "I didn't think this was gonna lead to *church*."

Denny understood. "I've been there, Michael. Church is just a place where people like you and I hang out. Like a gang—only for believers."

Michael snickered, but he seemed to respond to the unconventional explanation.

Their conversation ceased as the plane's wheels slammed, then bounced against the runway. The passenger to Denny's left—the lady in the aisle seat—leaned over. "You're quite the 'Billy Graham,' young man," she said without looking up from her needlepoint. "Can't say I've ever heard anything quite like it."

"I just show up, and God does the rest."

"Okey-dokey," she replied, putting her needle aside. She reached for the gate information in the seat pocket in front of her, obviously nervous. Maybe she was worried that Denny might start in with her about God and church.

He chuckled. *Double duty.* The woman had overheard the entire conversation. *And God's Word does not return void,* he thought joyfully.

Before deplaning, Denny and Michael traded phone numbers. The rest was in God's hands. Reluctant to bid farewell to Michael, Denny grabbed his own luggage and stuffed the pocket Bible in the kid's hands. "Take good care of it, okay?"

"Sure." The boy's eyes shone with gratitude, his earlier surliness gone.

Next challenge: Ryan and Melissa.

Ryan stood near the catwalk, waiting. Denny emerged soon enough, and Ryan was struck again by his friend's large and muscular build, wrapped in gray slacks and a red-and-blue polo shirt, topped off by that perpetual exuberance. The image of the Jolly Green Giant came to mind. Sans the green, of course.

They greeted each other as only good friends do, though pretending they were meeting under normal circumstances. "So . . . you've still got all your hair," Denny commented with false chagrin, releasing Ryan after a bear hug. "Uh! Wait a minute!" He pretended to examine Ryan's head. "I see some signs of hope . . . an emerging bald spot."

Ryan chuckled. "In your dreams."

"You know, it's an insult to flaunt that hair when you're around follicly challenged people like me."

"How do you think *I* feel?" Ryan shot back good-naturedly. "Standing next to you, I look emaciated."

"Jealousy will get you nowhere, my friend," Denny replied, releasing his grip.

They shared a good laugh and headed directly to the parking lot, since Denny preferred to carry on his luggage. No need to put up with baggage-claim madness.

Locating the SUV, Ryan opened the back and tossed Denny's bag inside. They negotiated the noncongested parking area, heading for the highway. Ryan steered the Bronco onto Interstate 95, southbound.

Small talk occupied their attention, at least for several miles, but the unspoken concern over Melissa created tension in the air. It was Denny who finally broached the subject heavy on Ryan's mind. "Did Melissa finally call?"

Ryan shook his head. "Still waiting." He picked up his cell phone. "All my calls are being forwarded to this."

"Any new ideas since we last talked?"

"No. I've called everyone I can think of—including the police."

Denny sighed audibly. "What're you going to do now?"

"Nothing I *can* do, but wait."

"Did she ever pull this kind of thing before? Just up and leave?"

Ryan hesitated. "Well . . . yes. Before we were married."

"Really?"

"She got spooked or something. I didn't know where she was for a couple days."

Denny looked surprised. "What happened?"

Ryan shrugged. "She finally called. And

we worked everything out."

Denny didn't say anything for a moment. "Has she run off since you've been married?"

"Just that one time."

"Ever threaten to?" Denny persisted.

Ryan turned to his friend. "C'mon, Den, cut me some slack here."

Denny said nothing.

Eventually, Ryan's apologetic tone ended the silence. "Sorry. Guess I'm a little on edge."

"My fault. I'm like a bull in a china shop sometimes," Denny replied. "She'll call soon." He turned to look out the window, quiet for a moment, then—"I sure missed the trees here."

"I miss *your* mountains."

"Missed your ocean, too," Denny added.

"And your desert sand."

Denny laughed. "Yeah, right!"

"Just trying to keep up," Ryan replied. Denny grinned back. But as the miles passed, a subdued mood prevailed, and for the remainder of the drive to Lord's Point, neither said another word regarding Melissa. Ryan, however, thought of little else.

# Chapter Ten

RYAN RESISTED the urge to hope. Melissa would *not* be waiting for him, sitting on the back steps when he arrived home from the airport with Denny. Foolish thought. But then again . . . what if she *were?*

He imagined the moment clearly, as if the vision might materialize by the sure force of his will. Pulling into the driveway, he'd catch a glimpse of her. Denny might point and grin at Ryan. "Well, whadaya know!"

Mellie might stand timidly, brush off her jeans, and watch him leap out of the car. Their eyes would meet and then . . . all hesitancy would melt away as they embraced like lost lovers who hadn't seen each other in months.

"I'm so sorry," she'd whisper over and over, asking his forgiveness for creating such a silly misunderstanding. He would hold her face in his hands, gently kiss her sweet lips. "Shh, my darling. It's okay now, everything's okay." All would be forgiven and their short nightmare—a mere twenty-four hours— would soon become a blip on the screen over the next fifty years or more, a lifetime of love.

Not normally given to flights of fancy, Ryan sighed. As they turned the final corner, their home appeared, and he drove into the driveway. His chest tightened in anticipation, hoping for a miracle. But Mellie was not waiting on the porch.

The cliché *It doesn't hurt to hope* crossed his mind. But he dismissed it, discouraged. *Yeah, it does hurt. Hurts a lot.*

"You okay?" Denny asked.

He caught his friend's expression of concern. "I'd better check on things in the guest room. Clean sheets, stuff like that." One more reminder of Mellie's absence. She would have been the one to prepare the room for Denny's stay.

"There's a bed, right?" Denny joked.

Ryan chuckled. "And some new paintings, too. Mellie was eager for you to see them. In fact, one of them is yours to take home. It was supposed to be a surprise."

"When did she—?"

"Finished it about a month ago." Ryan registered Denny's uncertain look. "She wanted you to have it—a special gift."

"Sure, man. Just seems so . . . weird."

*Weird, all right,* thought Ryan as he grabbed Denny's bag and led the way up the brick walk to the house. He was strangely aware of Melissa's flowers, well tended and blooming profusely. The lawn, edged and well manicured, was a mere backdrop for the colorful array.

Daisy was barely able to contain herself with delight, meeting them at the door and following close on their heels as they headed upstairs. Down the hall, past framed pictures recording their happy days, Ryan led his guest to the back room—Melissa's pride and joy. A breezy seaside retreat, nestled under the eaves, the roomy place was set up for their occasional guests, as well as another showplace for more of Mellie's art.

The bed, angled against two white-paneled walls, was draped with an airy comforter that resembled old-fashioned mattress ticking. Abundant pastel blue and cream-colored pillows vied for attention against the white wooden headboard. Windows on either side of the bed appeared wider, with louvered shutters that opened flat against the walls. Mellie's idea. She thought the room seemed larger by emphasizing the diagonal line.

Starfish, spray-painted white, stood along a plate rail a third of the way down from the pale blue ceiling. A see-through white bird-cage graced the room as walls sang with Mellie's floral paintings.

One of her best paintings hung to the left of the dresser—a young woman surrounded by rosebushes, growing wild on a grassy mound near the beach-bordered ocean.

Denny seemed drawn to the image, gazing at the art as he inched closer. "This one's for me, isn't it?"

Ryan nodded. "She wanted you to take the ocean home with you."

Denny raised his finger to the canvas, delicately tracing the faint symbol in the clouds, a product of the shadows and light, "Is this—"

"She thought you'd appreciate it."

"Beautiful," Denny replied, transfixed by the unmistakable outline of a cross.

"I only wish she were here to present it to you herself."

Silence reigned for a moment. Then Ryan gestured toward the north-facing window overlooking the garage. "Not much of an ocean view, I'm afraid."

Denny shrugged. "The whole *house* has an ocean view. The beach is what . . . twenty paces away?"

"About that." Ryan opened the closet, showing Denny the available space and extra hangers. "Make yourself at home."

"Won't take me long to unpack." Denny was staring at the painting again, seemingly reluctant to take his eyes off it. Then he turned a worried look on Ryan.

"What is it?" Ryan asked.

"Shouldn't we go looking for her?"

"Where?"

"I don't know . . . but somewhere. Aren't you worried?"

Ryan sighed. "Of course I am. But where do we start? She has one friend, Ali, and she doesn't know anything. Mellie's mother died when she was young. Her father abandoned her, left her to be raised by a neighbor. No one knows where he is now. No other living relatives."

"No other friends?"

"Not here. None that she talked about," Ryan replied.

"Didn't she have some favorite places?" Denny sat on the bed, gingerly testing the box springs.

"A few. Watch Hill . . . Napatree. We never took you there last time you came out. I met her there, in fact."

"Why don't we check it out?" Denny persisted. "Take your cell phone along."

Ryan forced a smile. "We could do a late lunch."

"Hey, I do lunch," Denny chuckled.

Ryan closed the door, leaving his friend alone in Mellie's blue-and-white paradise.

Denny opened his suitcase, removed his toiletries—shaver, deodorant, and tooth-brush—and placed them in the bathroom. One look in the mirror, and he knew another shave was in order. Plugging in the razor, he registered how quiet the house seemed this time, so empty without Melissa's eager pres-ence. Not that she was larger than life, no. She just had a warm and welcoming way about her, a knack for making a person feel at home. Last time, she'd gone overboard to make him feel comfortable, even going so far as to arrange her menus around his prefer-ences. Yet in spite of Melissa's obvious gift of hospitality, her outgoing nature, something had seemed amiss. At times she had struck Denny as . . . somewhat secretive. Just today Ryan had said of his wife that she had no liv-ing relatives, practically no friends besides Ali.

No friends or acquaintances from the past? Her estranged father out there some-where, never bothering to contact his only daughter. Seemed strange.

He finished shaving, splashing on some aftershave, still absorbed in his overactive imagination. Melissa's leaving surely pointed only to a lover's spat—she and Ryan had sim-ply had a misunderstanding and needed a few days to sort things out. That was all.

Suppressing his curiosity, he put away his shaver and finished unpacking.

♦ ♦ ♦ ♦ ♦

The last thing Lela wanted to be was pushy, but her Connecticut houseguest looked a little peaked this morning. "Would you care to eat lunch with me?" she asked. "There's plenty here, and I'd like the company. No extra charge." She let out a little chuckle, altogether glad she'd opened her door last night, in spite of the hour.

Melissa smiled back faintly, then rose from the sofa in the sitting area just off the kitchen. "I'd love to have lunch with you. Thanks."

Grateful for the positive response from her first boarder, she thought Melissa's face seemed downright thin, her eyes, though clearly blue, were drawn and pain ridden. She had been surprised when Melissa had not packed up and left this morning, as she had indicated she would. Lela overlooked the check-out time, and along about breakfast, Melissa mentioned that she was expecting a phone call and would it be all right if she stayed on a bit longer.

Glad for the company, Lela had agreed that Melissa could stay on another night, or for the extra hours she needed. "Don't worry about paying for half a day or whatnot. It's no trouble to me."

Obvious relief spread over Melissa's face, giving her cause to sigh. But, then, of all things—and on such a heavenly summer day, too—she had gone and curled up on the love seat in the corner of the room, sitting there all morning, just a-gazing out the bay window that faced westward, toward the area of Hunsecker Mill Bridge.

*What could possibly weigh so heavily on her heart that she would sit nearly lifeless that way?* Lela wondered. Was Melissa holding her breath for the telephone to ring? She *had* kept her eye on the kitchen phone a lot, no question. Seemed so awful downtrodden, too. Even despairing. So much so, Lela had thought of offering her a Scripture or a prayer.

She guessed Melissa to be no more than twenty-five. Maybe a bit older, though it wasn't always easy to tell. She wore a tasteful amount of makeup and the typical attire that modern women seemed to feel comfortable wearing these days. *Designer jeans*, yes, that's what they were called, Lela was fairly sure. And a T-shirt that had some writing on it, but she hadn't bothered to stare long enough to see really. Anyway, the girl from Connecticut had the look of—how should she say?—

an up-to-the-minute woman. And it appeared that she was married, according to the wedding band and diamond ring on the fourth finger of her left hand. A married woman traveling alone? This idea was most foreign to Lela.

There was something else, too. Something she hoped she was wrong about; but Melissa appeared to be in some kind of trouble. The girl was more than anxious. Lela's concern for her guest increased considerably when Melissa asked to park her car "somewhere else."

"Where . . . do you mean?" she'd asked, confused, wondering why the driveway area outside the house wasn't just fine for a short time.

"Is there an out-of-the-way place?" came the strange request.

She hadn't had to think much about such a question. Why Melissa wanted to hide her car, Lela had no idea. "Well, I suppose you could drive on over to my sister and brother-in-law's place."

Melissa seemed eager. "How far from here?"

"Just up the road apiece, to the next farmhouse. I'll call up to the barn after lunch. That way I'm sure to catch somebody." She hadn't bothered to explain that Thaddeus

King, her brother-in-law, though raised in the Old Ways, had joined a church with less conservative Amish folk. He enjoyed his newfangled conveniences, such as a radio—"helps calm the cows at milkin' "—as well as a telephone in the barn.

"Thanks." The color suddenly returned to Melissa's cheeks.

"Well, first I'll have to see if there's room for a car in their old shed." She didn't go on to say that Thaddeus might not want such a thing as an automobile hidden away on his property, being that he and Elizabeth still preferred horse and buggy for their main transportation. But that sort of thing wouldn't make any difference to a fancy *Englischer*, probably.

Melissa stared out at countless acres of alfalfa, and, in the distance, verdant and rolling hills toward the south ridge. To occupy her mind, and out of courtesy, she offered to help Lela prepare lunch but was quickly turned down. Not rudely, though. She couldn't imagine the owner of this country cottage exhibiting anything but genuine courtesy.

Lela was the epitome of hospitality, the gracious hostess, in spite of the fact that Melissa was a paying guest. Lela had presented a lavish breakfast, so abundant that Melissa had felt almost too full. So she was content to simply while away the morning gazing out at the tranquil sweep of field and trees, waiting for the phone to ring.

## *Chapter Eleven*

TENDRILS OF ENGLISH IVY, trained along the windows in the kitchen, was the perfect touch for the dining area. Melissa marveled at such a unique window treatment. Something she had never thought of doing. "What a great idea," she told Lela.

"I decided there was no need for curtains in this room," Lela explained happily over homemade chicken noodle soup and grilled cheese sandwiches.

"You could be an interior designer," Melissa remarked. "Who would've thought to eliminate the need for curtains by using strands of ivy?"

"Well, I've always loved natural light." Lela smiled, glancing at the windows. "Even as a girl, I liked to bring the outside in."

"I know the feeling."

They ate in silence until Lela remarked, "There's really no need for privacy what with the courtyard out back, you know."

"And all those beautiful trees."

"Oh yes, I do love my maples."

Melissa had a sudden urge to share her tree-hugging experiences. College years had spawned impulsive behavior. Yet she'd saved some enormous ponderosa pines in her life- time and was proud of it. Taking another bite of her grilled cheese, she decided against the urge to reveal too much about herself. She must use caution.

Still overly anxious about her car, Melissa asked Lela when she might be able to move it.

"I'll call my brother-in-law as soon as the table is cleared off and the dishes are washed and dried." Which she did promptly and without accepting Melissa's offer of help.

"Hello, Thaddeus," Lela said when he answered.

"Well, how *are* ya, Lela?"

She filled him in quickly, so as not to call too much attention to her suspicions. After all, Melissa was sitting right across the room, curled up on the same sofa as before. "I have an overnight guest who needs a place to put her car. Somewhere out of the way," she told him.

"That's no problem. She can park it in

our shed for the time being." Thaddeus fell silent for a second, then asked, "When didja decide to take in boarders?"

"Just last evening."

"Does Elizabeth know anything 'bout it?"

"Well, not yet she doesn't."

He sighed into the phone, probably mulling things over.

Before he could question her further, she said, "Then you won't mind about having a car parked in the shed?"

"Don't mind if it ain't too awful long," said Thaddeus.

"We'll be on over, then."

After hanging up the phone, she invited Melissa out on the front porch and pointed to the sprawling farmhouse up the way. "My sister and her family live over there. Her husband, Thaddeus, says it'll be all right to put your car in their shed."

"Thanks, Lela. This means a lot to me." Melissa pushed her hair behind her ear and turned toward the house. "I'll go in and get my car keys."

When she returned, Melissa asked Lela to ride along.

"Well . . . that's nice of you, but I don't mind the walk." She didn't want Melissa to think she was hesitant to trust her. But she wasn't sure if she ought to. The younger woman *was* a stranger, after all.

"Please, I insist," Melissa said. "You're doing me a big favor, and I'm very grateful."

Papa had often said if a person was gracious—thankful—you could most likely trust him or her. Melissa certainly was that. "All right, I'll ride there with you."

Melissa's eyes widened. "So, it's okay? I mean, you're allowed to?"

She laughed softly. "Of course, I may ride in a car. I'm not Amish, if that's what you're thinking."

"I couldn't be sure," Melissa said with a grin. "I'm not at all familiar with the customs here. I've heard there are many varieties of Plain folk."

"That's for sure," she replied, not wanting to go into all that just now.

They drove together, Lela in the front seat, telling Melissa where to turn into the long dirt lane. "See that sign there—says *Amish Quilts & Sundries*—that's where you turn. Then keep going till you come to the barnyard."

Melissa did just that. And when the car came to a stop, Elizabeth and the children came running out to greet them. "Here comes my sister and her brood. They'll be more than happy to meet an Englischer. They probably haven't seen or talked to a modern lady like you in the longest time."

When Melissa didn't seem to understand, Lela explained further. "In Plain circles, if you're not Amish, you're viewed as an outsider—an Englischer."

"Oh," said Melissa.

Lela wasn't at all certain if the woman eager to hide her car had any idea that she was actually considered worldly in the eyes of Elizabeth and the youngsters gathered round. But, really, she was more concerned how Elizabeth and Thaddeus would react to her taking in strangers as boarders.

Melissa was careful not to stare at Lela's Amish relatives. She recalled seeing from her bedroom window this morning the dark dresses and little white caps on the women riding in the horse-drawn carriages. But now, as she encountered the lineup of bare feet and the long brown dresses and black aprons worn by Lela's sister and her girls, and the peculiar black trousers, suspenders, and cropped hair on the boys, she felt terribly awkward. Still, their rosy cheeks, bright eyes, and genuine smiles soon captured her heart, and she felt strangely warm. Accepted.

"Melissa, this is Elizabeth King, one of my three sisters," Lela said, introducing them. "Elizabeth lives the closest of all my siblings."

"Hullo," said the soft-spoken woman. "Nice to meet you."

The children were next, beginning with Mary Jane, followed by Timothy, Linda, and John, the baby.

When Elizabeth invited them inside for lemonade and cookies, Melissa felt herself tense up. "Do you mind if I put my car in the shed first?" she asked, feeling the urgency to hide the vehicle from prying eyes as soon as possible.

"Not a'tall," Elizabeth said, exchanging curious glances with Lela.

Relieved, she scurried off to the car and pulled it forward, noticing an Amishman motioning to her. Tall, blond, and exceptionally tanned, the man nodded and smiled as she drove her car into the shed. Getting out, she called her thanks to him, deciding that he must be Elizabeth's husband.

"Name's Thaddeus King," he said, extending one hand and removing his straw hat with the other. "Are you new to the area?" He held his hat flat against his chest.

*First question . . . How many more?* she wondered.

"New England's my home." That was enough.

"Just passin' through, are ya?"

How far would he press?

She turned and scanned the farmland with her eyes. "I'd heard about Lancaster County from friends of mine. I wanted to see it for myself." Not entirely true, but this would have to suffice.

"Well, then, Lela will just hafta bring you over again sometime. We'll show you all around the farm."

She didn't have the heart to tell him she wouldn't be staying *that* long. Yet he seemed kind enough. Helpful, too. Still, people like Thaddeus made her feel uncomfortable. She just didn't know how to take him. Was he as considerate as he seemed?

"Slide over just a little," Elizabeth said, waving her hand at young John. "Your auntie can scarcely squeeze herself in."

"Oh, I'm fine," Lela said, giving John a quick hug. "There's plenty of room."

They were assembled in her sister's big kitchen, all of them, sitting around the long trestle table. Mary Jane helped her mother carry plates of cookies to the table. And there was a tall pitcher of fresh lemonade, the kind Elizabeth was known to serve her guests.

From across the table, she eyed Melissa, who seemed entirely out of place, what with her blue jeans and trendy T-shirt. Lela hoped the fancy woman didn't feel uncomfortable.

"Care for some chocolate chip cookies?" Elizabeth offered a plate of warm treats, all smiles.

"Thank you" was all Melissa said. Silently, she reached for a single cookie, displaying rust-colored fingernails. Several flashy rings, too—two on each hand. Her Connecticut boarder was clearly well off, wearing diamond-studded rings.

She tried not to dwell on such thoughts. The Lord was sovereign, giving good gifts to whom He saw fit. It was not her place to judge. Yet she wondered what Melissa was all about. The woman renting her second bedroom seemed as *naerfich*—nervous—as anybody she'd known. Why so?

The walk back to Lela's cottage was pleasant enough, though Melissa felt uneasy about being out on the open road. So vulnerable. Too accessible . . .

Even with Lela at her side, she felt the old apprehension settle in. Wild strawberry vines grew in the grassy ditch and occasional roses bordered the road. The setting reminded her of some of Ryan's favorite haunts in New Hampshire and Vermont, where winding narrow roads led to delightful destinations such as ancient covered bridges and cider mills. The song of many birds gave her courage, sounds reminiscent of her New England home by the sea.

*Home* . . .

Ryan was and always would be her home. Where he was, there she longed to be. He had found her at a time when she was lost, disconnected from the world. Young and terrified, she had welcomed his love, making his heart her home.

*I have to let him know I'm safe,* she thought. *He deserves to know that much.*

She walked a bit farther, reluctant to strike up another conversation with Lela. The smell of honeysuckle, the abandoned road, the patchwork land as far as the eye could see—all this offered her a chance to catch her breath. Desperately, she needed to soak in the serenity, because the minute the phone call came, most likely she would be on her way.

"Such a pretty day," Lela commented.

"Yes."

"I dislike staying indoors on days like this."

She wondered what Lela did for a living. Surely she worked somewhere. "Do you rent out your second bedroom all year long?"

"I suppose I would if someone needed it" came Lela's quick reply. "But I just got the notion yesterday to put out my room-for-rent sign."

Melissa was taken aback by this information. "So I'm your first renter?"

"God dropped the idea in my heart," Lela surprised her by saying. "Yes, you're the very first."

"Well, I'm honored."

Lela continued. "I'd been reading my Bible and praying, asking the Lord what I might do to help someone in need."

Melissa hardly knew what to say. Hadn't *she* herself made a prayer to God last evening, as well? A reckless one, at best. She'd asked God to help her get away from that monster in the gray sedan.

"I do believe God answered my prayer," Lela added.

*And mine*, thought Melissa.

"You believe in Him, don't you?"

The question was completely unexpected. She thought how she might answer. Lela's face was indeed earnest—the good woman was waiting for an honest response. She deserved as much.

"I'm not much of a prize for God, I'm afraid," she admitted softly.

"Well, now, you don't have to be," Lela said. "The Lord doesn't look on your heart and expect it to be neat as a pin. That's what

*He* wants to do for you."

She wondered how a stranger could know anything about the state of her heart. Broken was the best word to describe her heart at the moment. Wounded and bleeding.

"The Lord loves you, Melissa. Just as you are."

She didn't feel she had to respond to Lela's comment. Instead, she focused on the bungalow with its gingerbread and wooden posts along the front porch, in the near distance. They made the turn at the bend, and the flower gardens arranged in perfect symmetry around the front yard came into view. Parallel rectangular beds divided by a flagstone walkway marked the path to the house. Black-eyed Susans bloomed en masse in a mixed perennial garden, outshining the other flowers.

"Is there taxi service out here?" she asked, not weighing the consequences.

"Well, I suppose there is, yes." Lela looked puzzled. "Why do you ask?"

She knew she owed the woman an explanation as to why she wanted to call a cab when free transportation—her own car—had just been concealed in Thaddeus King's shed. "I have a quick errand to run," she said. "I wouldn't want to bother your sister and husband again."

Lela's eyes widened. She was clearly confused.

Quickening her pace, Melissa worried that she'd missed her phone call.

"Are you in a hurry?" Lela asked as they approached the sidewalk leading to her house.

"Just a little." She stopped to admire the garden, hoping Lela wouldn't pry.

"Shall we cut some flowers for a bouquet?" Lela suggested, her voice higher in pitch than before.

Picking flowers in Lela's garden would be a delightful experience, but she wanted—*needed*—to send an e-mail to Ryan, risky as it was. She had to make contact with him, even though she'd been warned against doing so. He would receive the message on Monday morning when he turned on his office computer. She'd use his personal e-mail address at work.

"I'll take a rain check on the flowers," she said, hoping she hadn't offended her kind hostess. She could hardly wait to call a cab and get to town, locate a place to rent some Internet time. A short message would soothe some of Ryan's pain.

*Love always finds its way home*, Mrs. Browning used to say. Now, fondly recalling the woman who had served as her second mother, Melissa was surprised to have forgotten the often-repeated words. Remembering gave her permission to follow through with her plan, despite the perplexed look on Lela's face.

*Something's awful wrong*, Lela thought as she watched the yellow taxicab pull away. She thought of calling Elizabeth and confiding her growing concern about the woman who'd rented her spare bedroom. One minute Melissa wanted to hide away her car, or so it seemed. The next she was willing to pay good money for a taxi to drive her all the way into Lancaster. Well, she didn't care to think what a pretty penny such a trip might cost. Yet, why did she care? She'd encountered strangers a-plenty through the years. None as scatterbrained and restless, however. Just what Melissa's story was, she didn't know.

Suddenly, out of the blue, a strange feeling of foreboding clouded Lela's mind. A feeling of . . . *what?* Fear? Danger? Puzzled by her own emotions, Lela went immediately to her bedroom, closed the door, and knelt beside her bed. "Lord, I don't understand why Melissa is here. But I know you have a purpose in this. . . ."

She continued to pray for her guest, but the inexplicable fear only deepened in her heart. The fervency of her prayer increased in response, and she stormed the gates of heaven with her petitions for help and peace, until Lela felt like Jacob of old, who had wrestled with an angel.

She lost track of time as she interceded. And gently, quietly, the psalm came to mind: *The angel of the Lord encampeth round about them that fear him, and delivereth them.* A ray of hope pierced the darkness, and with it came renewed peace of mind. Ready to let the quiet embrace her, Lela collapsed on the bed, exhausted.

## · Chapter Twelve ·

HE STARED AT THE SCREEN of the small portable computer, took another drag on his cigarette, then ground the butt into the table. Sitting in a motel room specifically designated for nonsmokers, he waited patiently for the modem to dial the number. He had all the time in the world.

Once the connection was made, he punched the keys, bringing up the Global Positioning Satellite Tracking Web site. He entered his password, ID, and the vehicle control number. Seconds later, he had what he wanted: a detailed local street map and a red star blinking beside the street address.

He smiled, lit another cigarette, then clicked the screen through several windows, cross-referencing the street address with a name.

*Thaddeus King, 1135 Hunsecker Road, Lancaster, Pennsylvania.*

"Gotcha, Missy James," he whispered, his smile turning to a full-fledged grin. The state-of-the-art tracking device—a transmitter—on the woman's Toyota Camry, about the size of a paperback book, weighed less than half a pound. Attached beneath the vehicle magnetically, it linked to the car's own battery system and harbored a NASA-developed stealth antenna. Undetectable to the casual observer, even a car mechanic could be fooled, assuming the small box performed a computerized automobile function. Accessing the United States Government Military Global Positioning Satellites, the device transmitted its exact location within thirty feet of accuracy.

*What would I do without my marvelous toys?* he thought, recalling the startled look on Melissa's face when he found her just outside Trenton, New Jersey, after she'd managed to elude him in New York. Finding the woman had been easy. A quick call to his GPS tracking service operator had alerted him to her location on Route 30, heading west, even reporting the Camry's precise speed at the time: sixty-seven miles per hour. Simple as that. *And now . . . she must feel safe again*, he thought, chuckling to himself.

*Secure as a mouse in a cat's paw.*

He was about to disconnect when the thought occurred to him to double-check the history of the transmitter—determining *each* specific location of the car during the past twenty-four hours. Clicking on *history*, he discovered Melissa's vehicle had *not* been parked at the King residence very long, little more than a few minutes. The first significant stop in Lancaster County—Friday night— had been a restaurant on Route 222, followed by another stop at 702 Hunsecker Road, overnight.

"Thought you could lose me . . ." he muttered.

He cross-referenced that location with the name/address software. Within minutes another name materialized: *Lela Denlinger.*

*So . . . that's where you're hiding.*

Closing the GPS Web site, he disconnected the modem from his laptop, then attached a portable telephone scrambler to the phone handset. Although he enjoyed taking chances, his partners were the nervous types. Without the aid of a scrambler, they would insist on speaking in elaborate Russian code, indecipherable to the most skilled translators.

Two short rings, then—"Yeah?" a gruff, apathetic voice answered in his native tongue. "Got something?"

"Found her."

The voice spewed profanity. "What are you waiting for?"

"Relax. We'll have what we want by tomorrow."

"What about the husband?"

"Oblivious," he replied.

"Then finish this . . . once and for all."

He hung up the phone and smiled once again. At times his work was pretty dull. Then there were times like this, when the thrill of the chase filled his soul with macabre delight.

## Chapter Thirteen

RYAN AND DENNY DROVE along scenic Route 1 toward Westerly, Rhode Island, and Watch Hill. Turning south on Watch Hill Road, they burrowed through a wooded and affluent neighborhood until the road became Bay Street, bordered by tourist shops on the left and a boat-congested harbor on the right.

Slowing, they turned right into a small parking lot and parked the SUV facing the dock. They sat for a moment, watching the tourists. In the harbor, moored sailboats rocked with the gentle waves. Sea gulls flew overhead, catching a warm air current and drifting lazily like paper airplanes.

Ryan gestured toward the Olympia Tea Room. "That's the place."

They got out, stretched their legs, and crossed the street. Entering the restaurant, they walked through glass doors into a crowded room dominated by dark wood and straight-back booths set in the middle of a checkered floor. Smaller booths bordered the walls near the windows.

They were greeted by the hostess, a pixie-faced brunette, who led them to a spot near the window. Settling into their seats, they waited for a waitress to serve water and deliver menus.

Ryan pointed toward the far end of the room, where the ceiling appeared to be made of wine glasses. "Four years ago, Melissa was over there wiping the counter. First time I saw her."

Denny twisted in his seat, eyeing the bar

and wooden stools at the end of the room. "Proverbial love at first sight, across a crowded room?"

Ryan remembered the day as if it had happened *yesterday*. Melissa's hair had been pulled back from her forehead and done up in a bun. She'd glanced at him quickly. . . .

"For a split second, our eyes met, and it seemed as if we already knew each other," he recalled.

Denny nodded and added glibly, "So you just *happened* to walk in here, instantly fell in love, and got married twenty-four hours later."

Ryan concealed a wry grin. "No . . . actually it was Bernie's idea."

"Your boss?"

"Yeah, he liked to eat here. Told me about this waitress he'd met. He was impressed with her and wanted to hire her as his secretary. Before we hired Marge, he sent me out here to talk Melissa into applying for a job."

"What happened?"

Ryan chuckled. "Well . . . for one thing I discovered Melissa doesn't type."

"Whoa . . . strike one." Denny laughed. "So the secretary thing fell through. But in the meantime, you fell in love."

"Who's telling this story?"

"Okay, okay." Denny put up his hands. "I'm listening."

"I didn't ask her out right away."

Denny frowned. "Why not?"

"I don't know. She seemed reticent at first. Afraid of her own shadow."

"Didn't seem so shy to *me*."

Ryan considered this. "She trusted you."

Denny stared at him, then grinned.

"So how did *you* win her over?"

"I just kept coming to the restaurant. Asked to be seated in her section. Asked her lots of questions about herself."

Denny nodded. "And?"

"She answered some of them." He forced a smile.

"I think I might've given up."

"I did," Ryan admitted.

Denny seemed surprised.

Their conversation was interrupted when the waitress came to take their order.

Afterward, Ryan observed the activity in the room—tourists and locals. His buddy looked out the window until the waitress returned with their meals. Ryan took one look at the chicken dinner and promptly lost his appetite. At Denny's encouragement, he attempted a few bites, mostly watching Denny eat. *Old friends are the best friends*, Ryan thought.

Eventually, Denny grew silent, studying him from across the table as if biding his time, waiting for the right moment to probe deeper.

They drank their coffee, and the tension mounted. Denny fixed on him an expression that conveyed, *I'm really sorry to have to ask you this.*

Finally, Ryan said, "Why don't you just say it and get it over with?"

Denny smiled apologetically. "You know me too well, ol' buddy."

Placing the coffee cup on the saucer, he felt uneasy. Denny's expression was serious, yet his manner seemed nonthreatening. "Last time I visited, I was bowled over by Melissa's generous hospitality." Denny's voice trailed off.

"She knows how to make someone feel . . . comfortable."

"And yet . . ." Denny continued, "the more I talked to her, the more she seemed to be . . ." He stopped, hesitating once again.

"Go on," Ryan urged.

"Well . . . she seemed to be hiding something."

Ryan shrugged. "Like I said, Mellie has a hard time trusting people. I think it has something to do with her past, with her father abandoning her."

Denny nodded agreeably, a glint in his eye. "You said you gave up on her. What did you mean by that? Did you stop visiting the restaurant?"

"You're really interested in this romance stuff, aren't you?"

"Just trying to help."

"None of this has anything to do with why she left," he found himself saying.

"So, humor me, Ryan. What do we have to do besides wait? Tell me the whole story. Start at the beginning."

Sighing audibly, Ryan felt tense. "All right, you asked for it. I'll even take you to our beach."

"Now you're talking."

They paid the bill and left the restaurant, crossing the narrow two-lane street. Ryan touched the cell phone in his pocket.

Beyond the parking area, they made their way toward a sandy ridge. Napatree Point lay in the distance. The shoreline was part of a long, narrow cape, jutting into Long Island Sound. On a clear day, you could see out past Fishers Island.

Temperatures had risen in the past hour, but sea breezes made the heat bearable. Scattered low-lying clouds hovered at the horizon line as Ryan hiked up a knoll. There, he and Denny peered at the ocean below. Ryan gestured to the stone jetty to their left, and they worked their way through the sand past wild rosebushes, then crossed a small section of the beach before picking their way across the boulders and rocks stacked methodically to create a breakwater.

When they reached the end of the quay, Denny appeared breathless with wonder, staring at the ocean as if he'd never seen it before. "Melissa told me about your wedding. This must be the place."

"We came here one evening. Said our vows before a minister we found in the yellow pages, then tossed white and red rose petals into the ocean."

"Rose petals?" Denny asked. "Another secret meaning?"

"Mixed together, they mean *unity*." He pointed to the west, to the beach that extended toward Napatree Point. "Mellie and I used to come here all the time."

Denny shaded his eyes, following Ryan's gaze. Several families played in the sand, tossing beach balls just a few yards away. A German shepherd barked and scampered around in a frenzy of delight as he chased a Frisbee thrown by a young boy. Farther up the beach, teenagers fished from the shoreline.

"C'mon, let's go closer to the water,"

Ryan said as he led the way.

Away from the rocks, they removed their socks and shoes and headed toward Napatree Point, struggling to walk through the porous sand. As they did, Ryan pointed out the driftwood, seashells, wild rosebushes, sea birds—all the ingredients that gave the beach front its character.

At last he turned to Denny and forced a smile. "When we married, I believed Mellie would open up more in time. And she did . . . in a way. In her *own* way."

Denny regarded him thoughtfully. Ryan turned to gaze out at the ocean, lost in the past, as the waves crashed against the shore. They stood for several minutes before Ryan spoke again, as if speaking from the past, removed from a distance in time.

"I still remember the day I found her here. . . ."

The day had been unusually windy from the start, the sun slipping in and out of clouds. Ryan had arrived at the Olympia Tea Room on a Friday, traveling from Mystic, where he worked. Several weeks had passed since last stopping by the restaurant. He had decided to back off a bit. Melissa, most likely, wasn't interested in romance. At least not with him. Time to move on.

He marveled at how little he knew of her. She liked flowers and art; never spoke of parents, nor brothers and sisters. And she hailed from Minnesota. That was the extent of it. A couple of months of conversations—sometimes a smile.

So what was he doing back here? *Wasting my time*, he thought, as he stood in line waiting to be seated. Finally, Suzie, the hostess, greeted him. She smiled at him as if he were a long-lost friend.

"Hey, stranger," she said. "Haven't seen you for a while."

He'd smiled sheepishly. "Been busy."

"Too busy to eat?" She laughed. "Listen . . . I'm sorry Melissa isn't working today."

*Just as well.* Then Suzie said something that got his attention. "Melissa was asking about you the other day."

He sucked in a breath, trying to act nonchalant. "Oh . . . really?"

Her smile broadened. "Yep." Then she added with a mischievous glint in her eye, "She really *loves* to paint at the beach." She nodded her head to her left, toward the public beach area, out beyond the parking lot. "In fact . . . she spends lots of time there. Especially on her days off." Suzie grabbed a menu. "Nonsmoking section?"

"How 'bout I come back later?"

Suzie smiled knowingly. "Good idea."

Taking the hint, he left the restaurant, making his way to Napatree. Climbing the rim, he searched the beach front and . . . sure enough, Suzie was right. There was Melissa, sporting a yellow sundress, a refreshing change. She was walking barefoot in the sand at the edge of the water. He spotted a tripod several yards back, supporting a wide easel. One white swan, on a sea of glass, was the focal point of the painting.

Still with her back to him, she tossed pieces of bread to a lone swan, who lunged for each bite. Watching her, Ryan was taken with her beauty, her shoulder-length, sun-touched hair flowing freely in the wind. Unaccustomed to seeing her hair like this, he observed her movements. Tanned and lovely, she leaned playfully toward the swan in response to the bird's fluid movements. The agile animal had met its match.

Ryan made his way down the hill and sat in the sand, pretending to contemplate the ocean. The beach was relatively unpopulated. Only a dozen or so people. Some jogged by the sea. Others played ball or sat on beach towels in the sand.

He waited, enjoying the moment. Eventually, Melissa reached the end of the little bag of food she had with her and held up her empty hands in apology. The swan waddled off for greener pastures. She crumpled the bag, carried it back to the beach, and tossed it into the community trash can. Then she stopped to scrutinize her painting, picked up a brush and dabbed some additional blue on the calm sea. She stood back, cocked her head as she peered at her work. Seemingly satisfied, she returned the brush to the palette and strolled toward the ocean, her ankles soon enveloped in the incoming tide. Her profile was now visible to him as she gazed toward the horizon with obvious wonderment. A gust of wind had the nerve to assail her, but she shook her head defiantly, clearing her face from errant strands of hair and pinning down her tresses with one hand.

With the sun on her face, illuminating her near-angelic features, she turned bravely to the zephyr. Smiling, she closed her eyes dreamily, as if lost in the ocean's beauty.

As he watched from his spot in the sand, Ryan thought he saw tears on her face, although he couldn't be sure. She brushed her cheek with the back of her hand, opening her eyes and squinting against the sun.

After a time she seemed tired and turned to head back to her easel. At that moment she spotted him. Butterflies took flight in his stomach as he registered the recognition in her face, embarrassed to have been caught mid-worship.

She broke into a full smile as he rose to meet her.

"Hi!" she said enthusiastically. "I didn't see you. How long have you been here?"

"Not long," he replied, mustering his best casual smile. "Nice painting."

"Thanks. Did you see the *real* swan? I've lived here three months, and I haven't seen anything like it." Without pause, she began packing up her palette and brushes.

"I hope I'm not interrupting your work."

She shook her head. "I've been painting for hours, so . . . no." She removed the canvas, then folded the tripod. "Sit with me?" she asked, sitting down on the beach, demurely crossing her legs. Ryan joined her as they faced the ocean together.

She turned to look at him. "I'm glad you came. Haven't seen you for a while." She broke into another grin. "Suzie must've told you I was here."

He let out a short, nervous laugh. "You must get a lot of guys asking for your number."

She shrugged and removed the canvas. "It happens. Just not the *right* guys." She wrinkled her nose. "Sorry. I'm not usually such a flirt."

Surprised by her openness, Ryan wondered what had happened to his shy, reticent waitress. "You don't have to flirt with me."

"Why's that?"

He wanted to say, *Because you had me from the first day I saw you. . . .* But he didn't. He just shrugged, tongue-tied.

She laughed softly, elbowing his arm. "You're kind of shy."

Humored by the irony, Ryan replied, "You wouldn't think so . . . if you knew me."

"I hope to have that chance," she said, not missing a beat.

He turned to face her, but she looked away, toward the clouds, at the fragments of sunshine peeking through. "I love New England, but I wish it were sunnier here," she remarked.

"More like Minnesota?"

She pushed a strand of hair behind her ear, then regarded him mischievously. "You remembered."

"I listened," Ryan replied.

"Actually, Minnesota isn't consistently sunny, either." Then she paused. "So . . . do you remember my nickname, too?"

"Sure . . ." He paused, too, for effect.

"Well?"

"It's Mellie."

"Wow! I *am* impressed."

Their attention was distracted by a large sailboat, traveling south toward the outer ocean. "Have you been sailing yet?" he asked.

"No, but I'd *love* to go. Do you sail?"

"Yeah, but you can't go with me, you know. You shouldn't trust strangers," he said with a wink and a grin.

She nodded, as if giving his remark serious attention. "Well then, we'll just have to go sailing on our *second* date." She raised her eyebrows. "What do you say?"

"Confident, aren't we?" He liked her spunk.

"Just hopeful." Her expression turned more serious and she appraised him gently, her eyes a soft blue green. "I *didn't* trust you at first, you know. I don't trust most people."

"Can't blame you for that," he said softly. "Why did you change your mind?"

She grimaced a bit. "It's silly, I guess."

But he prodded her, had to know.

She was coy but met his gaze as if searching for an appropriate response. "Maybe it was . . . your eyes." She bit her lower lip, stifling a giggle, gauging his expression.

He laughed. "You're flirting again."

"Maybe."

A knowing look passed between them, and Ryan realized he'd succeeded at last. He had won her over. Their natural rapport, so-called love at first sight—a bit of a sputter initially—roared into full-blown romance. From that moment on they became inseparable.

A few months later, after a whirlwind courtship, they married on the stone pier, just before sunset.

Ryan finished their love story, waiting for Denny's reaction.

Tossing a pebble into the water, Denny stood and brushed sand from his slacks. "Why the sudden change in her behavior?" he asked skeptically.

"I never knew exactly. She just decided to . . . trust me."

Denny nodded, apparently lost in thought. Then—"Maybe you should've wondered if you could trust *her*. You knew so little about her."

"Maybe so." He waved his hand nonchalantly. "Ready to go?"

"Sure."

Ryan led the way back, plodding toward the stone pier. They climbed the ridge and headed back to the car.

Reaching the Bronco, Ryan unlocked the

car, but Denny leaned on the door without getting in. "Listen, I didn't mean to pry, okay?"

"Yeah, you are a bit on the nosy side," he quipped, looking back toward the ridge. *Their* beach.

"So what's the next step in finding Melissa?" Denny asked, doing it again.

"If I haven't heard from Melissa by Monday, I'll report her credit cards and cell phone. Hopefully trace her location."

Denny frowned, reaching for the car door. "I guess I'm not very good at this waiting game."

He had to smile. "Sure you are. You've waited years for me. You know—Christianity and all?"

They got in the car. "I'm *still* waiting," Denny said.

"See? You have the patience of a saint."

"You're quoting Revelation, my pagan friend." Denny grinned and shook his head in mock disgust.

Ryan was glad to be heading home as he pulled out of the parking space and onto the road. There was little left to be said as dusk delivered a panorama of color. Perhaps a sign of hope. . . .

# · Chapter Fourteen ·

RYAN CHECKED the digital clock on his nightstand. 4:21. In a couple of hours, dawn. He pushed on his pillow, turning away from the window, struggling to recall what day it was.

*Sunday . . .*

His friend, Denny Franklin, was sleeping down the hall in the guest room. Daisy was . . . where? Sitting up, he peered around the dimly lit room. He spied the dog sprawled on the floor, her head draped over one of Ryan's slippers.

*Sleep on, girl.*

Melissa, on the other hand, was probably holed up in a motel somewhere. Did she miss him? Was she lonely?

*Mellie . . . call me. Pick up the phone, let me know you're okay.*

An image flickered in his memory, and stumbling out of bed, he located Melissa's note on the dresser. Holding it again, he re-lived the first moment of discovery, two days ago. He lay on the bed again and pushed back the covers, feeling as if *he* were the one awakening in a strange motel, in an unfamiliar town. . . .

Daisy roused a bit and pattered over to the edge of the bed. Placing her paws on the mattress, she hesitated as if reconsidering the height.

"Come on, girl," Ryan replied, patting the bed. "S'okay."

Suddenly confident, Daisy burst from the floor, landing awkwardly on his stomach.

"Umph!"

The dog went straight for his face, blanketing him with sloppy saliva. He covered his face with his hands, protecting himself from the barrage. "Too early to play," he said. "Go back to sleep."

Daisy stopped and began to whine. Following her gaze to Mellie's side of the bed, Ryan felt renewed sadness. "I know, girl. I miss her, too."

Still whimpering, Daisy snuggled into the cavity at his side, and Ryan stroked her fur, attempting to comfort his pet. Yet his own fears remained undiminished.

◆ ◆ ◆ ◆ ◆

Melissa sat at the window watching the rising sun wink through the trees. Birds twittered in a large oak tree just outside the window, and beyond Lela's abode, farmers finished up early-morning milking, no doubt their stomachs rumbling for breakfast.

Having slept more soundly than the previous night, she felt better. Hiding her car away had served to lessen her worries, and she'd written her message to Ryan at last—a loving memo that told him she was safe. He would be somewhat relieved, she knew, though he would still wonder where she was and why she had left him.

*Relax now*, she told herself, still wondering why the expected phone call had not come. Returning from town yesterday afternoon, she'd inquired of Lela if there had been any calls or messages. "Not once has the phone rung," Lela told her, removing two plump pies from the oven.

Concealing her disappointment, Melissa climbed the stairs to her rented room. The weekend was possibly the holdup. Surely by Monday she would hear something. For now she ought to use this time to unwind, take advantage of the gentle setting, this quaint society of people, seemingly set in the middle of the nineteenth century.

Reaching up, she slid back the Priscilla curtains slightly, seeing the many horse-drawn carriages going up the narrow lane— more of them than yesterday. Quite a parade of them, heading . . . where? To a common church building, perhaps. At breakfast, she would ask Lela where Amish folk went en masse.

Here she was, the second day away from home. Lela had seemed agreeable about allowing her to stay another night. In fact, she assumed that Lela was enjoying the company, since she seemed to be going out of her way to serve hot meals, home-baked goodies, and delicious cold drinks. For a woman thirty-something, it seemed strange that she had no work outside the home. So the extra income was surely welcome.

Kneeling beside the chair, Lela folded her hands in prayer. "Dear Lord, please make me a blessing to my houseguest this day." On behalf of her additional concerns, she prayed about her great-aunt's ill health, a friend's pending marriage, and a second cousin's need for direction in ministry. She also breathed a prayer of thanksgiving for God's abundant blessings. The earlier sense of doom had vanished completely.

Her father had taught her and her siblings to lift high the name of the Lord in gratitude for all He had done in their lives and in the lives of those around them. "We must never live unto ourselves," he would often say. "Yet we must surely recognize what a blessing our heritage is, a privilege, really, to serve the Lord."

"Now, Pop," her mother would some-times chide him, "we aren't any better for being Plain than the next person."

"Well, now that's the truth," Papa might say. Yet Lela felt her father was a little bit proud of his spiritual heritage, the fact that for more than four generations, there were God-fearing Mennonites on both sides of the family tree.

*All well and good*, she thought, getting up from her morning prayer. Yet she knew the importance of a person yielding his or her heart to the Savior—a personal relation-ship—not relying on the faith of others who'd gone before. With all her heart, she yearned for God and His ways. She longed to be a servant, as the Lord was to His own disciples while here on earth. In spite of her meager means, she wanted to be a giver, as well.

She remembered a poem Mama had taught her as a child, about the camel. He kneels in the morning to take the burden upon his back and kneels again in the evening to have it removed. Her prayer ritual went something like that, too, she sometimes felt. Not that she was weighed down with the cares of life like some folk, no. But she was a willing vessel, prepared to lay down her life if need be to show love for others. "Shake me, Lord. May I hurt for my neighbor who may not know your saving grace," she often prayed.

Today she wept on her knees. "Help me build bridges to a lost world . . . beginning with Melissa."

The dear girl was clearly perplexed, suffering. When Melissa had inquired about phone calls, Lela was sure she saw grave concern in the blue eyes. Who or what was the woman afraid of? And what was so urgent as to keep waiting for a call, not to mention hiding her car?

Sometimes in the past twenty-four hours, just thinking on it, Lela was tempted to give way to fear herself—having such an apprehensive person in the house. Truth was, she'd prayed Melissa into her care last Friday evening. So without a shadow of doubt, she knew the Lord had sent the woman her way.

◆　◆　◆　◆　◆

Hours later, sleep coming in snatches, Ryan slipped out from under the covers, leaving Daisy to nap in the bed. Tossing his robe aside, he showered, dressed, then headed down the hall, looking in through the partially open door to Denny's room. Bed made . . . room empty. Denny was an early riser. He found his friend sitting in the living room, reading his Bible.

"Are you up for some church after breakfast?" he asked, expecting Denny to fall off the sofa in shock.

"That's *my* line," Denny said, eyes wide. "You're not messing with my head, are you?"

"What else do we have to do today—besides wait by the phone?"

"Say no more." Denny grabbed the phone book, flipped through the yellow pages under churches.

Ryan headed to the kitchen to cook breakfast—fried eggs, German sausage, and whole-wheat waffles—the sort of food he and Melissa rarely ate. They preferred whole-grain cereal and fresh fruit. Healthy fare.

"What about the Village Church . . . in Groton?" Denny called from the living room. "Okay with you?"

"Whatever you decide." Typically, on other occasions when Denny had come to visit—if Melissa was around, that is—no one had suggested attending church. But this time things were so up in the air, it didn't matter to Ryan how they spent the day. To some degree time had ceased. He was merely marking it, hour by hour, till Mellie contacted him.

Unaccustomed to the aroma of rich food,

Daisy whined incessantly, begging for a bite. Ryan resisted Daisy's pleading, and sat down to eat. Denny, however, gave in, tossing Daisy a taste of sausage after Ryan nodded his reluctant consent.

"You have to know, she'll get fat," he cautioned.

"Maybe, but she'll love me for it," Denny replied. "Besides, after I leave, you can put her back on a diet."

Daisy nuzzled her head into Denny's leg as he rubbed her neck. Then she lifted her paws to his lap—a household no-no—glancing at Ryan as if to gauge his response.

"See, she loves me best," Denny said, giving Daisy a full rubdown.

"She craves people food. You just happen to be the delivery boy."

"No-o," Denny cooed at Daisy. "You love me for my mind, don't you? Want to come home with me and have people food every day?"

Ryan chuckled. "You're corrupting my dog."

"Sorry, chief."

◆　◆　◆　◆　◆

"Would you care to go with me to the Mennonite meetinghouse today?" Lela asked her guest, serving up hot scrambled eggs and bacon.

Melissa looked up from the table, a rather startled expression on her face. "Well, I . . . I don't know." Then, quickly, "No. I'd better stay here."

"To wait for your phone call?"

Nodding, Melissa spread rhubarb jelly on her toast. "Any other Sunday . . ."

"Just not today?" she said, hoping Melissa might elaborate.

"I wondered . . ."

"Yes?"

Melissa paused, frowning, before she continued. "Where were all the horses and buggies headed this morning?"

"Up mighty early, were you?"

"The clip-clopping of horses' hooves awakened me just after dawn." Melissa's face was drawn and serious, though she seemed a bit more rested than before. "I didn't count them, but there were far more than yesterday."

"Ah yes, I know just what you mean." She reached for her coffee cup and leaned back in her chair. Glancing up at the ivy vines encircling her windows, she explained, "It's Sunday-go-to-meetin' in Lancaster County, which means many of my Amish neighbors are heading out to house church."

"You mean they attend church at some-one's house?" Melissa seemed altogether surprised at this revelation.

"Two hundred and more in some cases." She explained how the Old Order folk removed various partitions in their living rooms, making it possible to accommodate that many church members. "Same with Amish weddings and funerals. They make room for their people. The Plain folk are a close-knit bunch."

Melissa nodded, but there was a faraway look in her eyes.

"The horses and carriages were hurrying off to worship services all over this area," she added. " 'Tis a common sight every other Sunday morning, round here." She went on to say that the Old Order Amish have what they call "off Sundays," when they don't gather for preaching but spend the day reading their German and English Bibles, visiting and resting.

"Do your sister and husband ever have house church?" asked Melissa, gaze intent.

"Sometimes. With so many folk per church district, a family doesn't have preaching service too often. But I think they're due to have a meeting at their place here pretty soon." She rose, went to the pantry, and looked on the back of the door at the calendar. "Yes, next month. September ninth, in fact."

Melissa was quiet for the longest time, then—"I really liked your sister."

"Elizabeth?"

"She reminds me of someone from my childhood." *Mrs. Browning's housekeeper,* she thought.

"Elizabeth's a sweet girl, and she loves her family, as anybody can see."

"She must have a little store back behind the house," Melissa remarked.

Chuckling, Lela replied, "Oh my, does she ever. Suppose you saw the sign."

"I couldn't help but be curious."

"Well, if you stay on another day or so, I'll be happy to take you over, give you a look around the country store." Lela sighed, thinking she ought to stop talking so awful much and eat her breakfast. She didn't want to be late for church. "Elizabeth and I keep the store well stocked with all sorts of hand-made items."

"So, you work for Elizabeth—making things?"

She nodded. "Quite a lot of crocheting and sewing, and sometimes I make quilted pillow shams and bed coverings to match."

"Then, you're an artist," Melissa said.

She felt her cheeks get warm. "Well, now I wouldn't go that far."

"But you *are!*" insisted Melissa. "I love to paint flowers, the sea. I like to think of myself as an artist, too."

"What else do you like to do—for hobbies, I mean?"

Melissa sighed, getting that distant look in her eyes. "Making scrapbooks is one of my big interests, but it's been a long time since I worked on anything new."

Noting her wedding band, Lela wondered how much she should ask. Wouldn't want to pry where she ought not to.

"My husband enjoys our vacation scrapbooks," Melissa said, opening up the subject Lela was curious about.

"Where do you like to go together . . . on vacation?"

"Vermont and New Hampshire, especially. We get off the main roads and stay in small towns. Go exploring, I guess you could say."

She might've posed another question, but just then, the phone rang. Melissa let out a startled sound, locking eyes with her, but Lela put her guest at ease. "I'll get that," she said, rising up from the table.

Turned out the call wasn't for Melissa, but for Lela. "Do you want a ride for church?" asked Sadie Nan, her church friend. "My brother's in town from Indiana. I thought the three of us could go out to eat after, if you don't have other plans."

*Paul Martin . . .*

She'd heard through the community grapevine that Paul's wife had passed away, leaving him a widower with a young son.

"Well, I don't . . . know, uh, really." She disliked stumbling around like this. Not with Melissa sitting across the room, no doubt wondering what had her so flustered all of a sudden.

"Oh, please say you'll come, Lela. We'll have the *best* time. Besides, my brother's been asking 'bout you."

She would've said, "What's he asking?" but held her tongue. No, it would never do for Paul and Sadie Nan to show up at her door, what with Melissa here. Still, she was more than curious about Paul. Just why was he in town anyway?

Looking out the window, she could see the sun shining nice and bright. Looked to be a pretty day. "I believe I'll ride my bike to service," she managed. "Maybe another time."

"Okay, but I'll hold you to it," Sadie said. "I'll see you at church."

Melissa tried to ignore the phone conversation going on uncomfortably near. She stared out the wide windows that comprised a good portion of the west wall in the dining area of the kitchen. Today, while Lela was at church, might be a good time to do some exploring. At least, she might venture out past the patio courtyard directly behind the windows, near the low stone walls where pink and purple clematis spilled over native stone, to the perennial borders and herb gardens and tall hedges so characteristic of English gardens. A rose-covered pergola reminded her of the years spent with Mrs. Browning, the gardener extraordinaire who'd mothered her well into college.

Turning back to her coffee and the delicious "sticky buns," she glanced up to see Lela's face turning a bright pink, brown eyes glistening. She was sputtering like a schoolgirl. Well, what was this? Did Lela have a boyfriend?

She continued to observe as the phone conversation ensued. From what she could gather, someone was inviting Lela somewhere, and now she was declining. Why Melissa cared at all about any of this, she didn't know. Sure beat racing around on the highway, though, trying to ditch the contemptible man who'd tried to bump her off the road.

He probably would have killed her—if he had gotten close enough.

The area behind the house beckoned her, and she found herself gazing with longing, eager to stroll around the grounds. She spied what she thought was a sundial centered in a bed of snow-white and rose-colored alyssum. Leaning forward, then getting up, she moved to the window and peered out. Yes, it *was* a sundial! She favored the sundial above all the garden trappings in her own backyard retreat.

She knew well the rewards, the pleasures reaped from spending time in one's garden. Of all her hobbies, frittering away the hours doing the quiet, contemplative work of pruning, digging, weeding, planting, watering—all the necessary tending required—gardening was her thing. She often wondered if her years with Mrs. Browning had fostered such a love, wondered if her own mother, long deceased, might not have had a green thumb, as well. From her own enthusiasm for lovely plants, flowers, and shrubs had come her passion for painting. Daddy hadn't seemed all that fond of her childish sketches, but as she grew and her interest changed, he'd shown considerable amazement for her watercolor renderings, especially of roses.

"If you'll excuse me, I better see to cleaning up the kitchen," Lela said when the phone conversation ended.

"Let me help," Melissa said, remembering her manners. "In fact, why don't you go and dress for church. I'll finish up here."

For a fleeting moment she thought Lela was going to reject her offer, but then the big brown eyes softened. "That's thoughtful of you. Thank you, Melissa."

"Please . . . call me Mellie," she said all of a sudden.

Lela nodded, all smiles. "Well, sure I will. How nice of you to say so."

Going to the sink, Melissa turned on the hot water. "Have a good day," she said softly.

"You too." Lela turned to go, then paused. "If for any reason your phone call is delayed, feel free to stay on, all right?"

She was taken aback by the woman's generosity. "I'll keep that in mind, thanks."

*Mutual admiration society*, she thought. All this gratitude exchanged. Well, it *was* a lovely reprieve from the nightmare she'd experienced two days ago. To think she may have found a trustworthy friend in this Plain woman. . . .

In no time the kitchen was spotless, the place mats shaken over the sink and replaced at the table. With one purpose in mind—she would give herself permission to relax all day—Melissa hurried to the back of the house, to the four-season porch overlooking Lela's backyard garden. Sure, it was the Lord's Day, as Lela had so aptly put it, but the day was also Mellie's. She would guard the notion, see to it that nothing marred the next carefree hours.

## *Chapter Fifteen*

WHEN RYAN PULLED INTO the Village Church parking lot, the area was so crowded he had to back out and park across the street. The church building itself was a white colonial—classic New England architecture—complete with columns and a tall steeple.

They entered through the large double doors to the sound of hymn singing. A young woman greeted them with a smile and offered each of them a bulletin. Denny told her they were visiting.

"Welcome—and make yourself at home," she said. "I think you'll like it here."

"I'm sure we will," Denny replied quickly, with a sidelong glance at Ryan.

Heading into the sanctuary, Ryan wondered how he would survive an hour of dull religiosity. He was only doing this for Denny, who seemed thrilled to have his company.

He sat through a few hymns and some brief announcements. Then the pastor told a story about Jesus meeting a woman at a well, adding humorous anecdotes and personal illustrations. To Ryan's surprise, he found the sermon rather interesting. No protracted conjecture on theology, no demands for money, not even a hint of condemnation.

After the service, while driving back to Mystic, Ryan said little. The minister's words echoed in his mind: *Drink the living water . . . and never thirst again.* He wondered what Mellie would have thought of the sermon, knowing the answer instinctively. She would have enjoyed it.

Yet in the past few years, he'd given little encouragement to her religious preference. Hadn't she purchased the picture of Christ, so out of place in their living room? She'd also painted the cross in Denny's painting— this, very recently. Yes, she was definitely inclined in that direction.

"How'd you like the sermon?" Denny asked, interrupting Ryan's reverie.

"Short and sweet."

"You're hopeless," Denny moaned. "Did you hear him recite Melissa's favorite quote?"

Ryan nodded, remembering her framed poster of homeless people standing in a soup kitchen line. Under the picture was the caption *The mass of men lead lives of quiet desperation.* Last year Mellie had decided to read the book *Walden,* sometimes even reading aloud to him.

"So you must think religion is the answer to man's feelings of desperation," he replied, glancing over at Denny.

"Not religion—"

"And not *everyone* feels desperate, right?"

Denny paused. "Listen, I didn't come here to pound away at you—not this weekend. I mean . . . what with Melissa . . . and everything, maybe this just isn't the right time."

"I'm a big boy," Ryan said. "Answer the question."

"About desperation? Okay. I disagree with you. I think *everyone* feels some degree of underlying despair. We just call it by different names. I mean, not everyone's thrashing around in a miserable state. But most of us do seem to be dissatisfied, discontented. And another thing . . . we're all *addicted.*"

"Addicted," Ryan echoed flatly.

"Yeah. It goes hand in hand with discontent. We're addicted to having *more.* Getting more. More with a capital *M.* But *more* is never enough. We're like rats on a treadmill. We never catch up with the cheese, but we keep chasing it anyway. We spend our whole lives running after something—anything—to give us fulfillment, to satisfy our longing, our insatiable desire. We think more money, new loves, more notoriety will finally make the difference."

He stared out the window for a moment before continuing. "More of anything *never* satisfies, because ultimately we're looking in the wrong place. Most of us grow old thinking that feeling lost and lonely is simply a part of being human . . . but it isn't."

"*Some* people seem pretty happy," Ryan objected.

"Are they? *Really* happy?" Denny's voice trailed off. "The rich and famous often come to the end of their lives still feeling lost and unfulfilled. It's not money or fame that satisfies, Ryan. It's Christ who offers the *more* we're all seeking—the water that quenches our spiritual thirst."

Ryan shook his head. "But most Christians don't act like they're drinking living water."

Denny shrugged. "We only get little sips, here and there. Brief glimpses of eternity. Not the full deal—yet. But, ah . . . those glimpses."

"So how is any of this proof of Christianity?"

"Well . . . think about it. As human beings, we have complex physical and emotional needs. All those needs have a corresponding fulfillment. You might say that experience has proven to us that if we *need* something, fulfillment of that need exists somewhere, somehow. For example, our bodies need nourishment to survive, which proves the existence of food and water. We need oxygen to breathe, which proves the existence of air. We need light and warmth, which proves the sun exists. We desire to procreate, which proves the existence of sex. We get lonely simply because friendship and community exists. But even with all these physical and emotional needs satisfied, we *still* feel unfulfilled. Why? Because we have a deeper spiritual need—a need for God. And that, my friend, proves the existence of a Creator."

"Now you're sounding like Socrates," Ryan said.

"Would our spiritual need be the single exception—our one need that *doesn't* have a corresponding fulfillment?" Denny asked. "That seems unlikely. Let me put it another way: If it's proof you want, proof is in the pudding—in the *tasting*. Come to Christ and you'll find the evidence."

"But people need the evidence *first*, don't they?" Ryan said, adjusting his grip on the steering wheel.

"Most people don't need proof per se. They need to be *willing* to repent. The demand for evidence is often a smoke screen for hanging on to sin. For every reason I give you, you can find another objection. If you *want* to believe, you'll find my reasons are sufficient—even *compelling*. If you *don't* want to believe, no amount of logic will convince you."

"Back up a sec. That's where you lose me, Den. The *sin* part. Remember our college philosophy class?"

"Sure, I spent years recovering."

"We were taught that sin is a myth," Ryan said.

Denny grimaced. "So you're saying that evil is simply—"

"Ignorance," Ryan interrupted.

"Most skeptics argue that evil and suffering disproves the existence of God. But you're telling me evil doesn't even exist?"

"Of course it exists. But as a human race we can do *better*. Better psychology. Better treatment centers. Better schools. The worst evil we commit is telling our kids how bad they are. If we loved our children unconditionally, imparting genuine self-esteem, our so-called sinful behavior disappears."

"I agree with you, but only to a point," Denny said. "Sin goes much deeper into the human psyche, far beyond superficial behavior. As a human race we're sunk in moral depravity. We're bad to the bone. And that's *why* we experience such desperation and insatiable longing. Because our sin separates us from God. We need *divine* redemption, not better schools or psychological Band-Aids."

Steering the car into the restaurant parking lot, Ryan replied, "I'm sorry, Denny. It's just not working for me."

"Which part?"

"The whole thing."

◆ ◆ ◆ ◆ ◆

Green fields, dotted with black-and-white cows, widened out to meet the sky to the north. Silhouettes of windmills and silos punctuated the landscape, and flocks of crows flew overhead, like great dark clouds.

Melissa paused at the screen door, a slight shiver running down her back in spite of the warm day. Set against the gray slate floor and white clapboard walls, the cozy porch tempted her to remain in the confines of its protection. She *was* safe here. How ridiculous to think otherwise.

Opening the screen door, she ventured out. She wished she had her palette and a canvas. Her eyes embraced a myriad of colors and textures—Cleome spider flowers, their slender stems rising four feet high, topped with a deep pink crown. Amassed in a bold grouping that ran along the stone walkway from the house, the tender annuals withstood the sun's strongest rays during summer. This she knew from her growing-up years at Mrs. Browning's house.

Stepping down into the garden area, she felt as if she were wandering back to that familiar place in faraway Colorado. . . .

"Come here and look at this, Mellie dear," Mrs. Browning called, motioning her to the rows of golden yarrow growing near the birdbath.

She scurried across the yard, blades of grass cool beneath her bare feet. Always, she was interested in seeing what Mrs. Browning was up to, what new bud or blossom she'd discovered. The woman was a master gardener, and everyone in the small town of Palmer Lake knew it. People would stop by or call for gardening advice, sometimes bringing a feeble vine or distressed cutting to her for help. Melissa had seen Mrs. Browning work miracles with her green thumb.

This woman her father had chosen to raise her, as designated in his will, was vivacious and full of energy when she worked in her garden. But housework didn't thrill her, and Mr. Browning, at one point, decided to hire a housekeeper, who made short order of the dusting and vacuuming, much to Mrs. Browning's delight. "All the more time to talk to my flowers," she said, going about her business in the yard.

"What'd you want to show me?" Mellie squatted down near the yarrow.

Mrs. Browning's eyes shone. "Just imagine what fun we could have drying these naturally."

"What for?"

"Oh, we can use them for crafts, you know, for presents."

She liked the idea and followed the woman to her rose gardens, where twenty different varieties bloomed, a difficult task in such a dry climate. Yet Mrs. Browning persevered, adding mulch and fertilizer, installing a drip hose, and as always, whispering her sweet talk.

Mr. Browning stopped to listen when his wife spoke of another "very special rose garden" in the southernmost section of the yard.

"That one's in memory of your father,"

Mrs. Browning said, pointing to the garden plot, reminding Melissa once again. "How your daddy loved his pure white roses," she said, leaning down to breathe in the sweet fragrance of dozens of ivory-colored blossoms.

"White roses stand for silence and innocence," Mellie said, remembering all that her father had taught her of the language of flowers.

"And secrecy, too, don't forget," Mrs. Browning said. "White roses have more than just a few meanings."

Mr. Browning was nodding his head as if to reinforce the importance of it all.

"More than any of that, always remember how much your father loved *you*, dear." Mrs. Browning gave her a little hug, then went about her work.

*Always remember . . .*

Lela was ever so glad for partly cloudy skies, a reprieve from the typical dog days of August, as she pedaled her bicycle to the meetinghouse down the road. Less than a mile away, the church was accessible either by foot or her favorite mode of transportation, her old ten-speed bicycle. The exercise was good for her, and besides that she liked to talk to God as she rode.

Arriving at the small brick structure, she parked her bike near the side door and hurried into church, feeling terribly uncomfortable knowing that Sadie Nan and her brother would be arriving any minute. She'd first met Sadie during elementary school days, both girls having attended the Amish-Mennonite school two miles in the opposite direction, over on Snake Hill Road.

Sadie's brother was a year older, a student at the same school. For a time, he seemed to care for Lela. So much so that during their last years of high school, she began to expect a marriage proposal from her dear Paul. Around that time a new girl with strawberry blond hair and a coquettish grin caught his fancy, coming between them, dashing Lela's hopes. Never interfering to save their relationship, she followed her mother's example of a submissive attitude and quiet spirit, and several months after Paul's graduation, rumor had it that he'd married the blond girl and moved to Indiana.

"Plenty more good fish in the sea," Sadie had offered in an attempt to comfort her. "You'll see."

Wounded in spirit, Lela's heart was so broken she never cared to hope for another love. She poured herself into her singleness, helping her siblings with each new babe as the little ones came along, tending to her gardens, and sewing her fine stitchery to put food on the table and tires on her bicycle. Thankfully, her house was paid for, the result of her oldest brother's wise investment. Another brother paid her yearly property taxes and the utility bill each month, so she was quite content to work for Elizabeth, helping keep the shelves stocked with handmade goods at the little country store. The money from her larger-ticket items—such as the quilted coverlets and pillows—easily paid for phone bills and groceries, with money left over to give to the Mennonite missions and benevolence fund at church.

On the left side of the church where the women sat, she found a spot next to several cousins, happy to be surrounded by loving faces. She bowed her head in prayer, asking the Lord to anoint their minister's sermon, that he might break the Bread of Life so needed for the week ahead. She prayed for wisdom and help from her heavenly Father regarding any possible encounter and renewed friendship with widower Martin.

And she prayed for Melissa, who'd decided to stay at home, waiting for a phone call. "Touch her with your grace and love today," she whispered, then felt the Holy Spirit prompting her to pray further. "Please send your ministering servants—angels—to watch over Melissa . . . over *both* of us. In Jesus' name, amen."

◆ ◆ ◆ ◆ ◆

Ryan and Denny drove to Noah's in Stonington Borough and ordered halibut for lunch. Later they stopped in at the Stonington Lighthouse, built in 1823 on Stonington Point. The stone tower—thirty feet high—had once supported a lantern with ten oil lamps and silver reflectors. Denny appreciated the maritime history, commenting on the numerous relics from Stonington's whaling and sealing ships.

They spent the afternoon watching a preseason game between the Patriots and the Bengals. Ryan tolerated the game while Denny phoned his girlfriend on Ryan's cell phone, keeping the main line free in case Melissa called. They chatted for a good half hour, then Denny made another call to some kid he'd met on the plane.

Meanwhile, Ryan paged through several of Melissa's recent journals, reading her latest entries, searching for clues. *Anything.* He opened the scrapbook she'd recently finished of last year's trip to Manchester, Vermont. Picture after picture of peak foliage. Besides painting, Melissa loved the creative process of making scrapbooks. "The preservation of family history," she liked to call it. Every one of their vacations was imaginatively detailed for posterity, including ticket stubs, pictures, and brochures.

He couldn't handle even a few minutes of this self-induced torture. Setting the vacation scrapbook aside, Ryan's depression deepened. His single strand of hope—that Mellie would eventually call—was beginning to unravel. He'd expected her to phone him within a few hours of her leaving. But the hours were turning into days.

◆ ◆ ◆ ◆ ◆

Ryan walked out through the sun-room door, following the short path past Melissa's rose garden to the dock, all the while replaying events from the past several weeks.

The sun had already set. Denny was napping in front of TV news. The moon's silvery glow cast an eerie reflection on the ocean stillness, accompanied by a corresponding sense of endlessness.

*Most men lead lives of quiet desperation. . . .*

"You don't know the half of it, Mr. Thoreau," Ryan whispered, sitting on the dock with his legs dangling over the edge. Minutes later Daisy joined him, padding across the sun-bleached wood to nuzzle his back.

He hugged his dog. Then, facing the vast sea, Ryan recalled the day he'd proposed to his darling girl, their subsequent private wedding ceremony on Watch Hill, and her tear-streaked face when he'd kissed her.

"I'm so happy," she'd whispered with upturned face, eyes shining. "I wish today would never end."

"I won't let it end, Mellie," he'd promised, only to fail.

## Chapter Sixteen

RUSSIAN-BORN DIMA IVANOV had been abandoned as an infant on the doorstep of an orphanage. Left in a crib for weeks on end with no attention and scarcely enough nourishment to survive, he'd suffered the kind of neglect that has been known to breed severe psychological disturbances, even psychopathic tendencies. At least, that's what his sympathetic psychiatrist had told him when he was sent to a Psikhushka, a psychiatric hospital for troubled youths. Secretly, Ivanov regarded his lack of conscience as a *gift*.

Escaping from the Russian institution, he lived on the streets of Moscow, joined a gang, and made money through scams and extortion. Bred from the deep pain of abandonment, anger dominated his every waking moment. The pleasure of settling a grudge became so empowering, he craved the thrill of revenge.

Ivanov was only twenty-one when he escaped the state police and stowed aboard a commerce ship bound for America. Once in New York, he took the American name "Jim" Ivanov, practiced his English compulsively until his accent was only slight, and joined forces with two other Russian exiles.

Thirty years later Dima kept close protective ties with his *krysha*—homeland compatriots who sent him their dirty cash for laundering. And though they had lackeys to do the dirty work, Dima was a reckless man. He enjoyed implementing the day-to-day details of his criminal operations. Especially . . . *enforcement*.

Ivanov and his "partners" ruled their underworld through the twin powers of *fear* and *greed*. In the Russian homeland, bribery was a way of life. But in America, bribery was much more difficult. Dima and his men were required to pay more for criminal complicity, to select their criminal participants more carefully, and to be more persuasive.

So they bribed policemen who were

struggling to feed their families on low wages. They bribed judges, jealous of exorbitant attorney fees, eager to exchange favorable rulings for briefcases full of cash. They located dishonest corporate executives and bribed them for insider corporate information. Lastly, they bribed disgruntled bank officials in exchange for laundering their Russian cash.

Ivanov insured the preservation of his criminal operations through the judicious use of fear. His numerous greedy participants, including the fools they couldn't bribe, were taught the consequences of noncompliance. Dima had been arrested countless times, but never had a jury convicted him. Witnesses either disappeared or jurors dissented in terror.

Now, at two o'clock in the morning, Dima surveyed the Denlinger home, barely visible in the distance. Satisfied that the situation was benign, he worked his way through the pasture to the dirt road where his gray sedan was parked and drove to within half a mile of Lela Denlinger's home. With the aid of binoculars, he spotted the gleaming porch light populated by mosquitoes and moths.

Inside the cottage, Melissa James lay sleeping, the single offspring of the man who had humiliated him in California, the scene of Ivanov's *only* failed operation. He had taken out his revenge on the man, but Dima's rage was not spent.

His pulse quickened, nerves heightened as addictive fixation set in. He placed the binoculars on the console and caught his breath, overwhelmed by his need for retribution. First, he would get her to talk; then when he had learned the location of the money, he would enact his revenge.

Focusing his binoculars, he swept the surrounding area, assuring himself again of his safety. Earlier, he'd considered approaching the small house from the back. Such caution seemed unnecessary. In fact, there was no reason why he couldn't simply park the car on the street, stroll up to the front door, and slip inside.

Setting the binoculars aside, he patted his shirt pocket containing the Sodium Pentothal, also known as truth serum. While it didn't guarantee complete "truth-telling," the drug effectively unhinged the recipient's inhibition.

His left coat pocket contained a bottle of a nervous-system drug designed to stop the heart—undetectable in an autopsy. And finally, under his left shoulder, his holster concealed the 10mm Glock pistol—his weapon of choice, equipped with a silencer. Unlikely he'd need the gun tonight. These women would be frightened into compliance with a nasty stare.

*Show time.*

Focusing the lenses on the Denlinger house for one last look, he gave a sharp intake of breath.

He whispered a curse, putting down the glasses, attempting to make sense of it.

He put the binoculars to his eyes again, squinting and frowning. Sure enough, two men lumbered about the front yard of the Denlinger cottage. Both were blond and bearded, wearing straw hats, tan suspenders, and wide-legged black trousers. *Amishmen*, he thought, profoundly irritated. He continued to watch them from a distance as they roamed about the front yard, seemingly performing chores. The more he watched, the more confused he became.

What were they doing at this time of the night? Was there some strange custom that compelled these Amishmen to work while others slept? Shifting in his seat, he decided to wait them out. Eventually, they would leave.

◆ ◆ ◆ ◆ ◆

Dima awakened suddenly with a jolt and looked at his watch. 3:30 A.M. Grabbing the binoculars, he focused on the house, deeply relieved. The Amish farmers were gone at last.

With no time to waste, he shoved the car keys into his pocket, reached for the door handle, and climbed out. The night was softened with starlight and a large splinter of a moon. The echo of crickets mingled with the distant bark of a dog. Wearing tennis shoes, his steps were muted, yet he walked with purpose, creating the appearance of a local on his way home.

Less than a block from the house, he stopped short, dumbfounded. The Amishmen had suddenly returned, busy with indiscernible tasks. Staring at the men in frustration, Dima considered his options. He could return to the car and come back tomorrow or proceed with his plan.

In the end, greed decided for him. He'd waited for years for this moment, and he mustn't wait any longer, no matter the human casualties. He lifted his right foot in an attempt to move forward but nearly stumbled, his legs unpredictably weak, like jelly. Recovering his balance, a wave of unexplainable anxiety washed over him.

Standing on the narrow sidewalk in the early hours of the morning, he stared at the men, trying to get a grip on his own ridiculous reaction to these strange, nocturnal farmers.

*What's the matter, Dima, losing your edge?*

Angry with his mental weakness, he patted his holster and quickened his pace to the house. He was within a few yards of the gate when his arms began to shake uncontrollably, then his legs. Fear embraced him so completely that each step was an enormous effort.

When he reached the gate at last, he slumped against it, then turned his back on the Denlinger house, hyperventilating. Against his better judgment, he drew his gun out in the open, barely able to hold the weapon in his sweat-drenched palms. Raising the gun, he turned toward the Amishmen.

They stood motionless, their hands at their sides, watching him, their expressions deliberate, serious, almost grieved. Facing their penetrating gaze, he felt like a deer caught in the headlights of an oncoming car, unable to turn away.

Then something peculiar happened. Unfamiliar emotions began to click through his awareness like dominoes in a chain reaction.

*Shame, guilt, conviction . . .* ending with a final emotion long since dormant through decades of denial—the proffer of *acceptance.* Something he'd last felt as a child sitting across the table from the compassionate psychiatrist, as the doctor tended him with comforting words. *"Let me help you, Dima. I care about you. . . . You are safe here. . . ."*

For a brief, mysterious moment, he felt drawn to these men, as if they held the answers to the anguish that had driven him to a lifetime of revenge.

He shuddered, and the gun slipped through his fingers, bouncing against the concrete sidewalk. He fell to his knees, scrambled for it, finally grabbed the weapon with both trembling hands. In that moment, his anger returned, but all resolve had vanished. Stumbling to his feet, he backed away to the sidewalk, then bolted in an all-out sprint for his car.

Taking one last glance up the block at the Denlinger house—the Amishmen were gone—he shoved the gearshift into drive. Seconds later he squealed a narrow U-turn in the middle of the block and sped down the street, not caring what sort of commotion he created.

# Chapter Seventeen

IVANOV COMPOSED HIMSELF during the drive toward Connecticut. Confused and shaken by the events of the night, he wondered just what had happened at the little house on the deserted lane. But his mind remained vacantly unaware, as if he were just now coming out of a trance.

He considered turning the car around, waiting for daylight, and making another attempt to approach the house. But thinking of the Denlinger home and the Amishmen caused a cold sweat to break out.

No matter. Ivanov was a resourceful man. In a few hours he'd be back in Mystic, Connecticut. It was time for a surprise visit with Melissa's husband.

♦ ♦ ♦ ♦ ♦

Silently, Ryan slipped out the back door, methodically working his way around the gardens to the peaceful cove, coffee cup in hand. The steam curled and rose into the unseasonable coolness of early morning as gray-backed terns flitted about.

In the distance, the sea was pewterlike—a

stunning contrast to last night's moon-dappled waves. Their sailboat, *Mellie*, shifted with the gentle lapping of waves, air still as death. Just as sunbeams winked over the horizon—a show of gold on Fishers Island Sound—an unexpected gust came up. He turned his face toward wind and sun, experiencing the dawning of a new day, a sunrise that held little hope.

Slowly draining his cup, he considered his next course of action. Three raucous terns interrupted his thoughts, swooping toward the dock and landing on posts. Waiting.

*She's not here,* he thought. *Come again another day.*

Overwhelming sorrow encompassed him anew, and he turned back toward the house. Where the rise leveled off, he paused to look at the sundial, the focal point in Mellie's miniature rose garden. Abundant with peach-colored thimble-sized blooms, each twelve-inch plant nearly smothered itself in tiny but perfect rose blossoms. Mellie had chosen this classification of rose because of its undemanding nature. "Anyone can grow these," she'd said, laughing out loud as they worked together.

The color, peach, had been Mellie's idea. "A peach-hued rose is delicate and stands for admiration. Its Victorian Era meaning was 'Please, believe me,' " she gaily informed him as they planted each one.

" 'Believe me' . . . about what?" he'd played along.

"Oh, *you* know." She stood, wiping her brow and grinning her irresistible grin.

Playfully, he'd run to her, held her close, and whispered, "Believe that I'll love you for always?"

She nuzzled against him silently. Then, stepping out of his embrace, she pointed to the circular bed where the sundial would eventually stand at center stage—*their* rustic sundial discovered in New Hampshire at the Americana Celebration Antiques Show months later.

The horizontal stone dial was etched with the equation of time, boasting a metal gnomon and, at the center, a single rose. He recalled her squeal of delight at finding such a prize, and on the drive home, she spoke of nothing else. "We own a true masterpiece," she'd said. "Nearly as ancient as mankind itself."

"Pretty profound," he'd teased. "Sounds like you're a poet today."

Mellie had laughed with glee, snuggling close to him in the car, humming a happy song and reliving their day in New Hampshire. "Can we go back sometime soon?" she asked.

"Just say the word." He would take her to the ends of the earth and beyond if she so desired. Whatever brought a smile to Mellie's face was worth any amount of hassle, aching feet, and empty wallet.

Returning to the house, he was met with sounds of Denny banging around in the kitchen. Apparently, his guest had decided to cook.

"So . . . you didn't like *my* eggs?" Ryan mocked.

"Don't make me answer that," Denny shot back. "I value your friendship." He dipped his head beneath the counter, searching for the frying pan, no doubt.

"Over there." Ryan pointed to the wide drawer under the range and left his friend, going to the living room to phone the office. He left a short message for Marge. "I'll be a half hour late today," he said, recoiling at what awaited him upon his arrival at work— having to fill Marge and Bernie in on Melissa.

When Denny called him to breakfast, Ryan was pleasantly surprised with the results. Denny had whipped up creamy omelets and plenty of bacon. The food was good, albeit lethal.

"A few more meals like this and I'll be dead by next year," he said, picking up his fork.

"Admit it. You like it." Denny grinned.

"That's the problem. I should get back to granola and fruit." He bit into his toast. "By the way, I have to make an appearance at the office, for a couple hours at least."

"Not a problem." Denny tossed a bit of egg Daisy's way. The dog seemed to inhale it in one sniff. Wiping his hands on a napkin, Denny regarded Ryan uncertainly.

"I thought she'd call by now," Ryan said flatly. "I guess it's time to pull a trace on her credit cards and call the cell phone provider. I'll do that from the office. You gonna hang around here?"

"Sure," Denny replied. "I'll read a little. Maybe I'll look around a bit, if you don't mind."

"Make yourself at home, Investigator Franklin." Ryan rose to clear off the table. Together they loaded the dishwasher and wiped the table.

◆ ◆ ◆ ◆ ◆

Ryan marched through the anteroom door to a cheerful secretary. Marge grinned, eyes sparkling.

"What's that look?" he quizzed her.

"How was your weekend with the preacher man?"

He exhaled audibly. "You know . . . we could all use a little church around here."

"Oh my. He *is* getting to you."

He shrugged. "Any calls?"

"Bernie left you a note."

He felt a surge of disgust, grabbed the folded note paper, and hurried to his office door.

Marge called after him, "Say, I almost forgot. How did Melissa like the necklace?"

"Don't ask." Not ready to broach the subject, he closed the door to his office. Seated at his desk, he removed the key from his pocket and turned the lock, opening the drawers. He rubbed his face with both hands. Already he felt drained, wished he could turn around and go home—forget the day.

A flick of a central switch and all computers and monitors in the room buzzed to life. He glanced at his watch. Twenty minutes till the market officially opened. Premarket was already in full swing. Clutching Bernie's note, he cringed. The stock tip was comprised of a mere four letters—a basic stock symbol—*the* stock for the day.

He'd come to despise this aspect of his job. Utilizing the keyboard at his desk, Ryan accessed information on the Internet for the stock's recent technical pattern and the company fundamentals. Last Friday the stock had closed at 98½. Contacting his market maker electronically, he placed an order to short twenty thousand shares.

Then, glancing at the corner of his home page, he saw what he had somehow missed upon first booting up. A single e-mail message—originating from his own address. *Strange.* Assuming it was a mistake, his finger involuntarily reached toward the delete key. But just before touching it, instead he clicked the icon.

The note was from Melissa.

*Ryan,*

*I had to let you know I'm okay. Someday soon I'll make you understand. I promise.*

*Miss you terribly,*
*Mellie*

He kicked himself mentally. Why hadn't he realized she might send a note via e-mail? At least he was relieved to hear that she was safe. Also that her leaving wasn't about *them.* But if not, then what?

◆ ◆ ◆ ◆ ◆

Lela thought surely she had time to dash over to Lapp's General Store, less than half a mile away, before midmorning chores. Hezekiah Lapp never turned away early-bird shoppers, even up to an hour or so before the store officially opened at nine o'clock of a morning.

She was planning a special dinner at noon for Melissa, who'd been in a strange slump before breakfast. The phone call she had been eager for had simply not come.

*Some rhubarb tapioca and Mama's old-fashioned chicken loaf with pimentos and melted butter might help*, she thought.

But she'd run out of a few of the necessary ingredients and decided, since it was another nice day, to bicycle down to the store bright and early. The sky was bluer than yesterday, hardly a cloud, though she could see some building up on the horizon to the north. Still, she was ever so glad to be running errands on behalf of a wounded soul.

Arriving at Hezekiah's grocery shop, she parked her bike in one of the parallel spots, putting the kickstand down. A shiny blue car was parked at the end of the row. She entered the store, the tinkle of the bell greeting her.

"Hullo there, Lela," called Hezekiah. "I see you're out right early today."

She smiled back. "Need some pimentos for dinner," she replied, spotting another customer, a man whose back was turned to her, in the bulk foods aisle.

"Let me know if I can help you find anything," Hezekiah said, glancing over at the man. "And you, too, sir."

That's when she noticed the familiar profile, though it had been quite some time since she'd laid eyes on Paul Martin. Nevertheless, he was as handsome today as he had been back in high school. Her heart twitched a bit at the memory of those long-ago days. The demise of their love, due to the woman he'd chosen over her. Deceased now. The irony of it all.

Refusing to stare, she kept busy with her search for the items she needed. Paul was only a small part of her past, a truly happy memory if one left out the way things ended between them. 'Course, now, what with Sadie Nan eager to play matchmaker, well, she just didn't know what to think about such a thing. And yesterday, after church, Sadie had tried mighty hard to catch Lela's eye. Yet she would have nothing to do with Paul's sister's scheming. The fact of the matter was, she didn't like the thought of playing second fiddle to the fancy blond girl who'd claimed him as her husband. Dead or not.

"Well, my goodness, is that you, Lela?" She heard his voice, and something in her froze.

Turning, she gave him a cordial smile. "Hello, Paul."

"I'd hoped to visit with you yesterday after church, but you slipped out before I could—"

"What brings you to Lancaster?" she broke in.

Tall and ruddy, he looked at her with shining blue eyes. His light brown hair was cropped around his ears, cut and styled as though he'd never grown up in a strict Anabaptist community. Still, she found his meekness appealing. "I'm here on business," he replied.

Somewhat relieved, she wondered how long he would stay, though she had no intention of asking. For sure and for certain, Sadie Nan would be all too eager to fill her in.

"I hope you'll consider having dinner with me." His voice was gentle, his eyes sincere. "I know I don't deserve a second chance."

What was she to say? Spurned in her youth, here was the man who'd rejected her for another. "That's awful kind of you," she said softly.

"May I call you sometime?" He wasn't mincing words.

"I don't know . . . how I feel about that," she confessed.

He smiled down at her, waiting.

"And . . . I'm real busy with a boarder presently."

"Oh?" He seemed surprised to hear it. "I didn't know."

Because she was *not* in dire straits, definitely not, she didn't want him to think she was vulnerable, in need of a man. "God nudged me in that particular direction just recently," she said, revealing nothing about Melissa or the young Englischer's desperation.

"Well, then, I'm glad to hear it." He stepped back, smiling his winning smile. "My sister tells me you're well."

"Yes, and you?"

"Very well, thanks."

She hesitated to inquire of his wife's fatal illness. The subject seemed rather untouchable. "I'm sorry to hear of your loss."

"Thank you, Lela. How generous of you to say so."

To think otherwise would have been erroneous on his part. Surely, he must have known how very painful their breakup was for her.

"God bless you, Paul." She said it quickly, turning away to tend to her shopping.

# Chapter Eighteen

SETTLING ONTO THE COUCH in the sun-room, Denny was glad he'd brought a long-sleeved shirt. A hint of fall hung in the air, though he knew the day would most likely warm up. After all, this was Connecticut.

He read the newspaper for a few minutes but had trouble concentrating. His gaze drifted to the corner of the room, where Melissa's easel stood poised, the initial stages of a floral painting on display.

Thinking back to his first visit with Ryan and Melissa, he recalled his earliest impression of Ryan's wife: she was simply beautiful. Further conversation more than confirmed his initial reaction. Not only was Melissa very attractive, but more important, she had a warm personality and a sweet spirit.

He'd announced to Ryan in her presence, "You definitely married *up*, my friend."

Ryan had laughed. "You aren't telling *me* anything."

Melissa only blushed, slipping her arm through Ryan's.

He also remembered the morning Ryan ran off to the grocery store, leaving him alone with Melissa in the sun-room. They had exchanged small talk until he broached the subject of faith, discovering her to be open and receptive to spiritual things. While he painted word pictures for her of a loving, personal God, she perched on her stool, painting her oceans and listening intently.

"That sounds so . . . intriguing," she replied, seemingly sincere. In answer to her questions, he used Scripture, to the best of his ability. Melissa was definitely searching.

Eventually, Ryan returned with several pints of frozen yogurt. After that singular moment, no other opportunity to discuss spiritual matters with Melissa had presented itself. Yet something about that day stuck in his memory. He had been talking about growing up in Colorado, then switched gears to inquire of her home state, Minnesota. Usually candid, Melissa had turned elusive. At the time he'd dismissed it, thinking perhaps she was uncomfortable discussing her childhood.

To a history and geography buff, Denny found it strange that Melissa was uninformed about the basic facts of her own state, as if ten thousand lakes, enormous mosquitoes, harsh winters, even outlandishly high state taxes were somehow foreign to her. Now, with Mellie on the run, the incongruity of their previous discussion haunted him.

Several scrapbooks were lined up along the top shelf of the bookcase. He reached for them and, one by one, perused the pages—mostly pictures of Melissa and Ryan at scenic or historic sites in New England, intermingled with poses at the beach or in front of quaint B&B's.

He examined each picture carefully as if something in Melissa's face, her expression might reveal something important. He was unsure what he was looking for, but he had a peculiar feeling about the whole situation.

The jangle of the phone interrupted his musing. He rushed to the living room in search of the portable. Finding it, he answered, "Hello? James residence."

"Denny—" Ryan's voice.

"What's up?"

"You're not going to believe this. Mellie sent me an e-mail message."

Denny breathed a sigh of relief. "Where is she?"

"She didn't say, but she's all right."

Still confused by Melissa's secrecy, Denny did not reply.

"Well . . . I wanted you to know," Ryan said. "See you later."

"Later," Denny said and hung up, puzzled, then headed back to the sun-room. Melissa was safe. *Thanks, Lord.* Carefully, he placed the scrapbooks back on the shelf, determined to focus on other matters. But a smaller album, tucked back in the corner, caught his attention.

*Let it go, man,* he thought. *She's okay.*

Something urged him on. He thumbed through the pages, a single photo to each album leaf. The small scrapbook contained childhood photos of Melissa. Photos of a giggling girl riding her bike, posing shyly next to a woman who was possibly her teacher, walking with several other girls on a pathway beside a small lake, opening Christmas presents. The excitement in the small child's innocent smile touched his heart. He was about to close the album when he noticed something slightly different about the final page. He felt its thickness—bulkier than the others. *Why?*

Clumsily, Denny poked the page protector, creating a gap for his thumb and forefinger to explore. Sure enough, another photo lay hidden between. Carefully, he pulled it out and studied the birthday picture. A current of energy shivered down his back.

The photo was of Melissa blowing out candles on a cake. Denny squinted to count them. Eight. Beside her, an older man stood nearby, probably Melissa's father, his hand resting protectively behind her chair. Neither Melissa nor the man in the photo caused him concern. Directly behind Melissa was a window, and through it a grove of trees. And not just any kind of trees. These were *aspen trees*.

Aspens didn't grow in Minnesota. They thrived at higher elevations, typical of Colorado. Even more disturbing was the color of the foliage. The aspens had turned *golden* . . . an autumn birthday. . . .

Denny tapped the photo. His mind flashed back to a phone conversation he'd had with Ryan last spring. For her birthday, they'd gone out past Fishers Island in their sailboat, taking along a "catered picnic lunch," a surprise from Ryan. But Melissa's birthday was supposedly in mid-May, not fall. *Is that why this photo was hidden?*

*Must be an explanation*, he thought. After all, why would anyone lie about their birth month? For that matter, why fib about your home state? The more he thought about it, the more it bugged him.

Wandering through the living room, he looked out the back window and checked his watch: 10:15. Ryan would be home in a half hour. He recalled his friend's invitation prior to heading off to his office. *Make yourself at home, Investigator Franklin.*

He knew Ryan's filing cabinet was just off the family room, downstairs. Hurrying for the stairs, he felt a twinge of chagrin. Was he crossing a line? Maybe.

Flicking on the light, he swept past the pool table to a tall black cabinet standing against the far wall. He reached for the top drawer and tugged. Unlocked, it slid open easily. He began to work his way through the multitude of alphabetized files. The label *Personal Information* caught his eye, and he opened it, finding Ryan and Melissa's marriage certificate. Examining the document, he found nothing unusual.

He continued his thorough search until he spotted what he had been looking for: Melissa's birth certificate and social security card. Reading the certificate, he noted the newness of the document and the word "re-issue" at the bottom.

Birth Certificate
Louis Weiner Memorial Hospital
Marshall, Minnesota

This certifies that
Melissa Leigh Nolan
was born in this hospital
at 2:21 P.M.,
on Saturday the 7th day of May A.D.
1975.

According to the document, Melissa was born in Marshall, Minnesota. The superintendent of the hospital had signed on the appropriate line, as had the attending physician. Below their signatures, Denny saw something that gave him pause. *Family History*. Mother's and father's full names, their birthplaces, and birth dates.

The question nagged at him: Was her birth certificate valid? Denny was somewhat familiar with the process of personal identification in the U.S. and knew that birth certificates were widely considered to be the basis of identity. Before God had nudged him toward becoming a teacher, Denny had worked as a security officer for a high-profile law firm—his size had made it seem a natural career choice. During that time, he'd heard of people wishing to escape some crisis who assumed a new identity by either forging a birth certificate, which was risky, or having a new certificate issued in the name of someone who died at a young age, thus assuming that person's identity. With a fake birth certificate, all the other pieces of identification could be obtained, including social security number, driver's license, even passport.

Anyone could verify the authenticity of a forged birth certificate by calling a local agency where records of local births were maintained. A forgery was detectable in minutes; the agency would simply have no verifying records of the forgery. But the assumption of a deceased person's identity was more difficult to trace. After all, that birth certificate would be registered in a local county office. Unless the country cross-referenced birth certificates with death certificates, this kind of assumption of identity usually went undetected.

*This is absurd,* Denny thought. *Who am I kidding? Would Melissa actually fake her identity?* Unassuming and sweet, the young woman's only real crime was fleeing her home, leaving behind a mysterious note.

He came close to dumping everything back into the file and just forgetting the whole thing. But Denny couldn't walk away, not knowing for sure. Closing the filing cabinet, documents in hand, he trudged up the steps to the main floor. From the kitchen phone, he dialed Information.

"What city?" the operator asked.

"Marshall, Minnesota."

"One moment, please."

A few seconds later, another operator's voice—"What listing?"

"The county records division, where birth and death records are kept."

"Just a moment." A computerized voice read the number, then immediately connected. The phone rang. . . .

"County recorder. Gwen speaking."

Denny identified himself and told the clerk what he was looking for: the birth and death record of a Melissa Leigh Nolan, born in 1975 at Louis Weiner Hospital. He could hear her keyboard clicking in the background. "Mr. Franklin? We have the record of her birth but not her death."

Denny thanked her and hung up. He sighed. Maybe he was wrong after all. Maybe Melissa was who she said she was—Melissa Nolan, born in Marshall, Minnesota, in 1975. Denny chuckled. *I must have a bad case of overactive imagination.*

But he wasn't finished with his follow-up. If a person died outside their home county, the place of birth may not have the death record, even if cross-referenced. One more lead to follow...

*Birth history. The mother and father.* Ryan had told him that Melissa's mother had passed away and that her father had abandoned her to the care of a neighbor. But was the story true? One way to find out.

He dialed Information again, feeling increasingly stupid. He checked his watch again: 10:30. When the operator in Marshall, Minnesota, came on the line, Denny read the names directly off the birth certificate. "Bill and Georgia Nolan, please."

Silence prevailed while the operator's computer searched for the listing. "I show no listing for Bill.... I have a William—"

"Let's try that."

Denny was connected, and he could hear the phone ringing.

"Hello?"

"Yes, I'm trying to locate a Bill and Georgia Nolan."

"Well, my name's Bill, but there's no Georgia here. Wife's name is Betty."

"Oh, sorry to bother you," Denny replied, discouraged. *Time to let it go.*

"But I know just about every Nolan in the area."

"Yes, sir, well, thanks—"

"We had a Georgia Nolan, now that I

think of it. Lived crosstown from us. Let me think . . . yeah, I think her husband's name was Bill. Like mine. But I'm thinking they moved away."

"Oh." Denny wasn't sure how to proceed. "I was hoping to get some information concerning their daughter."

"Daughter, you say?" The man paused, then—"Hey, the wife just walked in. Let me ask her if she remembers anything about the family."

He heard muffled voices in the background. Bill Nolan had covered the phone with his hand. In a moment he was back on the line. "Well, the wife remembers 'em better'n I do. She says their daughter lives in Minneapolis somewhere."

"Mr. Nolan, I've taken enough of your time—"

But Bill went on. "Guess their *other* daughter died real young. Didn't even make it to school age."

Denny shuddered at this revelation. "Do you happen to know her name?"

"Here, you talk to the missus."

Betty got on the phone and began chattering away as if Denny were an old friend. "Bill doesn't pay much attention to people—not like I do. I remember Georgia Nolan real well, but they moved away years ago. What a tragedy! I don't think she ever recovered."

"Excuse me?"

"From little Melissa's death," she said almost reprovingly. "What a wonderful child. I can remember her from our church nursery. Used to substitute teach for the regular teacher on Sundays sometimes. Too old now for youngsters, though."

"Where did their daughter die?"

Betty paused, considering Denny's question. "You know," she began again, "I don't think it was here. Near the Twin Cities, I think. We heard about it, though, through friends in the church. Snowmobile accident. Can you imagine that?"

Eventually Denny hung up, after suffering through Betty's lengthy recollections of the other Nolan family. Enough information to know he'd found the truth. Melissa Leigh Nolan of Marshall, Minnesota, born in 1975, died *years* ago. Ryan's wife had obviously assumed her identity and obtained a copy of the birth certificate. The information left Denny reeling. Questions continued to plague him. Who was Ryan's Melissa? But more importantly: Why had she taken on the identity of another?

Folks who assumed false identities were running from something in their past, either from creditors . . . *or from the law*. What was Melissa running from?

Denny returned the folder to Ryan's filing cabinet and was closing the drawer when he heard the sounds of the upstairs back door.

Ryan was home.

## ◆ *Chapter Nineteen* ◆

DENNY CLIMBED THE STAIRS in time to witness Daisy's jubilant reunion with her master. Struggling to keep his composure, Denny stood silently in the doorway.

Ryan tossed his keys on the kitchen counter and crouched to rub down his overeager pet. "It's too nice out to hang around here."

Ryan's gloomy demeanor of the weekend had faded somewhat. Having received the first bit of good news in days, his friend seemed hopeful . . . and now Denny had to deliver more bad news.

Giving Daisy another pat, Ryan said, "We could hit a donut shop."

"Sure, whatever." Wasn't his place to throw a damper on things.

They drove past Ryan's office building

and over the drawbridge. A banner, still advertising last weekend's Annual Mystic Outdoor Art Festival, extended across West Main Street. Ryan mentioned that Melissa often entered her work in the juried show.

*Not this year*, he thought. *Maybe never again.* "So how did everyone at the office take it . . . about Melissa?" he ventured.

Ryan begged the question. "I haven't told them yet. Thought I'd wait till tomorrow. Who knows? Maybe she'll be back by then."

Not sure how to open a can of worms, Denny fell silent. He was fairly certain that Melissa was never coming home. "Did you check back with the police?" he asked finally.

Ryan shook his head.

Denny struggled with his knowledge of the situation. What would Ryan think of his snooping around in his files, calling record bureaus of vital statistics? Even so, he couldn't just leave his friend in the dark. Ryan would *want* to know the truth, wouldn't he?

They found a parking space on Water Street, then walked toward West Main.

"There's a little coffee shop Melissa liked to visit. In fact, Brad Short, the owner, is a client of mine."

"A coffee shop owner has money to invest? Thought you guys took only *rich* clients."

"Let's put it this way: Brad doesn't run a coffee shop because he needs the revenue."

"Family money?"

"Exactly."

The storefront boasted signs welcoming the coffee drinkers of the world. Inside, the owner, an older man with silver-gray hair and white apron tied around his waist, stood at attention behind a chest-high glass counter. He was preoccupied with a trio of giggling girls trying to decide which of the many delicious donuts to choose from behind the polished glass.

Spying Ryan, Brad nodded and gave a knowing snort. "Hey there, money man, I'll be right with you." He turned back to the group with an impatient look. "Ladies, what'll it be?"

"We'll have three of those," said one of the girls, gesturing toward the glazed donuts.

Denny and Ryan waited for the young women to divide up the sale, then rummage around in their tiny purses. Placing his hand on Ryan's back, Denny leaned over and said, "Listen, man, we need to talk. Somewhere private."

Turning to face him, Ryan's expression

was one of bewilderment. "Something wrong?"

"Could be" was all he said.

Ryan frowned, glancing about the room. "Private enough?"

Surveying the shop, Denny noticed several patrons at one large table. Smaller tables for two were available near the back corner. "That one's fine," he said, moving toward the rear.

"Sure you don't want anything?" Ryan called to him.

"Some coffee. Make it black." He took the chair facing the windows while Ryan ordered. Outside he saw tourists clambering about, hauling their purchases in large shopping bags.

Over near the counter, the teenagers moved on as Ryan greeted the owner, making small talk. He overheard snippets of the conversation. Brad was saying something about the outrageous payroll taxes and how hard it was to get quality help.

"How's the market?" Brad asked. Then, without waiting for an answer—"Hey, I got a question about the last portfolio statement your office sent out."

"Problem?"

"No, no. Just curious. By the way, how's that wife of yours?"

Ryan covered well, casually sidestepping Brad's innocent queries, but Denny noticed that his demeanor changed, shoulders slumped. Ryan soon brought two coffees and several donuts on a tray. Sliding the tray onto the table, he sat down with his back to the front door and took a quick sip of coffee. "Speak to me, my friend."

Denny sighed.

"Hey, you look like you're carrying the weight of the world."

"I think I am." Forging ahead, Denny said, "You told me you didn't know Melissa very well when you married her."

Ryan regarded him curiously. "So? What's the point?"

"I have a feeling she's not coming back."

"What do you mean?"

"Maybe I should start at the beginning—"

"Good idea," Ryan said.

Denny began with an apology for poking his nose into their personal files, then about finding the hidden photo. He removed the picture from his shirt pocket and handed it to Ryan, pointing out the aspen trees "in fall colors."

Ryan seemed alarmed initially but said nothing.

Denny pushed ahead to Melissa's birth

certificate, revealing what he'd learned during his calls to Marshall, Minnesota. He shared the exchange with Bill and Betty Nolan, too, the startling disclosure of Melissa Leigh Nolan's untimely death at age five.

Staring blankly, Ryan remained silent, but his jaw dropped and his face suddenly paled. He sighed deeply, as if gathering enough strength to speak. "You're saying that Melissa lied about who she is?"

Denny nodded respectfully. Telling Ryan had been harder than he'd imagined. He felt his friend's anguish, the sting of disbelief. "She assumed the identity of a child who died years ago," Denny managed to say.

"How do you know you're not mistaken?"

"Well, we could follow up with the death certificate, contact the parents of the original Melissa . . . verify their story."

Ryan shook his head, defeated. "No . . . actually . . ." He stopped, eyes glistening. "I suppose I shouldn't be too surprised at anything, after all this." He shrugged, unable to continue.

*How many hits does a guy have to take?* Denny felt lousy being the one to deliver the blow.

A tray fell, clattering to the floor. They turned in unison to look. A long line of customers, eager for donuts and varieties of coffee, stretched nearly to the door.

The girl behind the counter came around sheepishly, bending down to clean up the mess on the floor. "Oh man . . ." she said, evidently embarrassed by her clumsiness.

"Just let it go," the owner hollered from another room.

Flustered, the young clerk straightened and scurried back behind the counter to take orders, then filled them single-handedly.

"Nice guy, this client of yours," Denny interjected, feeling sorry for the poor girl.

"A little rough around the edges" was Ryan's distracted comment.

Observing the clerk's attempt to juggle the crowd, Denny's gaze zeroed in on a middle-aged man sauntering in the doorway, wearing gray slacks and a white shirt. Standing in line, the man made a furtive sweep around the room, stopping at their table. Then he turned away, a look of recognition on his face. *Strange*, thought Denny, who was particularly struck by the lone tuft of gray in the man's full head of dark hair.

He returned his attention to Ryan. "Has anyone ever contacted you about Melissa?"

Seemingly preoccupied, Ryan shook his head. "No. Listen—"

Just then, Ryan's pager chirped. He

pulled the pager off his belt, scrutinizing it, then finding his cell phone, he punched in a couple of numbers and waited. "Cover twenty thousand shares immediately," he barked. When he was finished, he shook his head. "I need some air. Let's take a walk."

Finished with coffee, they rose from their seats well after the man with a splash of silver in his hair had strolled out the door.

"Take it easy," Ryan called to the owner.

"Hey, don't I wish!" came the crusty reply.

Outside the donut shop, Ryan turned suddenly. "I forgot, Brad had a question. Can you wait a minute?"

"No problem."

"See you in a few minutes." Ryan hurried back inside.

Waiting, Denny leaned up against the glass window, watching the hustle and bustle around him. Tourists gawking and shopping, young mothers pushing baby strollers, traffic backed up.

Everyone seemed caught up in the movement downtown, everyone except himself . . . and the man he'd seen earlier in the shop, now across the street, casually drinking his cup of coffee. For no particular reason, Denny felt wary of the man. But he dismissed his unexplainable caution and went back into the shop, where Ryan and Brad were chatting at the far end of the counter, going over some figures on a piece of paper.

Ryan spotted Denny and nodded.

"Take your time." Denny poked his thumb toward the door. "I'm going to check out the gift shop up the street."

"Yeah, sure. I'll meet you there."

Denny headed up the sidewalk, trying to shake his apprehension. But he had an odd feeling that he was being watched. He covered half a block before peering over his shoulder again. The man had disappeared. Denny scanned the area, wondering how the man had slipped away so quickly.

*Relax*, Denny thought, ignoring his sense of foreboding. *Stop playing detective. You've done enough harm for one day.*

He resumed his mission to buy a gift for Evelyn. *Something "New England,"* Denny decided. *She'll like that.*

## Chapter Twenty

"I DON'T KNOW WHEN I've eaten food this delicious," Melissa noted after the last bite of the noon meal.

"Well, thank you." Lela, sitting opposite her, smiled. "I wanted to cook up something extra special for you."

Lela was perhaps one of the sweetest women Melissa had ever known. The fact that the Plain woman was past thirty and not yet married was astonishing. The truth was, the hostess had everything going for her—great cooking skills, gardening talent, a well-kept home. Why hadn't she married? Any reasonable man would find Lela Denlinger an excellent choice.

But Melissa knew little of the dating and courtship practices in the quiet community, and she wasn't about to ask. She *did* recall the blush of embarrassment on Lela's face, the slightly flustered speech, just yesterday morning. So did she have a man friend after all?

Their conversation turned to Elizabeth and Thaddeus and their little ones. Lela, it seemed, adored her nieces and nephews. She was also quite fond of Elizabeth. "We had the most interesting childhood," Lela said. "Always together, till school issues separated us. But, nevertheless, we had our evenings . . . and the summers."

"What happened at school?"

"Elizabeth began dating Thaddeus, a young Amishman, so she dropped out of higher education, so to speak, preparing to follow in his Old Order ways." Lela explained that the Amish stop educating their young people after eighth grade. "Since Elizabeth was well past that level, she decided to honor her fiancé."

"She quit school for Thaddeus?"

"To please him, you know."

Melissa hadn't heard of such a thing. Women's rights had been the top issue in college. The notion of a woman giving up her plans for a man was foreign to her.

"Did Elizabeth ever second-guess her decision?" she asked.

"Never, so far as I know." Lela paused. "But, then, Thaddeus has always been a good, kind man. He and Elizabeth became the best of friends, even before their marriage. Still are, I suspect."

*Best of friends . . .*

She'd always viewed herself and Ryan that way. And they *had* been close friends, in spite of their occasional disagreements. The commonalities between them made up for other things. They both loved dogs—Daisy was proof—and they enjoyed their quaint abode on Lord's Point, the sea, the sailing, and all that the prime cove-front property afforded.

How she missed being there, Ryan at her side. By now he would've read her e-mail message, and he would know she was safe and sound. She wondered how he'd reacted. Did he long to return a note to her? Did he . . .

She couldn't follow in this vein of thought. Lela was dishing up dessert. Time to continue their visit, try not to think about the phone over there on the counter, the telephone that was much too silent today.

"Would it be possible for me to visit Elizabeth's little store?" she asked, accepting the rhubarb tapioca dessert and a warm-from-the-oven coconut oatmeal gem—a delicious cookie.

"Oh sure." Lela beamed, her eyes bright. "We can go over after bit."

She wasn't sure how soon "after bit" was, but she would be ready whenever the time came. "I'm curious about the type of quilts you make to sell."

Lela nodded. "I'd be ever so happy to show you some of my patchwork upstairs, if you'd like."

Anything to kill some time. She wasn't exactly thrilled about the idea of examining piecework, quilting, all of that. But she was curious about Lela's simple life in Amish country. The young Mennonite didn't own much, though her home was nicely furnished, her wardrobe pleasant, if plain. She hadn't cared or bothered to learn to drive a car, didn't own one either. Lela's greatest joy seemed to come from within. She had an amazing sense of herself, not so much self-assured as she was settled. At peace.

They worked side by side in the kitchen, and at one point, Lela began to hum a tune. The melody offered a reprieve from Melissa's angst, if only briefly.

While drying dishes, she made a decision. If her contact had not returned her phone call by two o'clock Eastern Daylight Time, she would phone him again. This waiting was impossible. She had to know what she was to do next. For both her sake and Ryan's.

Lela's sewing room was a tiny spot situated under the garret. Wall shelving accommodated many spools of colorful thread and other sewing notions. An electric sewing machine was positioned under a window, and there was a table on the opposite wall for cutting out patterns. She also had a small bookcase, where she kept extra tracts and devotional books. The room was her "quiet place."

"As you can see, it's small but efficient," Lela said, showing Melissa around.

Melissa was most interested in the quilted goods, and Lela was eager to oblige, showing her the original pattern. "I've used this to make hundreds of pillow shams," Lela said.

Marveling at the tiny quilting stitches, Melissa found herself enjoying this creative side of her Mennonite friend—a common thread that tied her to this woman and brought more than a small measure of comfort.

◆ ◆ ◆ ◆ ◆

When the two women set out later in the afternoon, the road to Thaddeus King's farmhouse was deserted. It was paved, but only a two-lane, and that hardly wide enough for cars to pass each other. The stretch of road was ablaze with the westerly sun, its dips and turns accented by tall, lovely trees scattered here and there along the wayside.

When they neared the large clapboard house, Melissa noticed three of the King children at play in the side yard. School evidently was not yet in session.

"Baby John's probably down for a nap," Lela commented, pushing a strand of hair under her prayer bonnet. "I daresay Elizabeth's taking full advantage of the quiet house, cleaning and baking and whatnot."

Melissa was a little surprised that Lela seemed to know her sister's schedule so well. "Isn't it hard to keep up with four children?"

she said, as they made the turn into the Kings' dirt lane.

"Not so hard, really. Elizabeth knows how to make the children mind. Besides that, Mary Jane and Timothy help the younger two. The more children, the less work a mother oughta have."

The idea of the older ones assisting the younger children was something Melissa hadn't known, being an only child . . . and a half orphan for the first ten years of her life.

In the Jane Austen novels she loved, there was a hierarchy of duties among children, she remembered. She had no way of knowing where Plain people got *their* ideas, not having had contact with any of them before. She did find the ordering of domestic duties fascinating. Things ran like clockwork at both Lela's and Elizabeth's homes, almost effortlessly.

"We aren't perfect," Elizabeth said after greeting them and serving up some shoofly pie. "Don't ever think that." Melissa's awe-struck comments had elicited the disclaimer.

Mary Jane came over and plunked down at the table across from her. "I sewed my first stitches just this mornin'," said the adorable child. "Wouldja care to have a look-see?"

"I'd love to," Melissa said, marveling at the girl's confidence. She herself had been lacking in such characteristics, especially at

Mary Jane's tender age. The years following her mother's death had left her unsure of herself and her future. Her loss had been so deep that the mere act of getting up and off to school was a daily burden.

Mary Jane came back, face full of eagerness to show the straight stitches she'd sewn into a scrap of fabric. "Mama helped me," she whispered.

"Your mama's the best one for the job," Lela agreed.

Elizabeth waved her hand, as if the compliments were not accurate. "Ach, I can't take much credit, really. Mary Jane's a born quilter, I should say."

Lela grinned at young Mary Jane. "We know who's one of the best quilters around these parts, don't we?"

Mary Jane and Linda, her wee sister, nodded their heads. "And Mama makes wonderful-*gut* food, too," Linda, just four, said, her eyes growing bigger by the second.

Baby John began to cry upstairs, and Lela slipped away from the kitchen to get him. Bringing him down, she soothed him, rubbing his tiny back gently. She was so comfortable around little ones. Melissa wondered if being at ease with children was something a person had to be taught. Or were there women who took to it naturally, like both Elizabeth and Lela?

"The honor system must be in use today," Lela commented about the little store behind the house.

"Jah," said Elizabeth, "and so far nobody's seen fit to steal from us, which is right nice." She paused. "Oh, by the way, I forgot to tell you I sold another set of your quilted pillow shams first thing this mornin'."

"So you must be down to about three sets?" Lela walked up and down the kitchen with John nestled in her arms.

"What's left will go fast, I daresay." Elizabeth prepared a snack of applesauce for the baby.

"I best be getting busy, then," replied Lela while the children contented themselves with coloring at the table. "I oughta make up a batch more of them, fast as they go."

Melissa enjoyed watching the moments unfold, as if observing a scene from an old-fashioned movie. She was impressed with the children's good behavior, as small as they were. She found herself wondering what it would be like to have youngsters around her. Ryan might not be interested, as busy as he was. But if she taught her children to help take care of each other, as Elizabeth had, Ryan wouldn't have to be concerned over his hectic work schedule interfering so much. Now, thinking about the possibility of being a mother someday, she wondered why she'd never discussed the idea with Ryan. And why *he* hadn't broached the subject with her.

Allowing her hopes and dreams to run wild was a mistake. Most likely she was going to be a very lonely woman, and for a long, long time.

◆ ◆ ◆ ◆ ◆

Elizabeth's store was a small but tidy portion of a shed, though it was as well organized as any shop Melissa had ever seen. There were quilted items such as pillows—square, round, and heart-shaped—on one long row, with prices pinned to each. Doilies, table runners, pillowcases, and linens of all kinds—each handmade—graced the Amish store. Kitchen items included potholders, mitts, and aprons.

There were crocheted sweaters and shawls of various colors for women, as well as sunbonnets in all sizes, some small ones for girls. Baby items—terry-cloth bibs with appliqués for both boys and girls, tiny hats, dresses, baby sweaters, booties, and blankets.

Above them, on a makeshift clothesline, were quilted wall hangings with appliquéd pictures prominently pieced in—a woman wearing a sunbonnet and hanging out her wash featured each small item of clothing hanging free, attached only at the very top. So clever.

"The '*Sundries*' part of the sign out front are *my* things," Lela said, laughing.

"Since Auntie isn't Amish," Mary Jane spoke up.

"I see," Melissa said, playing along. "But if she were Amish, what then?"

"The sign might just say *Amish Store*. Ain't so, Mama?"

Elizabeth nodded with a smile, straightening a pile of tablecloths, then moved to the area where faceless dolls were lined up on a shelf. "My youngest sister, Emma, makes these."

Going over to look at the cute little dolls, Melissa noticed that the boy dolls had tiny suspenders and black felt hats. "These look tedious to make."

"Oh my, are they ever," Elizabeth said. "I don't see how Emma does it, workin' all day long on 'em."

"She must have good eyes," Lela added. "I'd sure hate to have to fool with such wee things."

Mary Jane came over for a closer look at the dolls' clothing. She removed a hat from the boy doll's head and, inspecting it closely, said, "I think *I* could prob'ly sew up a hat like this someday."

"Jah, someday you will, dear," Elizabeth agreed.

Just then several cars pulled into the barnyard. Melissa felt the old panic return, but when the customers entered the little store, she realized they were harmless. Just tourists eager to load up on the "real thing," said one. They had come to buy souvenirs and Christmas gifts "to take back home."

"No one would believe this place exists," said another with a laugh.

*Isn't that the truth?* thought Melissa.

◆ ◆ ◆ ◆ ◆

When they returned to Lela's home, Melissa asked if she could do a small load of laundry, since she'd brought so few clothes with her. Lela cheerfully obliged, and when the clothes were dried and folded, Melissa asked her to please check for phone messages. There were none.

Her spirits plummeted, but her impatience bolstered her resolve. *I can't wait any longer.* "Do you mind if I use your phone?" she asked.

"Not a'tall." Lela discreetly left the room, going to sit in the living room while Melissa made her call.

She removed a slip of paper from her pocket, then dialed quickly, hoping to get through this time. No more leaving Lela Denlinger's phone number on an answering machine. She needed answers—now. She wondered what Lela would think if she knew who Melissa was calling. Would the young Mennonite woman be frightened and ask her to leave?

She heard a click. "FBI," a male voice answered.

*Finally . . . her contact.*

"This is Melissa James," she identified herself. "Why haven't you—"

"Melissa? Where are you?" came the suddenly tense reply.

She paused, bewildered over his strained tone. "I left a phone number last Friday night. No one got back with me."

"We've been calling the entire weekend," he insisted. "Tell me the number again, in case something happens or we get disconnected."

Confused, Melissa held up the phone and began reading off Lela's phone number. "Wait." She stopped after reading the first three digits. She saw her mistake. In her haste she must have given the wrong number last Friday night.

*Unbelievable.* After all this time, they *had*

been trying to reach her. She finished giving the correct phone number.

"Confirm the address."

Melissa told him, then paused. "I was followed, but I lost him."

The man exhaled loudly. "We've got to get you out of there."

"No . . . I'm safe here."

"Listen, your life may be—"

"I left my husband behind because you insisted I flee. You didn't answer my questions then, so now I'm asking again—why did I have to leave my home?"

"It was imperative you leave, Melissa. By your own admission, you may have been in imminent danger. Our nearest agent was an hour away. But now we must speak with you . . . in person."

*Something was horribly wrong.* Doom was palpable. She heard it in his voice.

Her stomach knotted up. She leaned hard on the counter, breathless with worry, waiting for her world to come to a complete end. "It's about Ryan, isn't it?" she said at last.

The agent ignored her. "We can be at your location within ten minutes."

"The truth," she said simply with resignation. "I must know about my husband."

Terrifying images swept through her mind. She recoiled in horror. The room began spinning like a time capsule. She was ten again, black-and-white police cars were flashing in front of Daddy's little house. A woman in a blue uniform gently but firmly sat her down, telling her that her father had gone to heaven. *What do you mean? I just saw him this morning. Daddy dropped me off at school. . . .*

The nightmare was happening again. She felt, for a moment, Mrs. Browning's loving arms about her, soothing her. *"There, there, dearie, I'm here. Your Mrs. Browning will see to you. . . ."*

*See to you . . .*

She shivered, thinking of the precious woman. But Mrs. Browning wasn't here to pick up the pieces of her life this time. Angrily, Melissa shook her head. Hot tears spilled down her face. She felt she might erupt with rage.

*You told me Ryan would be safe!* She directed her thought to the FBI agent.

Teeth clenched, anticipating the worst, she waited for the agent to continue. When he spoke again, his voice was softer, gentler, as if attempting to console her. "Melissa . . . I have some upsetting news. It's about your husband, Ryan James. . . ."

# Chapter Twenty-One

AS GOD AS HER WITNESS, Lela did not wish to eavesdrop on Melissa's phone conversation. Yet she *had* heard bits and pieces, and she was greatly troubled. Could it be that Melissa's husband was in danger? She refused to think the worst, though Mellie's angry words echoed through the house—"I must know about my husband. . . ."

Now Mellie was venting her anger into the telephone, shouting at whoever was on the line. Then a period of calm followed. Silence overtook the place.

Last came weeping. "No . . . no, it can't be. . . ." Mellie's voice carried into the small living room. "You must be wrong."

Not knowing what to say or do, Lela prayed silently. *Lord, please help Melissa with whatever it is . . . let me be a comfort.*

Suddenly, she heard Melissa shout into the phone, "I don't believe you! Just leave me alone!" Abruptly, she returned the phone to its cradle.

Worried, Lela rose from her chair. She went to the kitchen where the girl was sobbing inconsolably. "Mellie?" she whispered.

Making eye contact with her, Melissa stammered through her tears, "I need to get my car. I have to leave."

"Sure, Mellie, but are you . . . will you be all right?"

Melissa shook her head. "Nothing's ever going to be all right again."

Picking up the phone, Lela quickly dialed the number for Thaddeus King. Meanwhile, Melissa rushed upstairs, still weeping. Thankfully, Elizabeth answered on the second ring. Lela told her sister that Melissa would be over soon to get her car. She hung up just as Melissa reached the entryway with her overnight case, fumbling through her purse. Approaching her, Lela prayed silently for divine guidance, observing Melissa's obvious frustration.

Turning to face her, with plaintive eyes, Melissa said, "I forget how much I owe you."

"Oh . . . well, it's thirty dollars per night. You've been here three nights total."

Melissa shuffled through a number of bills in her wallet—more money than Lela had seen in a long time—handing over five twenties. "This should cover it. Keep the change."

Meekly, she received the money. "Can I help you in any way?" Lela asked, her heart going out to the disturbed woman.

Tears welled up, and Melissa's lip quivered as she shook her head no. She juggled her overnight case and purse and headed for the door, then stopped abruptly, as if someone had spoken her name, calling her back.

Lela's own tears kept her from seeing clearly, yet she was hoping, perhaps, that the poor thing had changed her mind. Oh, more than anything, she wanted to help.

Melissa inched forward, making another attempt to exit. Yet once again she halted. Sighing ever so deeply, she set her overnight case down with some degree of resignation. Hugging herself, she seemed to stare past the door. Her expression changed from fear to grief. A pallor descended over her. "I can't go back. Can't *ever* go back," she whispered.

Seizing the opportunity, Lela reached out a hand. "Please stay longer, Mellie . . . as long as you like."

The young woman turned, her face a contortion of pain and sadness. Lela did what she knew best—she opened her arms to the hurting soul, and Melissa fell into them, sobbing without restraint.

After a time Melissa said she was tired and needed to lie down.

"May I steep some tea for you to take to your room?" Lela offered.

Mellie declined, desperation on her face. She made her way up the steps, slowly, methodically, lost in her anguish.

Thinking it wise to follow closely, Lela kept an eye on Melissa as the young woman went to the spare room, where she finally lay on the bed, breathing heavily.

"Oh, Ryan," whispered Mellie again and again. "Not you, too."

Lela pulled up the handmade quilt at the foot of the bed, placing it over Mellie's quivering body. The swollen red eyelids had closed, shutting out the world.

Watching over Mellie just now, Lela was reminded of the times she'd stood silently near the beds of her sleeping nieces and nephews. As if her presence were somehow consoling, though she took no pride in it.

When it seemed Melissa's breathing had slowed to a steadier rate, Lela felt the Lord prompting her to pray. She reached down and touched Melissa's arm lightly. *Father in heaven, please comfort this your dear one. Enfold her in your loving arms, for Jesus' sake. Amen.*

Sleep came at last. Lela left the room. She must phone Elizabeth right quick, let her know that Melissa would not be needing her car. Not just yet.

♦ ♦ ♦ ♦ ♦

Periodically throughout the afternoon, Lela checked in on her guest, but Melissa, sleeping soundly, did not stir once. It was well past five o'clock when Lela made another round past the spare room. She found Melissa sitting at the edge of the bed, looking a bit groggy, a sad, lost look in her eyes.

"May I get some tea for you now?" she asked, tapping the door that stood slightly ajar.

Attempting a weak smile—perhaps trying to acknowledge Lela's generosity—Melissa's face was stony white. "I should go," she said blankly, "back to Connecticut."

Lela was filled with dismay. Melissa was in no shape to drive any distance, much less all that way. "I thought you said . . . you could never return."

Melissa looked up at her, eyes glistening anew. "You've been so kind to me, Lela. It wouldn't be right for me to stay longer."

"Well, why not?"

Melissa's eyes lowered. "My life's in danger. I can't put you in jeopardy. If I stay . . . he might find me."

"*Who* will?" Lela was stunned by Melissa's admission. Perhaps, though, the young woman was just confused. Lela sat on the bed, turning her gaze back to Melissa. "Does someone want to hurt you?"

Nodding, Melissa leaned her head into her fists, beginning to cry.

"Does that person know where you are?" she probed gently.

"I don't see how . . . but it's still too dangerous."

"I believe God will keep you safe here, Mellie. He is bigger than the evil around us," Lela said. "Our help cometh from the Lord," she whispered.

Melissa looked doubtful. "Can God stop bullets?"

Lela's breath caught in her throat. *What sort of trouble is Melissa in anyhow?* she thought, not letting on. Bravely she smiled. "Are you in some kind of trouble . . . with the law, I mean?"

Melissa smiled crookedly. "No."

"Should we call the police?"

"They'll do nothing. And he'd find me for sure."

"You'll be all right here till you decide what to do. We'll trust in the Lord."

"Why are you willing to take the chance?"

Lela felt the assurance rise up in her. "Truth is, I've seen the miracle-working power of God in this community."

Melissa's gaze held hers, as though searching, hoping for truth, then she shook her head, lying back on the bed. "God doesn't answer my prayers."

"Mellie—"

Melissa shook her head, then closed her eyes again, hugging herself tightly, as if hiding from the world. Lela reached down, pulled the covers over her guest, and left the room.

◆ ◆ ◆ ◆ ◆

The next morning Lela knocked on Melissa's door. The door was ajar, and she saw that Mellie was up, sitting in a chair, pale and listless. "Were you able to sleep much at all?" she asked.

"I think so."

"What would you like to eat?"

"Only some juice, thanks."

Lela headed downstairs to fix breakfast. Maybe if Melissa smelled the food cooking, her nose would prod her stomach. How important that the girl keep up her strength. Especially being so emotionally overwrought.

Pouring batter into her waffle iron, she kept an eye on the eggs frying and bacon sizzling. She set the table, placing a small cluster of flowers in a vase for the centerpiece.

When the table was ready, she heard

footsteps on the stair and caught a glimpse of Melissa coming through the kitchen, heading toward the sun porch. "It's another nice day," she called to her. "Go ahead, have yourself a look round the garden."

Melissa obliged and went outside. Lela could see her looking out over the pasture-land to the east. She seemed motionless, quite forlorn.

After a time Lela carried a tray of freshly squeezed orange juice outside, offering some to Melissa, who accepted it graciously. "This may help to make you feel better," Lela said, hoping it would.

Their eyes met. "You remind me so much of . . ."

"Who?" Lela asked, curious to know.

"My best friend . . . Mrs. Browning."

Lela was glad to see Melissa coming out of her shell a bit. "Did you know each other from school?"

"No, she was lots older. She took care of me after . . ." She paused as tears filled her eyes. "My friend was like a mother to me."

"Where is she now?"

Melissa bit her lip. "I haven't seen Mrs. Browning in years. I used to talk to her about everything. I miss her so much."

"Some people say *I'm* a good listener."

Melissa nodded, her face drawn. "I know you are."

"I don't mean to pry, but if you feel like talking, I'm here for you. All right?"

The poor thing looked away, out toward the distant horizon. "I wouldn't even know where to begin," she said, her voice low. "I don't even know who I am anymore. I've lost my identity . . . and my husband in the same lifetime. Everything important to me is gone. . . ." Her voice trailed off and her shoulders shook with fresh waves of grief.

Lela was stunned, allowing her guest to sob out her pain. She wished she might comfort the poor girl, but she was unsure of what to do, considering Melissa's secrecy.

After a time she headed back into the house to check on the breakfast in the warming oven. Eventually Melissa followed and sat at the table, preoccupied as she reached for her cloth napkin and placed it solemnly in her lap.

Lela served up eggs and bacon, along with the waffles. "Sometimes when I need solitude, I take long walks," she said. "There's a beautiful place almost a mile from here. I call it my sanctuary, but it's not mine, really. Still, I can go and sit on the banks of the Conestoga River and talk to the Lord."

"Where is it?" Melissa asked.

"Did you come in by way of Hunsecker Mill Bridge?"

"Is that the covered bridge?"

"Yes, that's the one. Sometime, we'll go for a walk there."

Melissa seemed remotely interested. "I saw the bridge by moonlight last Friday evening. "

"It's mighty peaceful and lovely with the willows along the river," Lela added.

"I know that feeling of tranquility." Melissa had a faraway look in her eyes. "I had a place something like that, too, when I was a girl. Actually, it was Mrs. Browning's flower garden, the whole backyard of the house."

Lela was cautious, didn't want to pry into Melissa's past without permission. "Tell me about your best friend, if I may ask."

"Mrs. Browning . . ." Melissa began wistfully. "I was seven years old when my father, a widower, announced we were going to move to a small town in Colorado," she began. "It's hard to remember much about that time of my life, I was so young, but I do remember the overall feeling I had—one of confusion. Why did Daddy have to take us away from everything we knew and loved?"

Lela sat silently, eager for Mellie to continue.

"It was difficult, relocating so hurriedly.

And there was a great sense of urgency." She sighed, leaning back in the chair, reliving bits and pieces of her little-girl fears. "My father never explained the reason for the sudden change in our location. We flew to Denver the next night, leaving everything we owned behind at our home in Laguna Beach, California, except for a few changes of summer clothes and two of my favorite stuffed animals. My father said we could buy 'all new things' at our new home."

"How strange."

"Yes, but Daddy and I had each other. In a few short weeks, we settled into our little rental home in Palmer Lake, a place where everyone seemed to know everyone else. A quiet little town with friendly people. Folks there truly cared—teachers taught because they loved kids, not for the paycheck. Postal workers walked their route, stopping to visit along the way. And there was Mrs. Browning, who lived down the block from us—she and her husband became our good friends, our very best friends in the world."

The first time she'd met the British woman, Melissa and her father were choosing roses for the backyard at Algoma's Nursery, a small garden center on the outskirts of town. Mrs. Browning was also there, purchasing bedding plants. "Welcome to Palmer Lake," the middle-aged woman called across a table of pansies and petunias.

"Thanks," Melissa's father said. "Nice to be here."

At the time, Melissa found it interesting that the lady with a strong accent seemed to know they were newcomers. She tugged on her daddy's arm, whispering, "How's she know about us?"

He took time to explain that folks in a town this small knew who was a longtime resident and who wasn't. Melissa, all the while, watched Mrs. Browning's cart fill up with peachy pink roses. Missing their rose gardens in Laguna Beach, she was intrigued by the nice lady with creamy complexion, nut brown hair, and emerald eyes.

"Can we make more rose gardens, Daddy?" she asked, hiding behind her father.

"That's why we're here," he said, setting about picking out a number of hybrid tea roses, in a variety of colors, striking up a conversation with the cheerful woman, exchanging names and discovering that they were neighbors.

The next day Mrs. Browning and her husband, a sprite of a man, knocked on their door bearing gifts—strawberry shortbread and a box of chocolates. They were invited inside to chat, and from then on, Mellie was allowed to spend time with the charming couple.

Before their move, her father had been hesitant to let Mellie out of his sight. Here, in Palmer Lake, he seemed to trust people almost instantly. Especially Mrs. Browning. And Mellie was glad, because their neighbor was both fun and creative. Mellie fantasized that her deceased mother might've had similar qualities, though her father was reluctant to talk of his childhood sweetheart, now passed away.

*Daddy always had time for me. . . .*

She was especially fond of their after-supper hours. Curling up beside her father, Mellie listened intently as he read aloud, everything from *Heidi* to the classic fairy tales. Sometimes they watched favorite videos, always together.

Emery Keaton was outspokenly opposed to the violence so readily offered up on television. Having only one TV in the house, and a closely monitored one at that, kept Mellie somewhat sheltered during her primary grades.

One Tuesday, the week after school was out for the summer, she asked to go to the zoo. The day was exceptionally bright and warm for early June.

"Which zoo?" Daddy asked.

"I like Cheyenne Mountain Zoo best." She explained, in her little-girl fashion, that the walkways were steep and "very exciting." Meandering pathways, interspersed with flowers and foliage unique to Colorado, led them through the aviary, lion house, and outdoor bear exhibit. "Best of all, there's a great big monkey house." The tiniest monkeys always made her giggle. She liked the way they'd swing about, then turn and look down, eyes shining and mischievous, as if performing for her alone.

At the drop of a hat, Daddy took her off to the zoo. She never realized at that time just how financially well off they were. The fact remained, on a typical day her father rarely left the house. Occasionally, he did "run a few errands," but Mellie never knew precisely where his office was or if he even had one. Much of his supposed work took place at home, over the telephone. And after school, when she arrived eager to talk about the day, he was always there, waiting with warm eyes and smile.

There were frequent visits to the Brownings' home, as well. Mellie especially liked to wander about in the vast gardens beyond the house, thinking surely the place was much like, even patterned after, the "real" secret

231

garden in the world of Mary Lennox and Misselthwaite Manor.

"Do you know the book?" she asked Mrs. Browning one day while the two of them weeded the small-blossomed roses Mrs. Browning called her "Joseph's Coat" masterpieces. Tricolored, they were low growing, similar to a small bush, their red, orange, and pink petals forming as sprays or clusters.

"Why, of course I do." Mrs. Browning, it turned out, had made a trip with her sister to see the rose garden in Maytham Hall, Kent, England—the source for the fictitious one, where the author lived during the late 1800s. Just as the garden in the story had a hidden entrance with a low arch and a wooden door, the real-life garden did as well. "I adored the book *The Secret Garden*, and I don't know of anyone who should say differently."

Books, flowers, and outdoors in general became the attachment by which the twosome explored the world and their relationship. By the beginning of third grade, Mellie liked to think of her neighbor as a relative of some kind. An aunt, perhaps. But when she'd gotten up her nerve to inform Mrs. Browning of her hope, the woman gently chided her, saying they were "the best of friends, yes," but Mellie shouldn't think of her as more than that.

Saddened for a day, Mellie sought out her father for advice on the matter. "She's as close as any relative might be," she insisted, thinking of Nana Clark, whom she hadn't seen in the longest time. "So why won't Mrs. Browning let me call her 'auntie'?"

Daddy was kind, understanding. "The truth is Mrs. Browning is your friend." He paused, looking over his glasses as he lowered his newspaper. "Isn't she?"

Mellie agreed. "My *best* friend."

"Well, then, I'd say you have more than a pretend relative in our neighbor."

"What do you mean?"

"To say that someone is your friend is a wonderful thing." Her father went on to explain that not just *anyone* might have such a title bestowed on them. He said that relatives were usually not chosen, only inherited, "except, of course, in the case of adoptions." But the truth of the matter was that her father believed in the beauty of true friendship. "If you find one or two close friends in a lifetime, that is all a person needs."

Promptly, she shared her father's opinion with Mrs. Browning, who said she couldn't agree more, and that was that. Mellie and Mrs. Browning *were* friends—a higher calling than any common aunt or cousin. They were gardeners and bookworms, too, and what was wrong with that?

Her father also liked to help their neighbors by working in Mrs. Browning's gardens, due to the fact that Mr. Browning's back sometimes gave him considerable trouble. The most and best he could do was dig with a shovel—bending over and weeding were definitely out of the question.

Mellie often volunteered her father's services, helping Mrs. Browning, who wasn't getting any younger. Her father liked to make up rhymes about flowers, especially roses, as he worked. This became somewhat of a game for the three of them. He began by chanting the first line of the rhyme, and Mellie would say the next, and so on.

Sometimes her father would see who could name the author of a particular quotation, including Mrs. Browning in the contest. "Who knows this one?" Daddy might say, eyes gleaming. " 'There is no duty we so much underrate as the duty of being happy.' "

Mellie didn't have to think for long. The saying was one of Daddy's favorites. "Robert Louis Stevenson," she announced, glad to know.

"Never forget it, Mellie," Daddy said,

nodding his head and looking at her with all the love in his eyes.

And they *were* happy those first few years. Happy—if it meant a young girl could run down the street and spend time learning the names of flowers with a fifty-year-old British woman and her ailing husband. Happy—if it meant going to the library in nearby Colorado Springs, hoarding fiction books by the dozens, reading aloud to either Daddy or Mrs. Browning whenever skies were gray or clouds surrendered rain. Truly, happiness was growing up under the cautious eye of an attentive parent, someone interested in every minute detail of her life. But their cozy paradise was soon to be shattered.

## Chapter Twenty-Two

THE DAY WAS NOT unlike any other school day. Daddy made a hot breakfast and drove her to the Montessori School only a few blocks away. He always took her and dropped her off, no matter the weather.

With a wave and a smile he called after her, "I'll miss you, Mellie."

"See you this afternoon," she called back.

"Be careful." At every parting, he offered her a warning. The words rang in her thoughts. They had become his trademark. She must never forget. . . .

She didn't think much of it when two police officers arrived during afternoon recess. When they came in search of *her*, being escorted by the principal, she began to feel frightened. Never before had she encountered such serious-looking folk.

One of the officers was a lady with blond hair and gentle eyes. "Something's happened, Melissa," she said, squatting down. "We're here to take you home."

Uneasy, she followed them into the school building, gathered up her things, and headed toward the squad car. Her classmates were wide-eyed as she left, and she felt as if everyone was watching, which made her very nervous. She had not been a child who drew much attention to herself. She preferred to be left alone, always working independently of others, studying at her own fast pace. Today, being ushered out of the school by police unnerved her. She had no idea what was ahead.

Fear gripped her as they drove down the familiar street and neared her house, which was now surrounded by police cars. A long yellow strip encircled the property, but she did not see her father. And the squad car did not stop and let her out. Instead, the police-woman said they were "going to see Mrs. Browning."

"Where's my daddy?" she asked, starting to cry. "Why can't I go home?"

There was no answer, not at that moment. But soon, all too soon, she discovered the truth.

Mrs. Browning met her at the door, gathering her into her arms. "My dear, dear Mellie" was all she said.

A short time later, a lady—a social worker in a navy suit—arrived at Mrs. Browning's house. She was accompanied by a policeman, also wearing a dark suit. The woman sat with her on the sofa, patting Melissa's hand, which made the little girl very afraid.

"Where's my daddy?" she asked.

"There's been an accident," the woman said slowly, putting an arm around Mellie's shoulder. "Your father's gone to heaven."

"Daddy's *dead*?" She was overcome with grief. "How? Why?" she cried.

No words offered her comfort. She had need of answers.

But so did the social worker, it seemed. After the initial revelation that Daddy had indeed died, the woman quizzed her about her father. She was shown several pictures of men while the man in a suit stood in Mrs.

Browning's doorway, observing.

"I've never seen any of them," she stammered through her tears. "And I don't know where Daddy works or anything about what you're asking."

Mrs. Browning sat nearby, a worried expression on her face. At one point she cut in, asking if the little girl couldn't be allowed to grieve for her father "alone and in private."

The social worker glanced over at the man. "Are we finished here?" she asked.

He nodded and the woman consented to end the interrogation. Mellie, relieved to see them go, flew into Mrs. Browning's arms. There she felt safe as her friend spoke in soothing tones for the longest time, stroking her head until Mellie had no more tears left to cry.

In the days following her father's death, Mellie stayed with the Brownings, after a scribbled will was discovered. A judge agreed to recognize it as the last will and testament, believing the appointment of guardianship to be "in the child's best interest, due to the pre-existing bond." Grandpa and Nana Clark were not considered an option because of health and other concerns of aging.

Mellie continued her education at the private school, with funds from her father's life insurance policy. But she kept to herself more than ever. The other girls treated her differently; some of the boys whispered rumors on the playground. One of those rumors she overheard at lunch one day. "Mellie Keaton's dad was murdered."

She wanted to shout back at the boy, who had no business spreading such horrid things. But she felt helpless to say a word. The truth was, Daddy was dead, but she didn't know, not for sure, what had happened to end his life. She stayed awake at night wondering how it could be that her father had died "accidentally." What sort of accident had killed a grown man in his own home?

The only way to avoid the cruel talk by her classmates was to pretend to be ill on occasion, and for several mornings in a row, she missed school. Mrs. Browning never questioned Mellie's complaints of headaches or stomachaches. Though her temperature reading was usually normal, Mrs. Browning seemed to understand. So she spent some days being read to, enjoying homemade soups and teas, and in general, being looked after with great compassion.

"I always wondered how the Good Lord would answer my prayers, my yearnings for a child," Mrs. Browning confided one day

when Mellie was suffering a throbbing head-
ache.

"You did?"

"Oh, most certainly, dear." Mrs. Browning's smile stretched across her face. "You are
the splendid answer to any woman's heart's
desire."

*Daddy had to die so Mrs. Browning could
have a daughter*, she thought innocently. *How
strange.*

Later that week Mr. Browning said that
he, too, "was very glad to have the honor of
helping Mrs. Browning raise our girl."

So Melissa felt thoroughly loved and
wanted, thanking God—if there was one—
for allowing her to live with such fine, compassionate folk.

◆ ◆ ◆ ◆ ◆

"Hickory, dickory, rose; the bug crawled
up the stem," she chanted.

"The rose looked down and she did
frown . . . hickory, dickory, rose," Mrs.
Browning finished the silly verse.

Mellie burst into laughter, recalling the
days when her father used to make up non-
sense rhymes as they worked in the garden
together.

On various occasions she had considered
calling her guardian by the name of

"Mother," but with her parents deceased, she couldn't bring herself to do so. Melissa had always thought of Mrs. Browning as a truly dear friend. And, as Daddy had often said, "one or two close friends in a lifetime, that is all a person needs."

Months turned to years, and her emotional recovery was slow. She made friends with more classmates, groping through life, learning to feel confident again. But her closest ties were to the Brownings and the life they had crafted for her. Hours were spent in the gardens behind the house, hours of deep thought and creativity. She liked to take her sketch pad and pencils and sit near the bed of ivory roses, missing Daddy, sometimes weeping. She threw herself into her drawings, illustrating her father's beloved roses, perfecting her drafts as she worked on them, erasing, reworking, and modifying during all her free moments.

Melissa also enjoyed the lake near the train tracks in town, where she and her German friend, Howard Breit, her first high-school boyfriend, liked to feed the ducks. He was handsome, with hazel eyes and a gentle spirit. They strolled around the lake together, Mellie doing most of the talking. Compared to other boys his age, Howard was shy. He spoke with a heavy accent, and his clothes, while always clean, were never brand name. Howard was his own person, though reserved. Melissa had befriended him because he was a newcomer to the community and didn't seem to fit in, especially at school. She knew that feeling all too well. So their friendship blossomed.

"What do you want to do when you grow up?" she asked one springtime day, their second year as friends.

He didn't know offhand, but he gave her his answer in time. It was while they tossed bread crumbs to one particularly rambunctious duck, he finally said, "I want to work at a job that makes good money."

"You're excellent in math, right? You could become a banker," Melissa offered.

Howard chuckled. "Yeah, I like numbers, especially with dollar signs in front of them."

"You can help me with my algebra. Okay with you?"

He smiled, his eyes dancing. "Thought you'd never ask."

Mellie wouldn't have thought anything was amiss with Howard. He was the nicest boy she'd ever known. He truly cared for her, didn't he? Even took her home to meet his sister and his parents, went with them to Denver several times to a play or to see the Broncos at Mile-High Stadium, and once, out to eat down at the Village Inn in Monument, a few miles away.

One day, while studying at the library, Howard fixed her with a serious gaze. "You never talk about your father," he remarked.

She was silent, not prepared for the question.

"How did he die?" Howard persisted.

"I'd rather not talk about it," she said abruptly. Howard looked hurt, and she felt guilty.

Later, on the walk home, she tried to smooth things over. "I'm sorry . . . I honestly don't know how my father died."

Howard looked at her as if eager to pursue the topic. "Are the rumors true?"

She stared at the ground. "What are people saying, exactly?"

"That your dad was hooked up with the mob."

She was stunned. "That's the dumbest thing I've ever heard."

But Howard wouldn't quit. He continued to pry, until she broke into tears.

When they arrived at the Browning home, she left him on the front lawn, running up the steps and into the house. She couldn't bear to look back. Why had Howard taken this sudden interest in the most painful part of her life?

Later that week Howard called to apologize. Gladly, she forgave him, even invited him for dinner on the weekend. Mrs. Browning cooked an authentic German meal of onion soup au gratin, beef roladen, potato balls, butter twist rolls, and Black Forest cake for dessert.

During the meal, things seemed normal again, until Howard excused himself to the rest room. When he was gone for more than a few minutes, Melissa began to wonder. She found the bathroom door wide open and no Howard. Down the hall, she pushed open her bedroom door only to discover her friend digging through her desk drawers. "Looking for something?" she demanded.

Howard turned, startled. Caught red-handed.

"I think you'd better leave," she said angrily.

Without a single word of explanation, Howard fled down the hallway and out the door. While she continued to see him at school, she never spoke to him again. With Howard out of her life, she just assumed the strange occurrences would cease. But she was wrong.

At one point Mr. Browning realized that some of his mail was missing, especially various financial statements. He began to watch the street more closely. One day he discovered Howard Breit poking grimy fingers into the mailbox. Mr. Browning shouted to the boy, but Howard ran off. Frustrated, he called the Breit residence but got only an answering machine.

Immediately he reported the stolen mail to the police. In the end, the boy was threatened with a five-hundred-dollar fine. But the mail was never returned.

The very next month Mellie was shocked when their trash was strewn about the yard, as if someone had been searching through it. "Must be your Howard," Mr. Browning quipped. But Melissa was not amused.

Eventually Howard dropped out of school, and Melissa never saw him again. But even more troubling things began to happen. On the day of her driver's test, after sealing her chance of acquiring a driver's license on her sixteenth birthday, she noticed a man following her from the town of Monument to Palmer Lake.

During her senior year, she often felt she was being watched, especially when she headed for her car after school. Sometimes she wondered if she was being followed as she drove home. At first she chalked up the tension to the lingering creepiness she'd come to associate with Howard Breit.

Unwilling to trust a new relationship with any of the boys at school, she decided she wasn't going to miss out on her own prom. "Let's go together . . . in a group," she suggested to three other girls who were also without dates.

They danced and laughed the night away. But coming home late—in the wee hours—she felt she was being followed again. The back of her neck broke out in a cold sweat, and she wished she hadn't offered to drop off the others. On the drive back to the Brownings' little home, she felt vulnerable and alone.

Slowly making her way down the narrow road, she thought of diverting the other car by pulling into another residence. See what the driver might do. Not feeling particularly courageous, she pulled up in front of her father's former rental house—the darling home she and Daddy had lived in for such a short time. Her heart leaped up when she realized that the car had pulled in behind her and was parked at the curb.

Not thinking, she gunned her car forward, hightailing it down the street, so frightened was she. Her need for safety had led the stalker to her very door. She burst into tears when she was safe at last, trying to make sense of it to dear Mrs. Browning. "Someone's after me!"

"Oh, honey, not in *this* town. More than likely the driver was a bit soused, just trying to find his way home from the tavern, that's all. No, no, you're perfectly safe here. No need to worry." Mrs. Browning seemed so sure of it that Mellie dismissed the night's events as a figment of her own imagination. After all, she was quite tired, her head filled with the music and the handsome tuxedoed boys. Maybe Mrs. Browning was right. There was nothing to worry about at all.

◆ ◆ ◆ ◆ ◆

Emery Keaton had set aside money for college in a trust fund for Melissa. After high school graduation in the fall, Mellie bid a fond but sad farewell to the Brownings, having enrolled in the Rocky Mountain School of Art in Denver. There she lost herself in the world of figure drawing, acrylic and watercolor painting, her greatest passion being landscapes and still life. The peculiar incidents of the past years faded as she poured herself into study, hoping to have her own art studio and gallery in the future, as both Nana Clark and Mrs. Browning had encouraged her to do. Nana, more recently in letters and phone calls. "Your grandfather and I are so proud of you, Mellie. Please keep in touch," Nana often said before hanging up. "We love you."

*Love . . .*

Where did love ever get you? Where did it lead . . . but to heartache?

In suffering the death of both her mother and father, and at such an impressionable age, she had lost a chunk of herself. What did she have to give another person when half her heart was buried six feet under?

## Chapter Twenty-Three

ON THE EVENING OF March twenty-first, during her final semester at the art school, Melissa received a phone call. She was delighted to hear Mrs. Browning's voice, but her spirits promptly sank when she was told the sad news. "Mr. Browning has passed away just this afternoon, God rest him. I hated to tell you so late in the day—"

"No, no, I'm glad you did."

"I worried that you might not sleep, Mellie."

"Forget sleep," she said, fighting back tears. "I'm on my way home." She promptly left, and in less than forty-five minutes was turning into the driveway.

Mrs. Browning was glad to have her; Mellie was a comfort, too, it appeared. Together they met with the funeral director to plan the local memorial service. Mrs. Browning held up amazingly well, but then she had always exhibited a cheerful spirit in the midst of trying times—one of the reasons Mellie was drawn to her in the very beginning.

After the burial, it took several days to answer all the sympathy cards and letters, thanking various friends and the Browning relatives for flower sprays and other remembrances. Mellie was glad to help with that particular chore, and while she was there, she also cleaned the little house from top to bottom, even rearranging some of the furniture and sorting through Mr. Browning's clothing and personal effects for donation to a Colorado Springs charity. Folks were generous with their condolences, bringing in home-cooked meals.

Melissa wondered what Mrs. Browning would do now. "Will you be all right here alone?" she asked, preparing to return to Denver the next day.

"I shall be fine. Don't you worry one lick about me. I have my gardens in spring and my books in winter."

"Are you sure?"

"Absolutely" came the firm reply. "I have my friends, too, a host of them. They'll look in on me." Mrs. Browning nodded her head, though the sheen in her eye gave her away.

Not convinced she should leave her second mother, not now—not this way—Mellie promised to check in, even spend weekends in Palmer Lake. Which she did, nearly every weekend until summer break.

❖ ❖ ❖ ❖ ❖

It was the day after graduation from art college. She was busy packing, hauling clothes and books and things out to her car. A middle-aged man approached her, came right up to her apartment steps.

"Are you Melissa Keaton?" He held up his badge briefly. "I'm Agent Galia, from the Federal Bureau of Investigation."

She nodded. "Yes . . . I'm Melissa."

*What does the FBI want with me?* At first she was startled, her memory jogged a little. The man seemed familiar, but, no . . . the more she studied him, the less she was sure. "Mr. Galia?"

"*Agent* Galia. I'd like to talk with you . . . about your father."

"My father?" Melissa said, confused,

then gestured toward her apartment door. "Let's go inside."

He sat in a chair facing her on the couch and began to weave a mind-blowing tale. He told her everything, starting with her father's true identity. The news struck her like an actual physical blow. He said that her father had been a high level "accountant" for an organized crime group.

Her mind reeled. *So . . . the rumors were all true. Her beloved father—a criminal.*

"At one point, he turned informant," Galia continued. "With the help of the FBI, both of you had to be protected, hidden away under the Witness Protection Program."

"Hidden?" Her vague memory of their quick escape to Palmer Lake.

"You were *both* given new identities."

*My real name isn't Keaton?*

"Your father wanted out, but once a gangster, always a gangster," the agent said with a sigh. He went on to share information about her background, her life in Laguna Beach, even details about her ailing mother, who was "completely unaware of her husband's wrongful activity."

And then the agent got to the point. He studied her, eyes narrowed. "Just before he fled, your father stole eighty million dollars, had it wired to a secret account. He didn't even tell us—the FBI—about the money. And, unfortunately, after he testified he was found and killed. His death may have been an accident; he may have collapsed under severe questioning concerning the money. There was evidence of torture. Either way, once they found him, his people wouldn't have let him live."

Melissa pondered this, speechless. She hugged herself, feeling alone, empty. She simply could not fathom such a horrible death. She was saddened anew.

Galia's expression was empathetic. "I'm deeply sorry about your father."

"I always wondered . . ." She fought the tears. "I never knew how Daddy died."

He sighed, as if reluctant to continue. "The money was never recovered. Overnight, eighty mil vanished into thin air."

"Eighty million dollars?" They had lived like anyone else, renting the little house down the street from the Brownings, scraping together enough money to buy rosebushes and occasional ice cream treats. Except for her private school instruction and the fact that her father was often at home, she never thought of them as more than middle-income folk.

"This is news to me," she managed, her voice sounding far away, even to her own ears. "I have no idea. There *were* some strange things going on several years ago." She remembered Howard's dishonesty, the mail incident followed by the trash episode. She told the agent about the day of her driver's test and the night of her prom—how a man had followed her both times. "He scared the living daylights out of me!"

Galia shook his head with disgust. "The kid was probably paid to snoop around. These are evil people, Melissa. Your father was a part of them, I hate to say. We have reason to believe they are presently on *your* trail. That's partly why I'm here today. This issue must be settled, once and for all, not only for your safety, but also because, rightfully, that money belongs to the U.S. government. Eighty million would go a long way toward efforts to eliminate organized crime."

"Are you saying that you think *I* know where the money is?" she asked.

Galia nodded. "Your father was a smart man. There's no question in our minds—he would have made provision for the money to be salvaged in the event of his demise."

Her father may have been smart but apparently not enough to protect his own life. She was aware only of monies that had been earmarked for her schooling, though a far cry from eighty million dollars. And she told him so.

"Think hard about it, Melissa. As long as the money is missing, your life is in danger." He put his note pad away and took out his business card. "I'll visit you again tomorrow. Meanwhile, here's my number. Call me if something comes up. The slightest clue may be helpful."

Just as the agent started for the door, something occurred to her. "How do you know the mob hasn't already recovered the money?"

Agent Galia smiled. "Good question. I'm afraid I can't answer that directly. But we know for sure they have not. That's all I can say for now."

Rattled, she accepted his card, twisting it in her fingers. When he left, she stood at the window, watching. *How can any of this be true?* she wondered. *My father . . . a criminal?*

Agent Galia strode down the sidewalk toward his car. She stood, still as a stone.

*Eighty million dollars . . .*

By late morning Melissa *had* thought of something. Not the location of the money but about Mrs. Browning's safety. She didn't want anyone, not even special agents, harassing her dear friend. In her hurry to pack, however, and in the midst of the shocking revelation, Melissa had misplaced the agent's card.

Looking in the phone book under the government pages, she located the FBI's Denver office. Quickly, she dialed the number.

"FBI," a male voice answered.

"May I speak to Agent Galia, please?"

"One moment." A pause. "I'm sorry, but no one by that name works in our office."

"But he was just *here.*"

"When was that, miss?"

"Just this morning. He came to my apartment."

"I'll check on Colorado listings." He was gone for less than a minute. "We have no record of any Agent Galia working for the FBI in this state, or anywhere in the country, for that matter."

Shaken, she pondered the strange information. "I don't understand."

"Has someone talked to you, claiming to be an FBI agent?"

"Yes." She gave her name and the gist of her conversation with the man claiming to be Agent Galia.

"I'll send someone out immediately."

Melissa was boxing up her dishes when the agent arrived. Her mind was in a frenzy of worry. *How can I trust anyone?*

She heard the bell ring and answered it. Another serious-looking gentleman, wearing a black pinstripe suit, stood before her, similar in appearance to the previous man in both demeanor and attire. When he had displayed his badge with the name "Agent Walsh" in plain view, she invited him inside, where he questioned her about "Agent Galia."

*This is like a sitcom*, she thought. *Only too ridiculous.*

The agent pulled out a photo and showed it to her. "Is that the man?"

"Yes," she breathed, feeling a pang of alarm. "That's Galia."

"His real name is Ivanov," Walsh replied. "He's been arrested before and brought to trial, but nothing sticks. It appears you may be in grave danger, Miss Keaton. I've been given authorization to reveal the complete story regarding your father. Typically, we would never confirm the existence of an informant . . . even to his own family."

When Agent Walsh described her father's involvement with the mob, all the details were the same—everything except for the money. He said nothing at all about the eighty million dollars.

When she revealed this information, Walsh was astonished. "Your father *was* a shrewd man," he acknowledged. "What we'd call a slick operator. I guess I shouldn't be surprised at all."

This character assessment was far from comforting.

"The Witness Protection Program was necessary for you and your father—for your survival," Walsh explained. "Your father had testified in court to no avail. The fear-ridden jury refused to convict, resulting in a hung jury. The Justice Department case against the organized crime group collapsed, and there were no additional witnesses to provide the evidence needed. Further investigation conducted through the years has been fruitless."

She listened, amazed at the information. "So without an 'informant' there was no case?"

Walsh nodded. "That's how Ivanov operates. Those he can't bribe, he terrorizes. Those he can't frighten, he eliminates. After your father's death, the FBI dropped out of the picture. Mistakenly, we assumed you were safe. But your father never told us about any money. In fact, that would have been a clear violation of our agreement." The agent paused. "But now we have something—impersonating an FBI agent is a crime. We need to pursue this."

"What do you mean?"

"Ivanov was going to return tomorrow, right?"

She nodded, fear gripping her in fresh waves.

"The next visit likely would not be a friendly one. In all probability, he would drop all pretense, resorting to more cruel means of obtaining information." His eyes softened. "It's a good thing you called us."

A dark shiver ran up her back.

"If we can find Ivanov, we'll arrest him and try him with *your* testimony. Can you locate his so-called business card?"

Within ten minutes she found the imposter's phone number. Agent Walsh dialed the number on his own cell phone and reached a Denver hotel. The man had already checked out. Instantly, the lead had vanished.

"We'll have to wait . . . watch for him. We can set you up temporarily, try to lure him out again."

"I'm not your bait," she broke in firmly. She thought of Mrs. Browning and her grandparents. How would they feel if she, too, just happened to die from an "accident"? Hiding out hadn't helped her father in the end. Ivanov had found him. Now they knew where *she* was. . . .

"We need your testimony, Miss Keaton.

We have a chance to catch the man who killed your father. "

"I'm sorry, but you don't seem to protect your informants very well."

"Miss Keaton—"

"And nothing will bring my father back," she replied coldly.

Walsh glanced at the floor, shaking his head as frown lines wrinkled his brow. "You have no idea who or what you're dealing with—just how treacherous these people can be. If Ivanov finds you again . . ." His voice trailed away.

"You mean that I might end up like Daddy," she said accusingly.

The agent looked embarrassed. "If he thinks you know something about the eighty million—more specifically, where it's hidden . . ."

Walsh seemed at a loss for words. "Melissa, if you won't help us, we can't force you," he continued. "Off the record, if you wish to be safe, your best bet is to find a way to drop off the planet. Go where you can't be found."

He offered his personal contact number. "If you change your mind . . ."

She accepted his card. "Will they bother my friend, Mrs. Browning, my legal guardian?"

Hesitating, Walsh said, "I seriously doubt

it. These guys operate in the shadows."

That was some comfort. But only a little.

She contacted a private investigator, doing exactly as the FBI agent had advised. The PI, in turn, gave her a quick lesson on the art of disappearance: Find someone who has died and assume their identity.

Melissa recalled an acquaintance at the art institute whose sister had died at a very young age. The deceased girl's name had been Melissa, as well; born in Marshall, Minnesota. Perfect.

After purchasing a short auburn wig, she attempted to make a radical change in her appearance. Only to save her life. She left in the middle of the night by taxi, checking in at a nearby Denver hotel, leaving behind her car and an apartment filled with her packed belongings. Mrs. Browning and others would think she was kidnapped for sure, but there was no other way.

While at the hotel, she was able to obtain a fake birth certificate and a new social security number. In a matter of days, she was Melissa Nolan, from Marshall, Minnesota, having appropriated the other girl's vital data. Miss "Nolan" paid cash for her plane ticket to the East Coast, traveling by car to Westerly, Rhode Island, where her father had often visited. There she began her new life.

In New England she established residence close to her waitressing job at the Olympia Tea Room in Watch Hill, discarding the wig and heavy makeup. But the pain and deep disappointment regarding her father and his criminal involvement remained, torturing her night and day.

Was there one good person left in the world? Whom *could* she trust?

She had abandoned her life in Colorado, leaving all that was precious to her, never having the chance to make good on her hopes and dreams of establishing her own art gallery. All this for a peaceable life. At least she was safe here in Watch Hill.

## Chapter Twenty-four

LELA SHIFTED IN HER CHAIR, eyes fixed on Melissa. "So how was it you came to meet your husband?" she asked.

"I'd always felt we were *supposed* to meet, if you know what I mean," she said, recalling wistfully that moment in time.

Some people were simply born gregarious. Ryan James was one such person. She'd first noticed him at the restaurant, stopping in for breakfast or lunch, about a week after she began working as a waitress at the Olympia Tea Room, one of the nicest places a person might ever expect to work or dine. Though a far cry from the world of painting she had planned for herself, the tip money alone more than paid for her rent and groceries. So, for the time being, she was set financially.

"It's only temporary," she explained to the tall and handsome man when he asked why a bright girl like herself was waiting on tables.

He took her answer in stride, steering their conversation to other things, speaking of his brokerage firm, "in Mystic . . . ever been there?"

She hadn't. And she had no intention of leaving the protection of the cozy small-town feel of Watch Hill. Not even when he offered her a job as receptionist was she interested in broadening her horizons. She was still getting her bearings, acclimating to the name Nolan instead of Keaton, reminding herself that her birthday was no longer in mid-October but rather early May. She'd also falsified her life story to exclude the Brownings and, most importantly, her father's dealings, telling Ryan that her mother had died when she was a baby and that her father abandoned them shortly after. As far as the handsome broker knew, she'd grown up in a small town in Minnesota, where winters crept in stiffly on the heels of autumn, where folk took long walks to cool hot tempers instead of resorting to domestic violence, where curling up with a good book or touring an art museum in the big city of Minneapolis was the rule, not the exception.

Week after week Ryan came to the restaurant, ordering full dinners over the lunch hour, no doubt to keep her coming back to his table, she came to realize. They talked, snippets of conversation here and there, when she brought his salad, more coffee, the dessert. Over time they got to know each other, though she'd never sat down across from him at the table, secretly longing to. She even wished he might ask her out, yet not knowing if she could follow through with a solid romance, the kind her heart longed for.

So she'd backed off, changing her work schedule, sending him an unspoken message. Suzie, however, kept her appraised of his comings and goings. More "no shows" than before. Must be that he was taking the hint, backing away from what might have been.

"The day Ryan found me on the beach was really amazing," Melissa said. She told Lela of the wild roses, dyed both red and white by genetic origin, growing in nodding rows near the shoreline. Scent so fragile, yet alluring, she ran to them, eager to embrace their beauty . . . uncultivated and free. Here they flourished where one would least expect such robust blossoms, recipients of wind and weather, competing for attention with the enormity of the indigo sea. Minuscule distractions, no doubt, to the swell and pounce of breakers, the dash and spray of tide, and the salty bouquet of the deep. For Melissa, these roses held a special meaning, all the same. Delicate and lovely, they grew amidst smelly seaweed and polluted sand, like an innocent child surrounded by evil.

"I was so glad to be off work," she said. "Tired of carrying trays and serving impatient customers."

She had set up her tripod a few yards from water's edge, determined to paint as long as she pleased. Here, along the shoreline of her favorite beach, she settled in for the duration, happy for the leisurely flow of the day. Be it sailboats, seaweed, or sea birds, she would paint to her heart's delight. Whatever captured her fancy.

Heaven knows she needed a day like this, after what she'd gone through to find her way to safety and tranquility. Yet she'd left all that was dear behind. Never sparing time to say good-bye to either her grandparents or Mrs. Browning, she'd flown off to her new life, like a warbler's migration. A season of change, in all respects. Yet the season was rife with summer, heart-stoppingly picturesque in every way.

A swan caught her eye. The gentle creature must have crossed the ridge, perhaps followed her here. She picked up her brush and made wide, broad strokes, composing the vision of grace before her on canvas. Oh, to share this moment with Mrs. Browning. More than ever, she missed the dear lady, having only been in Rhode Island for three months. Not a single day passed that she didn't think of the woman, reliving the good days, the happy times, before everything changed. The ivory color of the swan reminded her of Daddy's favorite roses—white as the moon.

"The farmer in the dell," she sang, remembering her father's nonsensical response. *Farmer's stuck in the well . . .*

How many times had she and Mrs. Browning laughed over that one? And all the other ridiculous, meaningless rhymes Daddy created as they tilled and weeded the rose gardens at both the Browning house and their own. This couldn't be the same Daddy that . . .

Sighing, she knew if she recalled the memories for too long, she'd wind up weeping. Not today. Not here where the beach seemed to belong to her and her alone. Where a friendly swan had decided to pose for her, lingering near the shoreline, having waddled or flown over from the harbor, no doubt.

She focused on the gossamer whiteness, its feathers a high sheen in the luster of sun and half shadow. The sinuous movements intrigued her, and leaving her palette and canvas, she wandered out near the water, pulling bread crumbs from a small sack she'd brought with her, flinging the morsels. She laughed softly, coaxing the exquisite bird closer . . . closer.

In afternoon's light, she stopped to listen, absorbing surf and sound, enthralled by the idyllic moment. She thought no more of her father, of loved ones, of her daring dash to safety. She put all of it behind her, caught up in the rapture of the swan, its tantalizing poise and amity beguiling her.

How long she remained there, feet stuck in wet sand and the ebb and flow of tide, she cared not. Her very existence she celebrated in that sweeping moment, when nature and beast reached into her very soul. She was alive! She'd survived the ordeal of her past. In one brush stroke of fate, she had been made new. The time had come to submit, give in to love fully.

*Turn over more than one leaf at a time,* she told herself.

She must, as this swan did, acquiesce to both sun and shade. Allow the sky, as broad and lucid as heaven, to spread its canvas of blue, red, or gold above her; it mattered not. And the handsome young man who continued to pursue her, stopping by the restaurant to make supposed small talk over soup and sandwiches, was a big part of it. So why not? She had every reason to cease worry and enjoy life for a change, without fear.

This was *her* time, at last.

◆ ◆ ◆ ◆ ◆

Melissa soon discovered Ryan sitting there in the sand. Not knowing how long he'd been there, *watching her,* she thought back to her interaction with the swan, blushing at her spontaneity. Nevertheless, Ryan had found her, observing her delight over the lone swan, soaking up the sunshine, rejoicing in her newfound life.

She had been wary of the dashing man since they'd met. Unwilling to trust, unsure of herself; too vulnerable, perhaps. This being the first time she'd ever gone so far from home, she felt she had better look out for number one. For too long now she had been looking over her shoulder, half expecting to come face-to-face with more of the insanity.

Something real changed in her that day at Napatree. It may have been the manner in which Ryan spoke to her, taking his time to let the moment unfold. Or perhaps it was that she sensed he was trustworthy after all. All the same, she'd met a man who, like herself, longed for a profound and meaningful companionship. Not just the flirtatious here-today-gone-tomorrow type of thing. No, Ryan James was solid as granite. And sure. She felt she could bet her life on him.

They began dating, falling into the swift current of a serious relationship. They saw each other regularly, nearly every day. She shared her love of art, told him about the secret meaning of roses, reciting the various hues and classifications. Before too many weeks they became engaged—she, accepting a ring, and Ryan pressing to set a wedding date.

But one morning she freaked and left her fiancé wondering what had happened to her. She'd awakened from a terrifying dream. A nightmare that involved the remnants from her past as Melissa Keaton, a dream so real, she nearly fell to her knees in prayer. Her father was being tied to a chair, asked repeatedly the same question: *"Where is the money?"*

He refused to reveal a thing to the men in the room, the living room where bedtime stories had been lovingly told to Mellie, where she had laughed and romped and played with her darling father, the very room that had become their refuge from the universe. That day their home had been violated, her faith in all things good and true shattered. And now her dreams were menacing reminders of what she was trying to escape.

*I can't let them touch Ryan*, she thought, throwing clothes into a suitcase. She felt she must be crazy to fall in love with someone normal, someone who was innocent to the malevolence that lurked in the shadows, threatening to find and devour her. No, she would not let them hurt Ryan, too.

So she fled, "losing" herself for two days in the city of Providence, where she could easily hide, crying herself to sleep, knowing she had given up all hope of happiness. And she would have followed through, sneaked back to Watch Hill and packed up the few items she called her own, never to see Ryan again. She would've done so had she not missed him so desperately. Not only missed him but longed to be his wife, to start anew, to put the past behind her. This she decided the afternoon of the second day, phoning Ryan at his office in a panic, weeping . . . sobbing her apology.

Soon after, they planned a private wedding on a ridge of rocks jutting out into the ocean. To the cry of sea gulls, they sealed their love, tossing rose petals into the water below. The setting sun splashed reds and golds onto the blue canvas overhead, a ceremonious canopy. And Melissa Leigh Nolan took Ryan's hand and his last name, embracing the covering of his love. Forever. . . .

## ◆ *Chapter Twenty-five* ◆

THE WATERFRONT HOUSE lay at the far end of the road, set apart from the other homes by ample landscaping and trees. Hand in hand, they strolled up the stone walkway, Ryan grinning from ear to ear. Melissa wasn't quite sure why her husband had brought her here, having picked her up from the florist shop, her new workplace, and whisking her off to Lord's Point. "Whose house is this?" she asked, innocent as to what Ryan had planned.

"Ours." He opened the door for her.

She was amazed at the spaciousness, the open, light feeling as she stepped over the threshold and into the home facing the water. "You're kidding, right?"

Leaning against the door, he folded his arms over his chest. "I bought it with you in mind."

She had no reason to distrust him; he'd never lied to her before. "But we don't have money set aside. . . ."

He caught her and pulled her close, kissing her lips. "We have money you know not of," he teased. Then, turning toward the kitchen, he led her through the house. "So what do you think?"

What did she think . . . well, she could scarcely get the words out. "The truth?"

"And nothing but."

Standing in the middle of the sun-room, windows wide and wonderful, she claimed the place immediately for her art studio. "I love this room," she whispered, tears threatening to blur her vision. "Are you sure . . . this is really ours?"

"Every square inch." Ryan crossed the room to her. "Wait till you see the backyard."

She'd already glimpsed the garden area, the rolling lawn, and the private dock not many yards from the back door. Together they meandered about the place, pointing out perfect locations for various flower beds and Melissa's dream come true—her very own rose garden. *I'll have gardens like Mrs. Browning's,* she thought, relishing the idea, wishing above all she could share the truth of her past with her dear husband.

On several occasions she'd started to tell him, but each time decided to wait. Once, while Ryan was watching a television program depicting the dealings of the Mafia, he had laughed out loud, discouraging her further. "Is this for real?" he said, obviously surprised at the facts presented by the commentator. So Melissa withdrew, waiting for the right moment, which never seemed to come.

They moved in promptly, decorating the house from a seemingly bottomless account Ryan said he was glad to share with her. "Been saving up for something like this for a long time," he told her.

She was frugal in her decisions, however, choosing colors and fabrics, furnishings that met her liking. She included Ryan in the decision-making process, though he wanted *her* to do as she pleased. He made it very clear that this was more her home than his, "only because I know you're an artist and a woman." She had let him sweep her into his arms at that remark. "Women have a knack for making a house much more than just a place to hang a hat," he whispered, his face buried in her hair.

Laughing, she freed herself, reaching for his hand and taking him upstairs. "I want you to see where I've hung some of my paintings."

He obliged, and she was proud to show him the canvas displaying the friendly swan. "I thought this wall was best for it," she said.

"It is." He paused, studying the painting.

"Remember that day?"

He drew her near to him. "How could I forget?"

So the framed canvas remained in the hallway, across from the door leading to the master bedroom. "You can't miss it, coming and going."

"It's perfect," said Ryan. "Like you."

◆ ◆ ◆ ◆ ◆

The Amtrak train to Manhattan was always prompt, and that day Ryan ran ahead, glancing over his shoulder to see that she was close behind as they approached the platform. They had planned a weekend in the city, making the rounds of various art museums. "It's your birthday, so we'll do what you enjoy today."

*May seventh*—her first encounter with the new birth date. Disorienting at best. Having been accustomed to an autumn celebration for as long as she could remember, the springtime event fell flat.

"What's wrong, honey? Aren't you having a good time?" Ryan asked as they grabbed a salad at a nearby deli.

She couldn't bring herself to tell him that the day was an ordinary one, in fact, *not* her birthday at all. The whole situation seemed rather silly now that she felt perfectly safe as Ryan's wife, living in an out-of-the-way place like Lord's Point. Their home was nestled on a promontory, bordered by Quiambaug Cove and Fishers Island Sound. The cape was sparsely populated, a plus for someone yearning for peace.

"I'm fine," she answered, presenting him with her most endearing smile. "What a fabulous place to celebrate a birthday." She considered the little girl, Melissa Leigh Nolan—the *real* girl—long-since buried. Not only had she stolen the child's name and birth date to escape to freedom, to a life worth living, she had chosen to continue the lie. Playacting, of sorts. But what else was she to do?

◆ ◆ ◆ ◆ ◆

It was a Friday morning in mid-August when her good friend Ali Graham called Melissa at work. "Can you get away for an hour or so?" Ali had asked.

Melissa knew she could. Her boss recognized a loyal worker when she saw one. Melissa was certainly all that and more, a conscientious florist's assistant.

"It's been forever since we've had salad and a good face-to-face," Ali said, using their catch phrase.

"A face-to-face, eh?" She laughed, glad her friend had called. "I'll meet you there."

S&P Oyster Company, located beside the drawbridge, was crammed with hungry noontime patrons. Melissa gave her name to the receptionist and was told the wait would be "about ten minutes." Okay with that, she and Ali chatted, catching up on each other's lives. She noted the maroon awning above the outside deck, where small white lights twinkled over flower boxes, night and day.

Expansive windows on the entire west side of the restaurant looked out to the river. Private yachts and the *Mystic Belle* were docked nearby. *The Sabino*, a steam-powered passenger vessel, formerly an island steamer in Casco Bay, Maine, transported tourists to and from Mystic Seaport, a maritime museum.

"Did you and Ryan get to the outdoor art festival last weekend?" Ali asked.

"Wouldn't miss it. Great stuff."

Ali said that she and her husband had gone to Boston for a play. "Sometime the two of you should go with us."

"Sounds like fun." Melissa felt a bit overwhelmed by the crush of the crowd waiting for tables. "Maybe we should go somewhere else to eat," she commented.

They were about to leave when her name was called. They followed the hostess down the step to a table for two near the window, overlooking the water. Once seated, she said, "Glad we stayed?"

Ali agreed. "With a waterfront seat? Sure am."

They quickly ordered from the menu, glad for the opportunity to visit.

Midway through lunch, Melissa noticed a man seated across the room from them. Curious, she stared at him. His angular, square chin and piercing eyes drew her attention. Then it came to her.

"Ivanov," she whispered. Here, on *her* turf, was the man who'd claimed to be with the FBI in Denver, using the name Galia.

"What?" Ali said, obviously confused.

Melissa watched him a moment longer. She didn't think he had seen her. But it was only a matter of time before he did. She turned in her seat, shielding her face from his view.

*Now what?*

"Are you okay?" Ali asked, frowning.

"I don't feel good. I . . . I'd better leave."

Ali looked worried. "I'll drive you."

"No." She rose from her seat, grabbing her purse. "I'll see you later. I'm sorry."

"Mellie . . ." Ali called after her.

Outside, she stood across the street, waiting . . . watching the entrance. From her position she could see the entire restaurant. Several couples emerged during the few moments she waited. But Ivanov did not.

When she could wait no longer, she turned and headed up the street toward her parked car. *How foolish of me!* she thought as the realization of her precarious situation sank in. Why did she have to handle things herself? Her way?

At home she wasted no time locating the business card for the FBI's Agent Walsh, the kind man who had offered her protection back in Denver. The man whom she had not so politely refused.

Fingers shaking, she dialed the agent. Thankfully, he remembered her. "I wondered what had happened to you," said Agent Walsh. "You were going to keep in touch."

277

Quickly, she told her story, that for three years she'd been living in the Mystic area under an assumed identity. "But today I saw Ivanov at a restaurant downtown. I don't know what to do."

"Did he see you?" he asked, his voice suddenly tense.

"I'm not sure."

"I don't like the sound of this. And I don't believe in coincidences. Do you think it's possible he followed you to the restaurant?"

"I just don't know. How could he have found me?"

"That's what troubles me," the agent replied. "Think carefully. Did he follow you home?"

"I don't think so. I waited for him to follow me out of the restaurant, but I didn't see him come out."

The agent sighed.

"Should I call the police?"

"That may not be the best course," he replied. "That would only make you an easy target. This man is very dangerous. Unfortunately, I don't have an agent in the area right now. Let's go over this again. . . ." He asked her a few questions, starting with her address, whether she had kept in touch with her old friends and relatives, and whether or not she had ever married.

"My husband works for New England Asset Management," she told him.

A sudden pause. "Melissa," he said, his voice rising slightly. "You must do exactly as I say."

The terror, that all-too-familiar response, rose in her chest, blocking her lungs, making it difficult to breathe or to think.

"You must leave the area immediately . . . don't say a word to anyone."

"I don't understand."

"We have no time to debate this, Melissa. Find a safe place, a *new* location. Make sure you're not followed. When you arrive at your destination, call me again. Do not use your cell phone, except in an emergency."

"What about my husband? I can't just leave him."

"Your husband will be safe. Trust me."

"But—"

"Listen to me," he said, his voice adamant. "Your life is in grave danger. I'll explain everything when you call."

She hung up, nearly hysterical, found her overnight case, and scribbled a note to Ryan. Saying good-bye to their dog, she hurried to the car.

Once on the highway, she gave in to her fear and desperation. More than that, though, was her concern for Ryan's safety.

"You poor thing," Lela said, brushing tears from her eyes. "What you've been through."

Melissa had surprised herself by sharing so much. Yet now, looking into the face of the Mennonite woman, she knew Lela would keep her secrets, guard the truth. In the very core of her, she knew.

"When you called the FBI agent yesterday, what did he tell you . . . about your husband?" Lela asked, her eyes compassionate.

Melissa folded her arms at her waist, holding herself against the sadness that swept over her. How could she voice the words? Breathing deeply, she leaned forward, revealing the startling information. "Ivanov wasn't the only reason I had to leave Connecticut."

"Whatever do you mean?" Lela frowned.

Melissa shook her head, tears falling fast. *Just like Daddy* . . . "It's about Ryan," she whispered, then stopped, unable to speak.

Lela touched her arm gently. "What is it?"

Struggling with the reality, she said softly, "Ryan is—is one of *them*."

"I don't understand." Lela's frown seemed to encompass her entire face.

"Ryan works for the same people who killed my father."

# *Part Two*

*It is only with the heart
that one can see rightly;
what is essential is invisible to the eye.*

Antoine de Saint-Exupery

◆ ◆ ◆ ◆ ◆

# Chapter Twenty-Six

THE DAWN WAS BRIGHT, the sky clear. Mystic River flowed effortlessly toward the ocean. Several ducks waddled to the edge, hoping for handouts. Ryan had none to give as he leaned against the railing, hours before he was expected to arrive at work.

He had come to Mystic River Park, as he often did, to ponder the past few days. To question how everything had gone so wrong; how he might make it all right again.

"Hey, Mister Ryan."

He turned to see Stevie, a brown-haired boy, holding two fishing rods in his right hand and a tackle box in his left. Several months ago they'd met at this very spot. Ryan had bantered with Stevie, and the lonely boy had haltingly invited Ryan to fish with him. Since then it had become an oft-repeated event.

Ryan smiled at him. "Haven't seen you for a while."

"I've been here. Every morning," his young friend replied with a slight tone of reproach.

"Sorry. Been busy."

"Too busy today?"

"Give me that pole, young man. Let's wake up the fish."

Stevie broke into a grin. All was forgiven. Together they attached their bait and tossed the lines into the water. They fished for over an hour, enjoying each other's company, talking about guy stuff.

"Catch anything?" someone said behind them. Ryan turned to see Jim Ivanov leaning up against the retaining wall.

Ryan was surprised to see him. "Thought you were coming next week."

Jim shrugged, staring at the water. "Something came up."

"Bernie know you're here?" Ryan asked.

"Not yet."

"Have you had breakfast?" Ryan asked, making small talk.

He glanced at Stevie, whose face was crestfallen. He twitched the fishing line.

Ivanov ignored Ryan's question. "You going to be in the office today?"

"For a few hours. Have to take a friend to the airport this afternoon."

"I need a meeting with you and Bernie. Say about nine o'clock?"

Ryan frowned. "Is there a problem?"

"Nah," Jim replied casually, walking away.

"That guy's creepy," Stevie said once Ivanov was out of earshot.

"He just doesn't have any friends to play with," Ryan said.

Stevie giggled, pulling back on his fishing pole.

◆ ◆ ◆ ◆ ◆

"God will help us," Lela whispered as early-morning rays danced on the kitchen wall. She bowed her head, thinking of Melissa, still asleep upstairs. "Dear Lord, I stand on the promises of your Word. I rest in your care, confident of your mighty power. Thank you. Amen."

Mellie's words echoed in Lela's mind: *"You're in danger if I stay here."* She felt the slightest shiver of fear again. But she remembered the Scripture: "The angel of the Lord encampeth round about them that fear him." Renewed peace flooded her heart. She was doing the right thing, encouraging Melissa to stay put. Whatever danger lurked outside her doors, God was in control. Both she and Mellie were safe.

Melissa had not slept well. Her thoughts whirled with memories of the man she had believed in, trusted, and married. How could it be that her beloved husband was in league with the same group who'd taken her father's life? Part of her rejected it, disbelieving that her support system, all wrapped up in one wonderful man, could have been false.

She recalled one event after another where Ryan was true and good. Always forthright and decent. Never once had she doubted him or suspected that he might be less than honest in his business dealings or with her. She wished she could phone him and ask him for herself, yet she dared not.

Pushing back the covers, Melissa rose to face the window. She stared past the curtains to the sky, blue as a robin's egg. Ryan's words came back to haunt her. *"I have money you know not of,"* her husband had playfully teased her when first they'd gone to Lord's Point to see their house. At the time she'd wondered about his comment, but only for a flicker of a moment. The shine in his eyes, that spontaneous look of expectation and joy, had erased even the slightest hint of doubt.

Finally, she had to face something she hadn't thought about in years. *Eighty million dollars.* Where *was* it? If only she knew the answer to that, perhaps then, and only then, would this nightmare cease. As long as men like Ivanov suspected she knew where her father had holed away eighty million dollars, as long as they were watching her every move, she would never be truly free.

*Does Ryan know about the money?* Melissa wondered. *Did he trick me into marrying him, hoping I might reveal something someday? Has everything about our marriage been a lie?*

◆ ◆ ◆ ◆ ◆

Marge was at her desk when Ryan entered the reception area. "Mr. Personality is in town," she whispered grimly.

Ryan smiled. "Yeah, I know."

Her eyes darted toward Bernie's office. "They're in there."

"Hmm." Ryan headed for his own office and began preparing for his daily trading routine, turning on his wall of monitors.

Several minutes later Marge peeked in. "Bernie wants to see you—ASAP." She jerked her head toward Bernie's office, giving Ryan a look that said, *Pretty weird, eh?*

Ryan stood up quickly, trying to remember the last time Bernie had called him to the executive office. He followed Marge across the reception room to the door with the words *Bernard Stanton* etched in gold.

Ryan rapped twice on Bernie's door and opened it. Immediately to his left, Ivanov stood up. "Have a seat." Ivanov gestured toward his now vacant chair, as if it were *his* office Ryan was entering. "I'll leave you two alone for a moment." The client slipped out.

Ryan quickly appraised the seat that Ivanov had just vacated, choosing instead to sit in the chair opposite Bernie's desk. Glancing at his boss expectantly, their eyes met, then Bernie dropped his gaze to his hands, rubbing them together, as if preparing a speech.

"You wanted to see me," Ryan ventured.

Bernie didn't speak at first, allowing an uncomfortable silence to fill the room. A room nearly twice the size of Ryan's office. The floor, covered in deep forest green carpet, accented the mahogany bookcases and desk that the boss seemed to hide behind. *No wonder he escapes here every day,* Ryan thought fleetingly. *It's a paradise.*

Bernie stood tentatively, turning his back on Ryan to look out his tall windows. It was obvious by his awkward movements that the older man was deeply troubled. The ever-lengthening silence only served to unsettle Ryan's nerves.

Ryan frowned. "Everything okay, Bernie?"

His boss turned to face him, tracing his finger along his desk.

"Did we lose a client?" Ryan asked, thinking of Ivanov.

Bernie sat down again, steepling his fingers. He paused again. "Do you have any idea what we've been doing here all these years?"

"What do you mean?"

Bernie met his gaze. "Don't play games with me. I'm talking about our *business* . . . those stock symbols I feed you from time to time."

Ryan, loath to voice the words, replied softly, "Insider trading."

Bernie snorted, dropping his hands to the desk and giving Ryan a look of disgust. "For starters, yeah. Throw in money laundering, and you've got a better picture. Don't say you didn't figure *that* out years ago. If you didn't, then you're not as smart as I give you credit for."

Ryan had tried to ignore the occasional suspicious nature of their transactions. "It was none of my business," he replied, hoping Bernie would drop it.

"Why rock the gravy boat, eh?" Bernie stood tall, considering Ryan cynically. "You've been well paid to look the other way."

"What's your point?" Ryan asked.

"I'm getting to that." Bernie angled his head toward the reception area and lowered his voice. "First off, Ivanov isn't just a client. He *owns* us."

Bernie's admission sent shock waves through Ryan. "He *what*?"

Leaning forward, his boss continued. "He and his partners run an extensive inter-state network. Our company, New England Asset Management, is only a front, with a few *real* clients tacked on to make things look legit." Bernie dropped his gaze to the desk again. "And . . . do you remember a little more than three years ago, when we were in-terviewing potential secretaries?"

Ryan shifted in his seat, uncomfortable with the direction the conversation was tak-ing.

"I sent you out to Watch Hill to interview Melissa for the job," Bernie said. "Did you think I'd merely picked out a cute waitress and decided to hire her as office dressing? Truth is, Melissa's *father* used to work for Ivanov. I figured the best way to keep an eye on her was to have her work for us. We never expected you to *marry* her."

Ryan's mind reeled with Bernie's rapid-fire revelations. *Keep an eye on her. . . .*

Before Ryan could respond, a single knock came at the door. Ivanov ambled in, carrying a coffee mug. He sat down and fixed Bernie with a smug smile. "My turn?"

Bernie shrugged and pulled out a hand-kerchief, mopping his brow.

Ivanov chuckled, seemingly aware of the crackle of tension in the room. He picked up the story without missing a beat, his slight Russian accent becoming more conspicuous. "Your wife's father and I were business associates. Then one day he got cold feet and betrayed me. He was an *izmyenik*—a traitor."

And then it came to Ryan, as if putting the pieces of a puzzle together. This "truth session" had to do with Melissa's disappearance. "Where's my wife?" he asked, sitting forward abruptly.

"Don't jump ahead of me," Ivanov said, taking a long drink of coffee before continuing. "Quite an amazing thing, you know. What's the word for it—irony?—that Melissa would flee from Colorado, hoping to hide from me, and instead she ends up here in Connecticut. In my own backyard! The gods do smile on me."

Ryan stared at the arrogant man with growing fury and frustration. Denny's tortured revelation about Melissa's fake identity now made complete sense. His wife had been hiding from Ivanov.

"You seem to have left out a few important details," Ryan said.

"Yes, it seems I forgot the most important

part. Your wife's father stole my money, and I want it back," Ivanov replied matter-of-factly.

"Well, ask him for it," Ryan replied.

Ivanov exchanged glances with Bernie. "I'm afraid the man's a little indisposed at the moment."

Ryan barely concealed a shiver of fear.

Ivanov smirked, as if registering Ryan's realization. "You catch on fast." He took another measured sip of coffee, seeming to enjoy the power he wielded. Lowering his mug, he looked at Ryan with false sympathy. "Your wife spotted me at a restaurant last Friday. I was hoping to have a friendly conversation with her. Instead she took off like a frightened gazelle. Luckily, I was able to track her down again."

"Where is she?" Ryan demanded a second time, his voice deliberate and controlled, unlike his emotions.

"She's fine," he said. "But I need your help—"

Ryan came uncorked. "You terrorize my wife, and now—?"

"I want my money . . . is that too much to ask?"

"And you think Melissa knows where it is?"

Ivanov smiled broadly. "Of course she knows."

"If you're so sure, why'd you wait so long to approach her?"

"Good question. Frankly, at first, I had my doubts about her. I briefly considered the possibility that she had no knowledge of the money or its whereabouts, unlikely as that seems to me now."

"She never said anything to me—"

"My point exactly," Ivanov said. "She didn't say *anything* about her past at all, did she?"

Ryan said nothing.

Ivanov looked amused. "Don't feel too bad. She lied to both of us. And that's what finally persuaded me that she was hiding the money."

"That's a big leap in logic," Ryan muttered. "I want no part of this fantasy."

Bernie shook his head sadly. "There's no getting out, Ryan."

Ivanov changed the subject abruptly. "Do I understand correctly that your parents reside in Montana? Your dad goes to town on Friday afternoons . . . helps a friend restore a '57 Chevy."

Ryan was beginning to comprehend.

"Sundays, they attend the community church, always sit in the fourth pew, in front of their neighbor, Doris Chandler, who annoys your mother with her constant chattering. Need I continue?"

"Need I be impressed?" Ryan said.

"Be convinced. I have friends everywhere." Ivanov cocked his head.

"You're threatening my family."

"I'm explaining the stakes."

Ryan fell silent. Ivanov added, "You might as well know the full story. Your wife's been in touch with the FBI. She knows you work for me."

Ryan frowned in disbelief.

Ivanov smirked. "My dear boy, if it walks on two legs . . . I can bribe it. I've got enough Feds on my payroll to start my own federal police force. How do you think I found Melissa's father?"

"What do you want from me?"

"Talk sense to your little woman. Lay out the red carpet of reason," Ivanov said calmly, as if explaining the theory of physics. "We don't have much time. If the Feds put her under their protection—*poof!* she's gone. Later, she betrays you in court, taking the rest of us down, too. Of course, I won't let that happen."

Ivanov's eyes turned cold as he leaned over to make a point. "Mr. James, witnesses have a way of disappearing long before they ever testify in court."

The evil truth registered in the Russian's merciless eyes. Ryan took a deep breath and exhaled. "Let's cut to the chase, shall we?"

"By all means," Ivanov said.

"Why don't you question her yourself? Why do you need me?"

Ivanov stared back at Ryan, and for the first time since he'd entered Bernie's office, his confidence seemed to falter. His face paled briefly, then he recovered his bravado. "I figured that you, as her husband, might be more . . . persuasive."

Ryan considered Ivanov's odd response. "And why should I believe you won't harm her once we find your precious money?"

Ivanov broke into a resounding guffaw. "Because I *need* you, James. You've made us exceedingly rich. You're like the goose laying the golden eggs. If I ruffle your feathers you might stop."

"You have a strange way of putting things."

"We're starting over, bringing you fully on board. Are you with us or not?" Ivanov demanded.

Ryan caught Bernie's eye, which registered an unmistakable look: *Don't be a fool.* . . . Ryan hesitated. The silence spun out agonizingly. Finally he nodded. "All right."

Bernie gave his own sigh, apparently relieved.

"Good man." Ivanov made an open gesture with his hands that encompassed the entire office. "I don't understand much of what you do here, but some of my financial people want to take a look at your files."

"My files?" muttered Ryan.

"We want to expand your responsibilities when this is over. And, of course, you'll make far more money." Ivanov stood, brushed off his coat, and extended his hand to Ryan.

Ryan shook it, as if sealing an ordinary business deal—not a life-and-death decision to save Mellie's life.

To Bernie, Ivanov scoffed, "You worry for nothing. This went well." He got to the door and turned back to them. "They'll give you a call, Ryan. You won't meet here, of course."

Ryan watched Ivanov swagger out.

## Chapter Twenty-Seven

EAST MAIN STREET was crammed with vehicles waiting for the drawbridge, allowing early-morning boat passage down the Mystic River. Ivanov stared at the line of cars. *Commoners*, he thought, despising them. *Dull, pathetic mortals. . . .*

He sneered, recalling his conversation with the weak-minded but easily manipulated Bernie Stanton. *Like taking candy from a baby.* He especially reveled in the pathetic expression on Ryan James's face as Ivanov expertly led him down the long narrow path that would eventually lead to execution.

*And to think I waited so long for this pleasure,* he thought, remembering how, three years ago, he had sent his lackeys to place the transmitter under Melissa's car. Then his men, posing as city utility workers, had placed bugs in the living room of the beachfront home, as well as in the sailboat. Finally, to insure complete surveillance, they monitored all telephone and cell-phone communications. All this to snag the moment when Melissa might reveal to Ryan the truth about the money.

But nothing had been revealed, so Ivanov decided to stir the pot. He allowed Melissa to spot him at the restaurant, taking great pleasure in her scramble for safety. Then he'd tracked her movements, following her, curious to discover her final destination. Perhaps she might even lead him to the money. But she hadn't.

No matter. Ivanov was finished with his elaborate spy games. In a few days, thanks to naïve but desperate intervention from her beloved husband, Melissa would reveal where her father had hidden eighty million, which, by now—if properly managed—should have quadrupled in value.

He held little trust in the whole bunch of "money-handlers," that echelon of society that controlled large sums of drug and extortion money. But Ryan had made a tremendous amount of money for the network through his legitimate activities, and his partners were reluctant to part with their "star" trader.

Ultimately, though, desire for revenge had trumped his greed. Ivanov had convinced his partners to analyze the trading methods contained in Ryan's computer records. They'd consented, and the last brick was in place. Time to eliminate the "goose," since the golden eggs could be purchased elsewhere.

Revenge! How sweet it would be, and to take it out on the daughter of the very man who'd made him out to be a fool, along with the underling who'd married her.

Ryan was shaken as he stared at the row of monitors in his own office. When a knock came at his door, the sound seemed but a distant echo. Slowly the door opened and Marge poked her head around. "Need anything?"

He didn't reply at first, then asked absentmindedly, "Has Bernie left for the day?"

Marge nodded. "That guy had some weird effect on both you *and* Bernie. Why don't you just drop him? Who needs clients like that?"

Looking up at her, as though in a dream, he watched her enter the room tentatively.

"Ryan?"

"I'd better head out," he managed to say. "Denny's at home, waiting for a ride to the airport."

"Hey, I'm worried about you," Marge said quickly.

His mind a fog, he forced a laugh. "Don't be."

"See you tomorrow?"

He ignored the question and reached down to twist the key to his desk, locking up for the day. That done, he shut down the bank of screens.

◆ ◆ ◆ ◆ ◆

Denny stroked Ryan's dog, then carried

his suitcase outside, tossing it into the trunk. He waited for Ryan to emerge from the house, holding the wrapped painting, the gift from Melissa.

A few more hours and he'd see his Evelyn again. Never in his life had he missed anyone so much. Coming to Connecticut, he'd hoped to help Ryan, but in the end he'd only made matters worse, it seemed.

Ryan eventually ran out to the car, wearing jeans and a blue golf shirt. He gave Denny a halfhearted smile, and they settled into the car for the drive to the airport.

"I left you a book," he told Ryan, "in case you feel like reading."

"Sure, thanks," Ryan muttered.

"I wish things could have been different," Denny said softly, determining whether he should press further. Denny waited a moment, then continued. "I also wish we could have prayed together . . . about this whole mess."

Ryan snorted. "And what would *that* accomplish?"

Neither of them spoke for a time; then Denny said, "Hey, pal, what's going on . . . besides the fact that you're worried sick about Melissa?"

"Sorry, I'm not in a party mood."

"No . . . it's more than that," he persisted.

"C'mon, Den—"

"Let me say this. I'm your friend, Ryan. We've been through a lot together. I know when things aren't right."

Ryan looked at him. "What do you want from me?"

"What aren't you telling me? Why did Melissa *really* leave? Help me out here."

Ryan shook his head as if disgusted but remained silent. Denny looked over at his friend, feeling the sadness that emanated from Ryan like relentless ocean waves. And then it came to Denny as if a whisper from a still, small voice. The thought didn't make complete sense, but he plunged forward, almost desperately, taking a stab in the dark. "God can forgive anything, Ryan."

His friend frowned, obviously surprised. "What're you talking about?"

"It doesn't matter what you've done."

"You think I ran her off?"

"Of course not."

"Then what?"

"I don't know. . . ." A Scripture floated into Denny's mind. "Remember the sermon on Sunday?"

Ryan said nothing, looking ahead to the road.

" 'Come to me all you who labor and are heavy laden, and I will give you rest.' That's what it's about, Ryan. Repentance. Forgiveness of sin. Peace of mind. Freedom from guilt. That's the gospel. You don't need proof. You need grace. And it doesn't always make sense, but it's free. It's not for good people. It's for sinners—"

"You're a broken record. You're stuck in one place."

"Yes, I am," Denny replied.

"Just *who* do you think I am?"

Denny pondered the question, then said, "I'm not sure anymore."

Ryan shot an angry look at him. "I have no use for your God. Melissa's lost and He can't find her."

Denny caught the expression in Ryan's eyes—the hurt and guilt, mingled with something new: *bitterness*. He'd seen the same look countless times on the streets of Denver's inner city. "Don't let time run out for you," he finally urged.

When they reached the airport, Ryan drove to the gate, braked, and got out. Denny went around to the back of the car, carrying the painting from Melissa. He watched as Ryan opened the trunk, removed the suitcase, and placed it firmly on the cement. "Still friends?" Denny asked, extending his hand.

Ryan offered no response but shook

hands as if finishing a deal. "Take care, Denny," he replied, with a tone of finality.

His heart heavy, Denny picked up his bag and walked into the building alone. Once inside, he looked over his shoulder, through the glass windows, intending to wave good-bye, but Ryan had already sped off.

◆ ◆ ◆ ◆ ◆

Daisy was exuberant, running to Ryan as he came into the house.

"Not now," Ryan snapped, tossing his keys on the kitchen counter. The dog dropped back, cowed by the unaccustomed rebuff.

Making his way to the living room, where the wide windows overlooked the cove, Ryan erupted in a fit of anger, grabbing the first thing he found—a pewter vase—and hurled it at the window.

*Crash!* The glass exploded, jagged shards landing on the carpet and the floor of the porch outside. Several fragments sprinkled onto Melissa's unfinished painting.

Daisy whined and scampered back, obviously stunned by the outburst.

Immobilized, Ryan stared at the bay through the broken window and, in a moment, felt Daisy whimpering next to him.

She squatted down, nervously clawing at his ankle.

"I'm sorry," he said, his eyes shifting to Mellie's painting.

He was startled by the jangle of the phone and answered it, expecting Ivanov. The call was not from the man who made his blood boil, but rather from his mother in Montana.

"Ryan?" she said. "I'm surprised to catch you at home. I was calling to thank Mellie for the lovely birthday card. How's everything?"

Composing himself, he felt chagrined at the damage he'd caused to his own home. With forced calmness, he replied, "Fine, Mom. How are you and Dad?"

"Oh, your father hasn't complained in the last hour, so I guess he's all right." She laughed softly. "We received your check. Can't say how much we appreciate your help."

"Forget it, Mom. . . ." His voice trailed off.

"How was your visit with Denny? Such a nice young man."

"He left for Colorado a few hours ago."

"Did he like Mellie's painting? She told me all about it."

"Yeah, he liked it. Uh . . . Mom, I need to get going."

"Oh, sure. But may I talk to Melissa real

quick? I want to thank her—"

"She's not here at the moment. I'll talk to you soon. Take care of yourself, okay?"

Ryan said good-bye and hung up, then placed both hands flat on the counter, breathing deeply, his mind a jumble of emotions. He stared at the broken window and then at Mellie's painting, marred by his own rage—a fitting symbol of their fairy-tale existence.

Rehashing the past, he recalled the first time, years ago, when Bernie had approached him with a questionable trade. At the time, he'd vacillated, torn between making more money than he'd ever dreamed of—that, or taking the high road. Something inside him, a core of decency and honor, told him to quit his job and pack his bags. But greed had a stronger, louder voice.

Bernie was right. Ryan had been paid very well to look the other way. But he'd never known . . . *this*—the extent of the evil empire that controlled his workplace. And yet his own thirst for money had brought him to this place. Now he was in too much trouble to get out. The very lives of his wife and parents depended on what he did next.

*How can Mellie ever forgive me?* he thought grimly.

# Chapter Twenty-Eight

EVELYN MET DENNY at the airport, and after they embraced and engaged in small talk for a while, he filled her in on Ryan's plight. "It's a sad situation," he said as she drove him to her home.

"I've been praying for them . . . and for you, too, while you were there," Evelyn said, looking exceptionally beautiful in a denim skirt and matching blouse.

"Thanks, I appreciate that," he said, meaning it.

"Well, I hope you're hungry," she said as they entered the front door of her town home. "I made dinner for you."

"You're always thinking of me." He took her in his arms once again.

She giggled with delight, then headed off to the kitchen.

"Mind if I check my phone messages from here?"

"Make yourself at home," she called back over her shoulder.

He reached for the portable phone in the living room and dialed the number. Punching in his code, he listened to the usual smattering of hang-ups and unimportant calls, until he heard something disturbing. "Denny? It's me, Melissa. . . ."

Sitting down, he listened with interest to the rest of the recorded call. At the end she had given a number where she could be reached. Quickly, he hung up. Then, using his phone card, he dialed Melissa before he forgot the number.

When Evelyn wandered into the living room, he covered the mouthpiece with his hand and whispered, "Melissa." Her eyes grew wide.

But it wasn't Melissa who answered. When he identified himself, the woman said, "I'll go get her."

Soon he heard Mellie's familiar voice. "Denny, is it you?"

"Hey, where are you?" he asked. "Have you talked to Ryan? He's worried sick." He glanced over at Evelyn. She was sitting across from him in a chair, her hands clasped as if in prayer.

"I need to talk to you, Denny," Melissa said.

"I'm listening."

For the next few minutes, Melissa wove quite a tale on the phone, as unbelievable as any he had heard. Coupled with what he'd learned of her while in Connecticut, he was dubious. He suspended his judgment, nevertheless, long enough for her to finish her side of the story.

"Melissa . . . I'll be honest with you. I'm having some trouble believing any of this."

She paused. "I guess I shouldn't expect you to believe me" came her soft reply.

"You're saying that Ryan's a member of a Russian Mafia group? How do I wrap my brain around that?" He didn't want to shut her out, because it was obvious that Melissa needed someone to talk to. But it sounded like Melissa was a couple of eggs short of a dozen.

Melissa sighed into the phone. "I've lived this nightmare for so long, I've forgotten how mind-boggling it probably sounds."

Denny was uncertain how to proceed. Silently, he breathed a prayer heavenward, asking God for guidance. Organizing his thoughts, he realized he may have jumped to some conclusions. He recalled his conversation with Ryan as they drove to the airport, his own suspicions. *What aren't you telling me? Why did Melissa really leave?* he'd asked Ryan. Then it came to him . . . the mysterious man at the coffee shop. Was there more to him than met the eye?

He looked at his fiancée, her eyes compassionate and understanding. He sensed she was praying, too. Then, slowly . . . deliberately, she mouthed the words "Believe her."

Melissa was sniffling into the phone.

Denny nodded. "How can I help you, Melissa?"

◆ ◆ ◆ ◆ ◆

Marge was putting away her purse and keys the next morning when Ryan arrived at the office. She seemed reticent to meet his gaze.

He mumbled a quick "Hello" and walked to his office, leaving his door ajar.

For the hours that followed, neither of them engaged in their usual offhand bantering. In fact, they scarcely spoke at all.

Just before noon, when Marge delivered several documents, he was standing at the window, watching traffic cross the bridge. His computers were deathly still. At midday, no less.

He sensed her behind him and turned, forcing a smile.

"May I get something for you? Coffee, maybe?" she asked.

"I've never asked you for coffee. You know that."

"Well, I certainly don't mind if—"

"Thanks, anyway."

She slipped back toward the reception desk just as his phone rang. Fifteen minutes into the conversation, Marge poked her head in his door again.

He covered his receiver. "Yes?" he whispered, offering her an expectant look.

"I'm sorry to interrupt," she said. "But your friend Denny Franklin's on the other line."

"Denny?"

She nodded. "He says it's urgent . . . sounds worried."

*He's calling to apologize,* he thought. *Or to preach some more.* Ryan was put off. "Tell him I'm busy," he said.

Looking rather bewildered, Marge nodded and turned to leave.

Ryan uncovered the receiver and spoke at last. "I can meet you tomorrow morning, ten o'clock."

"Blue Waters Motel. Come alone," stated the voice on the other end.

"Alone . . . of course," Ryan said and hung up.

# Chapter Twenty-Nine

THERE WERE TWO PHONE CALLS in the afternoon. One from Elizabeth, inviting both Lela and Melissa for supper tomorrow evening. "It's your birthday, ya know," her sister reminded her.

"Oh my, I nearly forgot."

Elizabeth chortled. "Now, how on earth can you forget your own birthday?" She paused. "So you'll be comin', then?"

Without consulting Melissa, Lela agreed that they would. Thinking of the dire situation Mellie was in, she was tempted to ask for prayer from Elizabeth and Thaddeus. But she kept her peace, knowing full well that one thing could lead to another. Best this way, keeping Mellie's confidence, not sharing one iota with a soul, though she knew beyond a shadow of a doubt that she would be talking to her heavenly Father, who sees and knows and cares.

The second call came from Paul Martin. "I was hoping to catch you at home, Lela," he said, not waiting long for her response. "A little bird told me it was your birthday tomorrow."

*Now, who could that be?* she wondered, guessing it was Sadie Nan.

"Would you like to join me for dinner somewhere?" he asked. "You know—to celebrate."

She found it almost humorous that the man—this man who'd left her for another—was nearly pleading with her to spend time with him. Offhand, she'd thought of inviting him to Elizabeth's tomorrow evening. *Safety in numbers*, Mama always said, growing up. Paul *had* been a friend of the family, a close friend at that. Years ago. She resisted the urge, knowing it was not her place to extend the invitation. "Do you mind if I get back with you on this?" she said, finding her voice.

"Why, no, not at all."

They went on to chat about the fair weather and the good sermon yesterday. Small talk, to be sure, but Lela sensed the undertow of interest. Keen interest, at that.

"If it suits, you may call me later this evening," she said.

Indeed, she had a plan.


"I daresay my sister's in over her head with that fancy boarder of hers," Elizabeth confided in Thaddeus while the two of them swept out the milk house.

"Now, we don't know that for sure, do we?" her husband chided. "Best wait and see what happens. Who knows but maybe the Lord's in it, just like Lela seems to be thinkin'."

"Jah, maybe you're right. After all, it's not like Lela's the impulsive kind. She lives her life pleasin' to God, follows His leading in most everything she does." Elizabeth thought of one aspect of her sister's life—the part that left hardly any room for a husband. True, Lela had been hurt something awful by Paul Martin, back when. Elizabeth couldn't blame her sister for choosing the single life, wholly committed to the Lord God Almighty.

Thaddeus broke into her thoughts. "What gets my goat, though, is this car we're hidin' out over here."

"I'm not surprised you feel that way."

"Then Lela calls up to say the fancy woman's coming to get it, only to call back in a minute that she isn't." He shook his head, then scratched under his straw hat. "Seems to me, that woman she's got livin' over there doesn't have the slightest idea what she wants, no how."

Elizabeth had to chuckle. " 'Least we won't hafta be hiding anyone else's car in our shed, jah?" She thought of their Amish neighbors farther up the road, whose son had been caught hiding his automobile behind a tree in his father's own pasture. 'Course somebody got wind of it and blew the whistle on him, hauling the young fella in before the brethren. Since he hadn't joined church yet, hadn't taken the oath before God and the membership, he was spared a shunning. Still, she wondered what anybody would say or think if they knew about the shiny white car veiled by the wide planks of aging wood in their own shed.

If Lela's plan didn't set well with Paul, that, of course, was his prerogative entirely. But she *did* think she would ask Elizabeth to invite him to supper tomorrow evening. If he decided to do so, sharing a meal with the family gathered there, he'd have to behave like a gentleman. 'Course, having known Paul well before, she didn't see how that should be a problem at all. The man hadn't committed a sin by becoming a widower. But, then again, a woman of her circumstances couldn't be too cautious.

While Mellie slept, Lela phoned Elizabeth and had to laugh a little when her sister decided it was a "wonderful-gut" idea, Paul coming for the birthday meal, and all.

In Melissa's dream, she was a little girl again, preparing a flower bed for planting. "Mellie, Mellie *not* contrary, how does your garden grow?" Daddy chanted.

"Water and sunshine and everything fine . . . that's what makes rose gardens grow," Mellie answered.

Mrs. Browning was tickled at the two of them. "Goodness' sakes, you ought to jot down some of those silly sayings."

"What for?" Mellie asked.

"Why, for posterity, that's what," Mrs. Browning said, looking pert and sweet in her work apron.

Daddy stopped his raking, smiling down at little Mellie as she reached for a fat brown worm he had uncovered, dangling it in mid-air. "She'll forget just like we all do when we grow up."

"I'm *never* growing up," Mellie insisted.

"That's right," said Daddy, laughing, then resumed his raking.

"And I'll never forget either," Mellie vowed.

◆ ◆ ◆ ◆ ◆

When she awakened, her thoughts flew to Ryan. Heartbroken at the thought of her husband's double life, she wept, realizing that she was never going back to Lord's Point.

Never again to be held in Ryan's arms, talking and sharing into the night to the music of Debussy's "Claire de Lune." Never again would she laugh as he comically scrutinized her artwork too closely, or bask on the sun deck of their little sailboat. Never again. . . .

◆ ◆ ◆ ◆ ◆

Not only was Paul Martin on hand at the Kings' house, but his young son Joseph was there, too, playing a game of checkers with Timothy King. Indeed, Lela felt peculiar arriving *after* Paul, coming into her sister's back door along with Mellie, seeing him there already. She tried to ignore the awkwardness of the situation, greeting him and going out of her way to introduce Mellie.

"Very nice to meet you," Paul said, extending his hand to Melissa.

"She'll be staying on with me . . . indefinitely." She felt she ought to be straightforward with Paul, in case he decided to call on her at home sometime. Having Mellie there was also a deterrent, perhaps, a safeguard against something romantic developing too quickly.

"Are you enjoying yourself here in Lancaster County?" Paul asked Melissa, offering a smile.

Nodding, Mellie said, "Very much, thanks."

Just then Elizabeth rang her tiny dinner bell, and the children scurried to the kitchen to wash up, taking turns as they lined up. Lela enjoyed watching her nieces and nephews, as well as young Joseph, vie for the soap and, later, the hand towel. She quickly dismissed any notion of becoming the tow-headed boy's new mama. No, she mustn't set herself up for more pain, though it was clear Paul's adoring gaze was hard to avoid.

*Best be careful not to lose my heart again,* she thought. Besides, no one asked—not once during the meal—just how long Paul was scheduled to be in town. No one inquired of the business that had supposedly brought him home, either. So she steeled her emotions, praying for divine guidance, quite unsure of herself all round.

When the birthday cake was brought out, Lela delighted in discovering that her sister had baked a lemon cake with rich chocolate icing. Not at all in the typical Amish style, but definitely Lela's favorite dessert and one their mother often made in her own Mennonite home. "Why, thank you, Elizabeth," she said, looking around the table at the dear faces surrounding her. "And thanks to each of you for helping me celebrate this day."

Young Mary Jane excused herself, along with Timothy and Linda, and they headed for the front room. John, the baby, sat in his high chair, waving a spoon. Lela figured they were up to something. And they were. Her nieces and nephew returned, bringing homemade presents. Mary Jane's was a white doily; Timothy and Linda had made colorful drawings of cows and barns. To top things off, Elizabeth brought out a platter of whoopie pies.

"Don't you think we've had enough sweets for one day?" Lela said, smiling across the table at the children.

"Ach, how can that be?" Timothy answered, reaching for the plate of goodies.

"All right, then." Lela was ever so pleased.

Melissa could not have counted the times she noticed a loving exchange, eyes glowing, between Elizabeth and Thaddeus King. They were obviously very much in love and quite content with their happy brood of four. She was also well aware of Paul Martin's excessive courtesy and attention toward Lela, who was seated across from him and his son. Ardent interest, yes. So *this* was the man, no doubt the reason for Lela's blushing cheeks on the phone the other day.

Observing both couples, her heart ached anew for Ryan, con artist and smooth talker though he had turned out to be. Yet part of her longed to know, from his lips, the truth.

When the time came to say their good-byes, she wondered if she ought to make herself scarce, leave ahead of Lela, giving the woman ample opportunity for a proper send-off. But, no, Lela wouldn't hear of it, implored her to wait "and we'll walk home together."

"Please, allow me to drive you," Paul said, his hands resting on little Joseph's shoulders. "I would be very happy to see you both home."

Melissa was careful not to smile at the man's insistence, though he was not unpleasantly so. She rather liked him, and was fairly convinced that Lela did, too.

In the end Lela gave in, and they rode the ridiculously short way home—Lela in the front seat, Melissa in the back, next to Joseph.

"We're moving back to Lancaster," the boy said suddenly.

"You are?" Melissa asked. "And where is it you live now?"

"Alone . . . all alone, in Indiana." The child's voice was so pathetic, she wondered if he had been coached by his father.

Melissa fully expected Paul to comment

at this point, but he directed not a single re-mark toward the backseat.

Wondering when she might hear Lela's take on the celebration—particularly this guest—Melissa hoped they might have op-portunity to walk to the covered bridge be-fore dusk. She stared up at the sky, glad there was still plenty of light. More than an hour left before nightfall.

◆ ◆ ◆ ◆ ◆

"Let's walk down to Hunsecker Mill Bridge," Lela suggested to Melissa after say-ing good-bye to Paul and his delightful son. "Now's a good time for me to show you my own personal refuge."

"That's what *I* was thinking." They laughed, both a little surprised that they were thinking along the same lines. "A walk is a good idea."

"Yes, and Hunsecker Bridge is a lovely spot at dusk." Lela's face still felt warm from her encounter with Paul, but she hoped Mel-lie hadn't noticed. "You'll see what I mean when we get there."

"I can hardly wait."

It never occurred to Lela that they might be in any danger, walking the back country roads. The way she saw it, if the Lord God of heaven and earth couldn't take care of the two of them here *today*, what good was it to trust in Him for things eternal? They would have their nice stroll down the road to the covered bridge and the lovely grounds surrounding it—evil mobsters, or no.

"I'm glad you shared so openly with me yesterday," Lela said as they walked. "Believe me, what you told me about your past won't go anywhere but to the throne of grace."

Melissa didn't respond, keeping pace with Lela's quick step.

"The weather's not bound to be this pretty too much longer," she said to change the subject. "Around here we often get sudden changes of weather, least expected."

"In late summer?"

"That's right." She went on to explain that sweater weather would soon be upon them, and that maybe they should look for a handmade sweater or cape for Melissa to wear. "Or I can have Elizabeth make you one."

"That's nice of you, but I'll manage just fine."

"Maybe you'll feel comfortable going in to town now and then." Lela paused, wondering if she should say more. " 'Spose I could go along with you, show you to the best stores and whatnot. But only if you want to."

"Sure, I'll go sometime."

Lela smiled. "You seem much better, more relaxed now."

Mellie nodded. "I don't know why, but I'm beginning to feel very safe here. I'm glad to be staying on."

Breathing a prayer of thanksgiving, Lela said, "I'm ever so glad to hear it."

"Your birthday was extra special this year, I do believe."

Lela couldn't help but laugh. "Oh, dear me, I hope it wasn't written all over my face."

"And . . . Paul's," Mellie ventured. "He's your—special friend, right?"

"He *was*, but that was a long, long time ago . . . before he married someone else." Lela sighed, not realizing till this minute just how much she'd hoped to open her heart to Mellie, seeing as how the younger woman fully understood the pain of rejection and disappointment. Strange as it seemed, a delicate yet common thread seemed to bind the two of them together.

They sat along the grassy banks of the Conestoga River, the covered bridge spanning the water to their left. Birds twittered here and there as the sun made its slow tumble through the trees toward the unseen horizon.

"So it appears that Paul Martin has come

back for me, now that he's a lonely widower," Lela said, glad for the solitude here and the opportunity to share openly with Mellie.

" 'Love always finds its way home.' That's what Mrs. Browning used to say."

Lela didn't know what to think. "Easier said than done, I 'spose."

Mellie was quiet for a while, then—"I think I know what you mean."

Silently, they soaked up the beauty of their peaceful surroundings. Not speaking, yet joined in complete empathy.

"I did love Paul, very much," Lela said softly.

"I'm not surprised. He seems like a nice man."

"Paul was the joy of my life, but when he chose someone else to devote his life to, a good part of me died, I'd have to say," she confessed.

Mellie said she could understand that nothing could fill the void. "Nothing ever will."

"Well, now, that may be where we're different," Lela spoke up.

"How do you mean?"

Lela hugged her knees through her long dress. "After Paul and his wife left the area, I felt all my hopes were dashed to pieces. But very soon afterward, I decided to lay down my burden . . . at the feet of Jesus." She told Mellie how she'd grown up in a conservative Christian home, how her parents had instilled various worthwhile character traits. "My father liked to think he was passing down 'good gifts' to his children. Things like purity, generosity, sincerity . . . you know."

Mellie nodded. "My father encouraged me the same way, but we never attended church. Neither did the Brownings, but they were good people."

Lela was careful not to sermonize, yet she felt Mellie's heart was opening to spiritual truth. "Church attendance is all well and good, but walking with Jesus every day makes life joyful, even in spite of the pain of disappointment."

"I talked about this with someone once," said Mellie thoughtfully. "When my husband's friend Denny Franklin came for a visit. He always seemed so happy and full of life. I guess I'm searching for what both you and Denny have."

"Today's as good a day as any to find it," Lela said softly, turning to face her new friend. "Wouldn't you like to give your burdens to the Lord who loves you?"

Tears sprang to Mellie's eyes, and she gripped Lela's hand. "Yes . . ." she said. "That's exactly what I want to do."

An easier witness she'd never given. Lela was more than happy to lead Mellie in the sinner's prayer. There, amidst the flowing green willow boughs and the rush of the Conestoga River, Melissa James became a child of God. And Lela Denlinger her elder sister.

Melissa brushed tears from her eyes, thankful despite the circumstances that she had found her way to Lela's little house. Grateful that the Mennonite woman had cared enough to bring her to this sacred moment.

She thought of the picture of Christ the Good Shepherd, the one hanging in Ryan's and her living room, and as she did, she followed the river's current with her eyes, drinking in the tumble of water over rocks, mossy banks profuse with wild flowers, and thick ivy cascading about. She celebrated the moment, breathing in the freshness of the air, allowing the sound of finch and swallow to cloak her in this tranquil place.

*At last, I belong to God,* she thought, yearning to share this divine peace with Ryan. Yet knowing she could not.

# Chapter Thirty

BEFORE DAWN, LELA ROSE, dressed, and began sewing more pillow shams for Elizabeth's country store. Nothing fed the spirit like working with one's hands—baking bread daily, mending and sewing, putting up pickles and preserves, tatting pretty edges around ordinary-looking pillow slips, and the like. She hummed and prayed as she worked, anxious to catch up a bit, for she'd fallen behind on any number of house chores since Mellie's arrival. Still, she wouldn't have traded the hours and days spent with her boarder-turned-friend. Leading the young woman to the Savior had been the highlight of Lela's year. Oh, the light in Mellie's eyes as she sat there in the grass, having just opened her heart to Jesus!

"Thank you, Lord, for planting all this in my heart," she whispered. It had become very clear to her, the reason for Melissa James's arrival last week. She recalled the prayer she'd prayed, how eager to serve she had been. And she'd felt compelled to make the advertising signs to rent her spare room.

So much good had happened because she had been willing, unafraid to branch out from her comfortable and familiar life. And with God's help she would continue to share the love of the Lord Jesus.

Somewhat unexpectedly, she thought of little Joseph Martin. Surely, the bright-eyed boy must be as lonely as he sounded in the car, awful lost without his mother. 'Course, Lela would not allow herself to become romantically involved with Paul merely for the sake of his son, no. But there was no harm in thinking about the boy. For how she loved children, and Joseph would certainly be easy to love, given his sweet manner and seemingly obedient ways. Who couldn't fall in love with a child like that?

She thought of her own nieces and nephews, Elizabeth's children, as well as her other siblings. A growing number to be sure, yet she continued to remember each one with a crisp one-dollar bill on their birthdays, a tradition she'd started years ago when her oldest brother's first baby was born.

Yes, for one reason or another she was beginning to have a mighty good feeling about Paul's renewed affection for her. Didn't know precisely why that was, except that she'd given it over to the Lord. Now, it was up to Him to work His will and way in their lives.

Mellie awakened with such an overwhelming urge to call Ryan, she could scarcely think of anything else. But Agent Walsh's startling revelation continued to trouble her. Denny had called back to say that Ryan had refused his phone calls. If she wanted to hear the truth from his lips, she'd have to talk to Ryan herself. She had secretly wondered how any of it could be true, though she mourned the statement as if it were. Her darling—on the side of evil? How could that be?

All the endless days stretched ahead. The years—interminably long and lonely. Having enjoyed Lela's young nieces and nephews so much, she entertained a strong desire to have a baby of her own. With Ryan sharing her joy, the rebirth of their union, perhaps. And for the first time in years, she longed to celebrate her actual birthday in the fall, in October, the month it *ought* to be observed.

She reminisced of autumn's pungent flavors, of pumpkin carving, home-baked pies, and dried cornstalks propped up on the front porch, accompanied by a scarecrow or two. Christmas, too, soon followed. The best thing about Christmas, she decided, was that it was forever predictable. The lovely sound of traditional carols, the icy-sweet smell of falling snow, brightly colored packages beneath the tree, good will to men. Twigs of evergreen decorating a window, where glowed a new, tiny spruce tree, glittering with frosty flakes and white lights—their own first Christmas tree, she recalled. Ryan had taken the tree outside on the day after Christmas and planted it in the backyard, where it continued to thrive to this day.

She and Ryan painstakingly decorated their long dock each year at Lord's Point. Stringing strands of white lights along the pier, they tied sprigs of greenery with red bows here and there. Their parties were festive get-togethers. There was music and dancing and good food, always catered.

How would Ryan celebrate this year? Or would he celebrate at all? Knowing him as she did, she wondered if he'd feel so lost and alone that he might merely endure Christmas. She ached with the thought of him missing her so. On the other hand, perhaps she didn't know the real Ryan James. Perhaps she never had. . . .

◆ ◆ ◆ ◆ ◆

Glad to have caught up a bit with her sewing, Lela dusted the front room, going over the mantel with a damp rag. She wiped down each of the tiles surrounding the fireplace, singing hymns of praise. Carefully she dusted each shelf of her pine corner cabinet, lifting out the various china cups and saucers. Some of the nicest pieces she owned. Having given up the notion of a hope chest long ago, she had to smile at herself. Paul Martin's return to Lancaster certainly had stirred things up in her.

Dismissing the thought, she decided to offer tea, along with some raisin bars she'd baked yesterday—a recipe Elizabeth had shared with her recently—to the five ladies who would be coming this afternoon for the weekly Bible study. She couldn't help but hope that Mellie might join them, too.

*What a good time we'll have together*, she thought, taking the dust rag outside and giving it a good shake.

She was quite beside herself to see Paul Martin's car parked in front of her house, and here he came with a handful of red roses bobbing their heads as he made his way to the gate and up the walkway. "I hope it's all right to drop by," he said. "Just wanted to say hello again." He seemed slightly self-conscious, glancing down at the flowers, then holding them out to her like a schoolboy.

Their fragrance was so tempting, she

leaned forward and breathed in their aroma before even greeting him. "Oh, they're lovely! Thank you, Paul."

He stood tall and lean before her, his eyes enormous, their blueness astonishing. "May I talk with you, Lela?" he asked.

She hesitated, glancing up the street, unsure of herself. At last, she said, "Come on around to the back. We'll sit on the porch."

Placing the long-stemmed roses in a vase on the small table, she sat in her white wicker rocker. Paul found a spot in the cushioned settee. She wondered what had brought him here to her today, but she waited, hoping he'd strike up the conversation.

"I hope you won't think it bold of me, but I'd like to tell you about my life . . . outside the Mennonite community—the years I spent in Indiana, while I was married."

She didn't reply to this at once but waited, her hand resting on the uneven wicker weave of the rocker. He waited, too, and after a little while, she said, "It must've been a bit difficult for you, so far from family and the church you'd grown up in."

"That's not the half of it." He sighed, leaning forward for a moment, then back again. "I was warned not to marry my wife. More than a handful of folks said I'd live to regret it, leaving my Plain roots behind. My own mother said I ought to 'think twice about marrying an outsider.' "

Lela didn't know what to make of this. She was ever so uncomfortable hearing such things. She rubbed her hands against the arms of the rocker. Yet she had not the heart to stop him.

His face was earnest, eyes sincere. "My life changed radically the day I married. I did my best to make my wife happy, working hard to give her the things she desired. To the best of my ability, I loved her, yet nothing I ever did seemed good enough."

He paused, staring out across the yard toward the tall trees that formed a border between the gardens and the pastureland beyond. "When Joseph was born, our lives were taken up with a new baby and all the extra duties required. Soon after his birth, my wife became seriously ill. I tended to both her and our son until the day she passed away."

"I'm sorry things were so difficult."

"Well, it seems I've been making mistakes all my life. God allowed me to follow my own path for a time. Thankfully, I have my Joseph."

Her heart went out to him, this man whom she'd loved so dearly. "You've come through a dark tunnel, suffering so. But Joseph *is* a wonderful child. God knew what would bring a smile to your face."

Leaning forward, he covered her hand with his. "You always knew what to say to cheer me, didn't you?"

She smiled. It was true. She'd known how to treat him special, all right.

His voice came softly then. "I've come to ask your forgiveness, my dear Lela."

"Oh, Paul, I forgave you a long time ago."

He was still for moment, then released her hand. "I've been praying about the second chance God has given me—us—if that meets with your approval."

She gave him her most assuring smile, though she could not say just now whether Melissa's staying on with her might possibly put any thoughts of romance on hold.

"Red roses stand for true love," Melissa told Lela when she'd arranged the roses in a larger vase and placed them on the kitchen table after Paul had departed.

"Well, now, is that so?" Lela said.

"Absolutely. Ask me about any rose color and its meaning. My father taught me all about them." Even now, the thought of him both stung and sustained her. Like thoughts of her own true love. . . .

Lela hurried about the kitchen, cleaning up from lunch, but Mellie could see the woman's gaze straying often to the red roses.

♦ ♦ ♦ ♦ ♦

When the women arrived for the scheduled Thursday Bible study, Lela felt nearly giddy with joy. Sadie Nan seemed to notice and came into the kitchen, eyeing the bouquet. "Did my brother happen to stop by today?"

Lela was discreet—after all, the other women were only a few steps away, visiting in the living room. "Well, now, what do *you* think?"

"You mustn't play games with me." Sadie Nan scolded jokingly. "Aren't the roses from Paul?"

Pulling her aside, Lela lowered her voice. "I had a most interesting visitor this morning."

Sadie's eyes lit up. "Well, I do declare. When's the wedding?"

"Let's not rush things, now, all right?"

"What's to rush . . . you've got so many years to catch up on. Don't be waitin' too long, you hear?"

Lela hugged Sadie Nan. "We just might get to be sisters after all."

The other woman grinned. "I'd like that very much."

Lela went back to pouring tea while Sadie

Nan arranged the raisin bars on a plate. "Your boarder, Melissa, seems mighty hungry for the things of the Lord."

"Yes, she's just become a Christian. Yesterday evening, in fact."

They talked briefly about how to include Mellie in their church and community events. Yet Lela never once divulged the circumstances by which Melissa had come to Lancaster County. Neither did she say how the fancy Englischer's staying on might actually put Paul's hopes and plans on hold.

## Chapter Thirty-One

RYAN TURNED HIS VEHICLE into the parking area of the small motel, located several miles west of New London, and pulled to a stop in front of room #12. The place was a flat concrete structure with the typical neon sign out front and a number of cars parked nearby. Not a trash motel, by any means, yet a second-rate meeting place, to be sure.

He sat for a moment, then grabbed the satchel containing his digital financial files and got out of the car. Quickly, he knocked on the door. It opened slowly, revealing a tall, muscle-bound man wearing a solemn expression. Behind him, two other men sat at a small table, their suit coats bulging from hidden shoulder holsters.

At the back of the musty room, another man emerged from the bathroom, drying his hands on a towel. It was obvious to Ryan who was in charge. The man approached him with a smile, extending his hand. Nodding, he shook hands. Pleasantries seemed pointless now.

The man introduced himself as *McGuire*. "You know, like the baseball player," he said with a wink. He clasped his big hands together, as though eager to get started, gesturing to the table. "Have a seat."

One of the men locked the door, crossed his arms, and stood in front of it, legs spread, like a sentinel guard. The other guy sat on the bed, across from them. Ryan eyed them nervously. *You've seen one too many gangster flicks, pal,* he thought.

"Well . . . Mr. James," McGuire said once they were seated, the tone in his voice suddenly somber. "Where shall we begin?"

◆ ◆ ◆ ◆ ◆

One of the many facets of morning, Melissa had realized in the past few days, was her ability to cling to that delicate interval of time between sleep and awakening. One could appeal to the memory, relive a past precious moment at will. This day, she longed to experience again the Christmases spent with Daddy at the Brownings' home in faraway Colorado. Through the mist of preawakening, the scenes burst into her brain like sleet skipping against the pavement. . . .

Christmas was the smell of gingerbread cookies baking in the Brownings' kitchen, the tempting aroma of bacon, eggs, and sausage. Nearly every December twenty-fifth morning, Mellie and her father were invited to share a mouth-watering brunch with their neighbors. And what a spread it was. The tangy smell of freshly peeled tangerines filled the house, even as Mellie entered the Brownings' home, hand in hand with Daddy.

They walked the snowy sidewalk that led from their house to their neighbors', only a short block away. Before ringing the doorbell and being greeted with "Merry Christmas!" Mellie liked to look for the lights in the front window. Mrs. Browning loved to decorate in a rather big way, putting up a small tree in each room of the house. All except the living room, where a tall spruce often dominated one corner.

This tree captured Mellie's attention first

and foremost. Taller than Daddy, and most beautiful, it was decorated with ornaments illustrating Clement C. Moore's poem "The Night Before Christmas." Dancer, Prancer, a sleigh, and even tiny mice embellished the tree, nestled inside a large red drum.

Mr. Browning pointed out the fact that each ornament was hand painted, and Mellie went over to inspect them, seeing if she might someday mimic such pretty things for her own tree. After she'd married her Prince Charming and had her own little house, of course.

But the large bouquet of white roses, sent over each year by the florist from Daddy, was most often the topic of conversation—just before time to dive into the presents piled beneath the tree. Mrs. Browning always made a big to-do about thanking Daddy for his "generous and handsome gift." Mr. Browning did, too.

Daddy winked at Mellie and pushed his nose into one of the elegant blossoms, breathing deeply of what he called "the perfect perfume." Mellie frequently followed suit, having to be boosted up to the table to smell the sweetness. "Anyone remember what white roses stand for?" Daddy said, a twinkle in his eye.

"Secrets!" Mellie clapped her hands,

eager to see what wonderful gifts lay in store.

Each year her father repeated the same ritual. Mellie enjoyed the solid traditions, but given the chance, she would've chosen a bouquet of velvety *red* roses at Christmastime, or double red-and-white amaryllis blooms. Flowers with color made better sense on the Big Day. Yet Daddy insisted on the white roses, his favorite.

Plumping her pillow, Melissa decided that this Christmas would be far different from those of the past. *This year* she would find her way to a church, where the organ played "Oh, Come All Ye Faithful," and choirs sang "Joy to the World, the Lord is come!" This year, she knew the joy of such a heavenly coming. Embraced it totally. God had made himself real to her on the banks of the Conestoga River, with a little help from compassionate Lela. Yes, this year she would definitely commemorate the Holy Days in a new and different way. Although, perhaps in Daddy's memory, she would present a bouquet of white roses to her dear new friend.

"Wait a minute," she said to herself, throwing off the covers and getting out of bed. Until just this moment, she had never thought of her father's gift of white flowers and the talk of their *meaning* as anything more than a mere game. A new thought, impossible to shake, nagged at her brain.

Searching her memory for additional clues, she decided to break her own rule. Risking her false identity no longer intimidated her into silence. She must make a phone call to Mrs. Browning. After all this time, the sweet lady would probably think she was truly hearing from the grave.

Immediately after breakfast, Melissa called for a taxi and had the driver take her to the nearest pay phone. "Please wait for me," she told the cabbie. "I won't be long."

Dialing the familiar area code and phone number, she felt a resurgence of hope. If she could just figure out where the eighty million dollars were hidden, she could be free.

*Free from the life of a fugitive. . . .*

The phone rang several times before she heard the soft voice say, "Browning residence."

She gulped back the tears. "Please don't be alarmed, Mrs. Browning. It's Mellie."

There was silence for a moment, as if the line had become disconnected. Then Mrs. Browning spoke. "Oh, my dear child, whatever happened to you? I've worried for so long!"

Melissa wasted little time filling the woman in on the past several years. She said how very sorry she was for not saying good-bye, for not contacting Mrs. Browning at all. "There was no way I could reveal my where-abouts," she said.

"Are you safe now?" came the inevitable question.

"I'm all right, yes."

"How I've missed you, Mellie, my little lamb."

The choking sensation made speech im-possible. At last she managed, "Someday, I promise, I'll come visit you." *When this night-mare is over.* "We'll have a long visit, just the two of us."

"Yes . . . yes, you do that."

"Do you still live in the same house?" Melissa asked.

"The very same."

"And your gardens . . . do you still grow roses?"

She heard the chuckle. "What would life be without flowers?"

"What about the white rosebushes? Is Daddy's flower garden still. . . ?" Melissa couldn't go on. Hard as she tried, her heart was in her throat.

"I shouldn't think of doing away with your father's favorite roses—never!"

*Dare I say it?* she wondered. It was im-perative now. She had to know. "Can you get someone to dig up that garden . . . today?"

"Why, dearie, whatever for?"

She was at a loss as to how to make the woman understand. Plunging in, she told Mrs. Browning her strong hunch that there might be something buried "under Daddy's white roses."

"And what might that be?" came the vague reply.

"I don't know . . . something . . ."

"And . . . if I should find anything?"

"I'll call you back in a few hours."

"Whatever you say, Mellie." Mrs. Browning was clearly confused. "I'm doing this for you . . . whatever it means. . . ."

"Thank you, Mrs. Browning. Thank you so much."

◆ ◆ ◆ ◆ ◆

Lela was certain that Melissa was up to something mighty important. The girl had sprung out of the house at first sight of the taxicab, nearly forgetting her pocketbook. For goodness' sake, she was in a hurry!

In less than thirty minutes Melissa had returned, her face flushed. She had been crying. "I'll be leaving the house in a few hours," Melissa told her as she came inside.

"For good?" Lela asked, hoping not.

"No, to make another phone call." Melissa explained that she didn't want to take the risk of calling from Lela's phone. "It could easily be tapped."

That concerned Lela, but only a little. God was powerful enough to wipe out a phone tap if necessary, to protect them. She fully trusted in the Lord God of Abraham, Isaac, and Jacob. "That's all right," she said. "You do what you must."

Lela returned to her sewing room and cut out several more large pieces of fabric for additional pillow shams. All the while, she either sang or quoted Scripture. "My heavenly Father sees the tiniest sparrow. . . . 'Fear ye not therefore, ye are of more value than many sparrows.' "

◆ ◆ ◆ ◆ ◆

Melissa waited impatiently to leave the house again and get to a pay phone, but she wanted to give Mrs. Browning enough time to find or hire a neighbor to spade up the singular garden. It was past noon when she phoned for a taxi again. She was relieved to see that the driver was not the same man, and she played it safe and asked to be taken to a different pay phone, having inquired of Lela where another one might be.

Once there she looked about her cautiously, then closed the phone booth's doors behind her. Praying for God's help—that she could actually pull this off—she dialed Mrs. Browning's number.

"I'm glad you rang me again," Mrs. Browning said breathlessly. "I should say you knew what you were talking about, my dear."

"You found something?"

"A small metal box, and inside, a laminated piece of paper."

"Is there a number on the piece of paper?" she asked, shaking with anticipation.

"Yes . . . the name of a bank in Switzerland, the word *rose*, and an account number, to be sure."

"Please read it to me, very slowly."

She wrote down the number, reading it back for verification, then asked Mrs. Browning to burn the piece of paper. "Put it in the sink and light a match to it."

The dear woman promised to "see to it right away," without further question.

"I'll visit you soon," Melissa said.

"Very soon?" asked Mrs. Browning.

In her mind's eye, she remembered her second mother's smile. "It won't be long, I promise."

◆ ◆ ◆ ◆ ◆

From where Elizabeth stood at the kitchen window, she could see their alfalfa fields shifting in billowy patterns, swaying in the breeze like sea green velvet. Out in the barnyard, Thaddeus and several other men from their church district gathered to cut the alfalfa for the second time this summer, since early June. When that chore was finished, the whole family would be going out to Ohio to visit with Elizabeth's second cousins. She could hardly wait to see her Mennonite relatives again. Wouldn't be but a minute before she and Cousin Henny would be all caught up in their chatter—"catchin' up on our lives," they'd tell the menfolk, and be off to the kitchen, exchanging recipes and whatnot all.

She turned back to making chow-chow ahead for the evening meal, hoping for some time to spend with Lela this afternoon. In the past week, since Melissa had arrived on the scene, Elizabeth had hardly had a chance to pay her sister what was coming to her from the country store. *I'll take her the money I owe her and some strawberry jam, too,* she decided, thinking back to the interesting birthday supper for Lela. She had a feeling there was most likely goin' to be a new member in the family, and mighty soon at that. She'd seen the way Paul Martin looked in earnest at her sister. Funny how the Lord God heavenly Father answered prayer, and sometimes so awful fast!

◆ ◆ ◆ ◆ ◆

Melissa strolled down the road, alone this time, past Thaddeus and Elizabeth King's farmhouse, in a new direction. After the startling conversation—the discovery made by Mrs. Browning—she'd decided to go for a walk, taking Lela up on her offer of a cotton summer dress. The hem of the dress nearly skimmed her ankles as she walked, and she began to feel something like a Plain woman herself. As though she were living in a haven of sorts, far removed from the troubles of modern life.

Pondering the unearthing of her father's money, she recalled her previous phone conversation with Denny. He'd urged her to trust the FBI. But trusting was difficult. Yet what choice did she have? Ivanov would find her again, in just a matter of time. She had to do *something*.

A black-and-white warbler chirped his high-pitched solo, and Melissa smiled, glad for the distraction and for the way things had fallen into place so far today. She had spent the lunch hour over a hearty meal of apricot salad, ham loaf, and green beans, getting to know Lela even better. The woman was definitely in love, and Melissa was glad. Such a kind and caring person, Lela would surely be a good wife to Paul. Melissa had thought often of the little boy, the widower's son. A more precocious child she had never encountered, but then, she hadn't had much opportunity to engage herself with children. Never in college, and certainly not at the florist shop in Mystic.

Strangely enough, though, she could easily imagine herself caring for and raising children. Two, maybe, although Elizabeth King made child rearing appear almost effortless. Something about the Plain style of living made hard work seem altogether natural.

The countryside had a calming effect on her. She enjoyed every little wild flower, maidenhair fern, and tree along the way, the sky an appealing blue that reminded her of walks along the beach with Ryan and their golden retriever.

She was glad to be alone. Lela had taught her, through word and deed, that a little solitude each day was essential to good health and emotional well-being. Lela was big on having what she called a "quiet time" each morning. "Too many people are afraid to be alone with their thoughts," Lela had said just this morning. "There's always something—television, radio, family, and friends—vying for our attention, filling up the empty space, keeping us from feeding our inner person."

Melissa had never thought of it quite like that. Yes, she'd regretted not having her mother growing up, yet she'd had Mrs. Browning. She'd hated the thought of her grandparents living so far away in Grand Junction, but they were only a phone call away. She'd suffered great loss, it was true, but in spite of her loneliness, she had never learned to feel completely comfortable with herself. Until this day. The past and the future were eliminated as she breathed in the fresh air, infused with the subtle smell of alfalfa. Only the present remained as she talked to God, the first real prayer she'd prayed since her experience on the banks of the Conestoga River. "I'm not very good at this," she began. "But my friend Lela tells me that you listen and understand, that you hear the heart's cry of your children. I'm glad about that, because my heart's rather torn up these days." She prayed that God might change the souls of men like Ivanov, and she prayed for Ryan. "Help him find his way to you, Lord." But most important, she prayed for wisdom, as Lela put it—"Help me make the right decision."

She felt a peculiar lightness in her step. Her eyes were once again opened to the beauty around her. The euphoric flutter of a monarch butterfly caught her attention, and she walked more briskly, following its meandering path as it stopped to alight on shell pink pasture roses that covered a small slope. She was aware of the vivid, broad blossoms of the species roses, but she kept her gaze fixed on the butterfly's orange-brown wings, its black veins and borders, missing her palette and brushes. Orchard orioles and vivid goldfinches darted here and there, from one tree to another, as she made her way up the narrow country road—and she painted the picture in her memory instead.

## Chapter Thirty-Two

THE PHONE RANG late in the afternoon, after Elizabeth had dropped by for a short visit, bringing along peach and pineapple preserves, as well as some money she owed Lela for her many quilted pillow shams.

Melissa was curled up on one of the sofas, reading Lela's Bible, when the jangle made her glance up as Lela scurried to the kitchen.

"Denlinger residence." Lela paused,

listening for a moment, then replied, "Who may I say is calling?" She came into the living room, eyes too wide, the phone cord trailing behind her. Lela covered the receiver with her hand and whispered, "You have a phone call."

"Who is it?" Melissa mouthed.

"Your husband."

A thousand questions spun through her mind, and renewed panic seized her. For a moment, she considered denying that she was here and bolting for the door.

"What do you want to do?" Lela whispered, still holding the phone.

Finding courage, she said, "I'll talk to him."

Lela's expression conveyed hesitancy, as if asking, *Are you sure?*

Melissa nodded, getting up, and taking the phone. "Hello, Ryan?" she said, a lump already forming in her throat.

"Mellie, honey . . . are you okay?"

"How did you know where to reach me?"

"Sweetheart, you must listen to me—"

"Please, answer *me*, Ryan. How did you know where I was?" She looked at Lela, who was standing near, arms folded, eyes closed. She appeared to be praying.

"The FBI," he replied softly.

Melissa's breath caught in her throat, and

she reached for a chair to sit down. "I don't understand. How can that be?"

"There's been a huge mistake—"

"But . . . Agent Walsh said . . . no, don't do this, Ryan. Please don't lie to me." Tears welled up, and she fought the confusion and the fear.

"Don't hang up. Let me explain."

"I'm listening."

"Melissa . . . I *work* for the FBI as an informant. I'm on your side," Ryan said. "My job was to help the government break Ivanov's network. That's why I couldn't tell you the truth before. But it's over now. Ivanov and his crowd don't trust me anymore. That's why he showed up at the restaurant in Mystic last week. He was making a final play for your father's stolen money."

Her husband's explanation was, at best, astonishing. She struggled to understand. Even so, a new emotion surfaced. *Hope.* With all her heart she wanted to believe him. Was this the answer to her prayer on the road?

"I want to believe you," she said, her voice trembling, her heart longing for assurance. "But how do I know you're telling the truth?"

"You simply have to trust me."

"But I . . ." She was more confused than

ever. She breathed deeply, contemplating his words.

"Mellie, I know everything about you and your past. This one time, you must trust me."

*This one time . . .*

"But you lied to me, Ryan. If what you tell me is true . . . all those years . . ."

"I was sworn to secrecy. That's different, isn't it?" He seemed to have an answer for everything.

But he was right on one count. She had never entrusted him with her deepest secret, and she'd made a terrible mistake, panicking after seeing Ivanov at S&P Oyster Company. Now she felt foolish. Her walls of suspicion were beginning to crumble. "I've missed you, darling. I'm so sorry," she whispered.

She heard him sigh. "I've missed *you*, Mellie. You have no idea."

"What do we do now?"

"First of all, we stop this madness. These people will never be satisfied until we settle the issue about the money. I know you don't know where it is, but—"

"No . . . I *do* know, Ryan."

A disturbing silence fell between them.

Then—"What did you say?"

"I figured it out," she said. "My dad put the money in a Swiss bank account."

"Do you have the account number?"

"That, along with the code word."

"Listen, Mellie, what's the nearest restaurant to you?"

She turned to inquire of Lela.

"The closest place is Best Western Eden Resort Inn," Lela said, eyes serious.

Relaying the information to her husband, Melissa felt nervous, yet excited about seeing him again.

"Meet me in the parking lot there, tomorrow morning at eleven o'clock. An FBI agent will accompany me. From there we'll go to the bank and transfer the money to the government, get things squared away once and for all."

She was glad he was taking charge of things. For too long she'd carried her burdens alone. "I'll see you tomorrow."

"It's going to be okay, Mellie. This nightmare will soon be over. At last we'll be together, and no secrets between us anymore." His voice was tender and sweet to her ears.

"No secrets," she whispered. "I love you, Ryan."

"I love *you*, sweetheart."

She hung up the phone, her heart lighter than it had been in *ever so long*, she thought, lapsing into Lela's quaint speech.

# Chapter Thirty-Three

"*DURAK!*—fool!" bellowed Ivanov as both he and Ryan replaced their receivers. "Why didn't you get the account number?"

Ryan looked surprised. "I thought she would suspect something. I'll call her back if you wish." He reached for the phone again.

"No," Ivanov spit out. "You're right." Then he paused, composing himself. "That was quite the performance. You're a better liar than I thought you were."

Sitting in the swivel chair, looking exhausted, Ryan leaned his elbows on the desk.

Ivanov began pacing the floor, rehashing his plans. Tomorrow they'd meet up with Missy James and take her to a Philadelphia bank. There they would transfer the money, not to the federal government, as Ryan had told Melissa, but to Grand Cayman and other offshore accounts hidden around the world. Once the money transfer was complete, he'd be on his way to the Caribbean for a much needed rest. He had a penchant for hot, balmy weather.

"Are we finished here?" Ryan asked rather impatiently.

"Got a plane to catch?"

Ryan regarded him coolly, then looked away.

"Betrayal doesn't set well with you, does it?" Ivanov said, feeling amused, and for one tantalizing moment, he visualized the look of terrified shock on both Ryan's and Melissa's faces when they discovered Ivanov's own treachery. He had no intention of letting them live, not once he extracted the money. *A two-for-one deal*, he thought. *I get both my revenge* and *the money.*

"I'll get over it," Ryan replied.

"Good man. You two can go on a second honeymoon when this is over. Plenty of time to charm your way back into her good graces," he said. Then he clapped his hands once loudly, rubbing them together. "Better get some sleep. We've got a busy day tomorrow."

◆ ◆ ◆ ◆ ◆

Melissa waited outside, standing by her car in the parking lot of the Eden Resort Inn. She anticipated seeing her beloved again. So much so that she'd scarcely slept, too excited at the unexpected turn of events.

At 10:55 she spotted Ryan's white SUV

pulling into the parking lot. Catching a glimpse of him, her heart leaped up. She noticed the shadowy man in the backseat of the vehicle and assumed the FBI agent had come along, just as Ryan had said.

Rushing to the parked vehicle, she opened the passenger door. "Ryan . . . darling!"

He smiled tentatively, reaching for her as she jumped into the car. She snuggled next to him, returning his tender kisses. "I missed you so much," she whispered, tears blinding her. "I thought I'd never see you again."

She was startled by the sound of the car door slamming behind her. The FBI agent had gotten out and closed her door. Why? Confused, she turned toward the man, just as he slid into the backseat.

"Miss me, too?" he replied, leering at her.

She nearly choked. "*You?*" Horrified, she turned back to Ryan. "What's *he* doing here?"

Her husband's smile had faded. Yet something in his expression communicated compassion. "It's okay, Melissa. Let me explain."

"You tricked me," she said, the truth sinking in. She grabbed for her door, pushing on the handle with all her strength.

*Locked.*

"Melissa . . . please."

She pushed again, to no avail. Now Ryan's hand was on her shoulder. She twitched in horror, and he quickly removed it. Then, slumping against the door, she closed her eyes, overcome with both grief and terror. Helpless . . . defeated, she prayed. *Please, Lord, help me.*

Turning to Ryan, she unleashed her fury. "You said I could trust you!"

Ryan was silent, his eyes intense, yet empathetic.

"We're wasting time here," the man grumbled in the backseat. "I'll take the account number *and* the code word."

She stared at Ryan. "So . . . it's all about the money?" she blurted. "For that you betrayed me?"

Ryan shook his head. "You don't understand—"

"The number, please!" the man behind her roared.

Angrily, she shot him an icy look. "It's up here." She tapped her forehead.

Reaching into his coat, Ivanov withdrew a pocket-size notebook and tossed it over the front seat. "Write it down," he barked.

"And if I won't?"

"You should know the answer to that,"

Ivanov replied, his greedy eyes dancing with confidence.

She studied him, despicable man that he was. "And lose your precious money forever? I don't think so."

Ryan looked over his shoulder at Ivanov. "I'll handle this."

"By all means, work your magic."

Ryan reached for her hand, but she withdrew again. "Please, just do as he says, Mellie."

She glared at Ryan.

"All he wants is the money. Then we can be together again," Ryan reiterated.

She shook her head, her rage out of control. "No matter what happens, it's over between us."

Ryan flinched as if she'd slapped him in the face.

Ivanov asked again for the bank number, but she refused.

"Listen, Missy, I call the shots here." Ivanov pulled his jacket away from his chest area, exposing his gun holster. "I've had enough of your games, young lady. I'm willing to gamble that deep down you still love your husband. So . . . how would you like to become a very young widow?"

There was a flicker of fear in her husband's eyes. Relenting, she took her pen and began to write the account number on the small notebook. Finished, she handed it over to Ivanov. "How do you know I didn't just make up a number?"

"Melissa—" Ryan said.

"No, that's a very good question," Ivanov said. "Which is why we're all going to the Philadelphia bank together. Anything goes wrong—the account number's false—and I'm the instant owner of waterfront property. Follow me?"

She stared back at the monster. *How can this be happening?*

He kept it up. "When the wire transfer is complete, you go your merry way, with or without your husband. It's no concern of mine."

To Ryan, Ivanov snapped, "Get moving."

She couldn't help keeping her eyes on Ryan as he pulled out of the parking lot. His gaze, however, was on the road. Silence fell over the car as they drove out of the parking lot. Melissa prayed from her heart, *Lord, I trust you.*

◆ ◆ ◆ ◆ ◆

When they reached the outskirts of Philadelphia, Ryan made a turn onto I-76, heading south. Within minutes they were in the congested downtown area. Ryan pulled into a parking garage connected to a bank, removing the parking ticket from the machine as they passed the entrance into a labyrinth of increasingly darker levels.

Melissa grew more nervous as Ryan pulled into an available space near the elevator.

"All right, you lovebirds, it's show time. We're getting out of the car and going inside," Ivanov said, glowering at Melissa. "*Without* drawing attention to ourselves. Catch my drift?"

Ivanov pulled the handle and kicked his door open. Once out, he opened her door. Ryan emerged from his side, and the three of them walked toward the elevator doors, Ivanov taking up the rear, glancing about the parking lot. They were alone. Seconds before the elevator opened, Ivanov grabbed Melissa by the shirt and shoved her against the concrete wall.

"Lord, help me!" she whispered sharply, catching her breath.

"Hey, easy!" Ryan yelled.

Ivanov shot him a loathsome look. Melissa caught Ryan's eye and saw deep concern etched in his face. Ivanov leaned close to her, his repulsive breath overpowering. "Anything happens in there, and Ryan doesn't walk out. . . ."

"I know what you're capable of," she said, looking at Ryan again. The muscles in her husband's jaw twitched. He returned her gaze but remained sadly silent.

"That's right. You *would* know," Ivanov taunted. "Your daddy made some very poor decisions. Wouldn't advise you to make the same mistake."

"You're not half the man my father was," she murmured.

Ivanov laughed at her comment. "Maybe. But I'm alive." He released her, removed his cell phone from his coat pocket, and punched in some numbers. "Yeah, we're here. Meet us at the fourth-floor elevator."

Ivanov hung up, gesturing to the open elevator. The doors swallowed them with a swish, and they soared to the fourth floor. She noticed the marblelike floors with low-growing plants in lovely urns and the occasional hibiscus tree in various corners. *All fake*, she thought. *It's all a façade.*

A man who appeared to be a bank officer arrived as they entered the hallway. His face turned ashen when he spotted Ivanov. "What are *you* doing here?"

"I'm handling this one myself. Too much on the line," Ivanov said.

Was he referring to the men who normally handled his criminal transactions? Melissa wondered.

The officer turned to face Ryan and Melissa, obviously scrutinizing them. "Relax," Ivanov muttered to him. "They're with me."

Melissa caught the knowing exchange between the bank officer and Ivanov. Why would Ivanov allow her to witness this event? Unless . . .

She dreaded the answer, knowing she was in grave danger.

"Follow me," the man replied, evidently peeved at Ivanov's indiscretion.

Ivanov grabbed Melissa's arm, and she and Ryan were led through an office area. Dozens of bank employees worked at well-polished desks. Unsuspecting souls.

They were ushered down a short hallway, then into a small windowless room. A lone computer perched on an executive desk. Several chairs lined the walls. Numerous wires ran from the computer to the right wall. Ivanov closed the door.

Melissa made a quick assessment of the situation and realized that her escape options were limited. This was to be the location of the money transfer.

"Have a seat," Ivanov ordered.

Ryan took the chair next to her. "Are you all right?" he whispered.

It was a little late for caring. "I think he's going to kill me," she said softly.

"Quiet!" Ivanov bellowed, causing the bank officer to jolt in his seat. He grabbed a chair near the wall and pulled it over to the desk, where he was able to oversee the phone call to Switzerland.

After a brief conversation, the officer recited the code word and account number she'd given to Ivanov. Moments later, the bank officer acknowledged, "The information is correct. They'll transfer the funds immediately."

Ivanov gave Melissa a look that said, *Lucky for you.* Then he reached into his pocket and withdrew another piece of paper. "Transfer the money to this account," he ordered the officer. "Others will disburse it from there."

The man in uniform glanced at Ivanov's paper and nodded.

The room fell silent except for the click of computer keys as the numbers were entered. A second bank officer opened the door and walked in. Ivanov whirled in his chair, a puzzled look on his face. "Gerald, I'm sorry to interrupt," said the second employee. "Can you take a moment to sign something for me?"

The officer making the transfer for Ivanov kept his focus on the screen. "Later. I'm busy at the moment."

Suddenly, six other men barged into the room, guns drawn. "FBI! Freeze, Ivanov! Don't move!"

In the midst of the melee, Melissa dove off her chair just as someone wrestled Ivanov to the ground. Three men restrained him, removing his gun and cuffing his wrists.

Stunned, she saw that Ryan was also being seized by two men who pinned his arms, shoving one high behind his back. She turned away, unable to watch.

"Are you okay?" a woman agent asked. "Let's get you out of here." She pulled Melissa quickly to her feet, taking her arm and guiding her toward the door.

Once safely in the hallway, she looked over her shoulder. Ivanov, his eyes flaring with fury, was being led away toward the elevators by half a dozen FBI agents.

"Come with me," the woman agent said, but Melissa resisted momentarily, watching as Ryan was also ushered away. For an excruciating moment, his eyes found hers, and a curious look of relief veiled his countenance. Then he was escorted down the hallway—the same direction that Ivanov had been taken.

"Are you ready?" the agent asked.

Tearfully, Melissa nodded, unable to speak. She submitted, turning her back on the sad scene.

The two agents flanking Ryan led him to a waiting vehicle. Ivanov, too, was being taken to a car, although a different one, parked directly in front of them.

At one point, Ivanov turned and glowered at his captors. "I'll be out on the street by tonight. You have *nothing*." But the agent shoved Ivanov into the backseat, cutting short his diatribe.

"Watch your head," one of the agents told Ryan as he ducked and lowered himself into the car. The door closed firmly behind him, and two well-dressed men slid into the front seat.

They pulled out of the bank parking lot onto the main street, which by now was filled with hundreds of spectators observing the commotion. Ryan lowered his head as the car maneuvered through the narrow streets.

Choosing to shut out the thrill-seeking crowds, Ryan's thoughts were of Melissa—and her alone. He recalled the pain in her eyes as she had been confronted with his betrayal. As long as he lived, he would never forget the look of disbelief on her face.

The car was void of all conversation as

they drove past City Hall to Market Street, heading toward I-95. Several miles outside of Trenton, New Jersey, the driver pulled onto a side road and followed it for several miles to a deserted park. Veering right, they drove several more yards, stopping beside another dark sedan.

The driver turned and smiled at Ryan. "Tired of the cuffs?" The agent got out of the car and opened Ryan's door. He fumbled with the key to the handcuffs and unlocked them. "Better?"

"Much." Ryan got out of the car, rubbing his sore wrists.

The back door of the sedan opened. A man in a dark suit got out, adjusting his tie. Then the front passenger door opened, and another man stepped out into the sunshine.

It was McGuire. *FBI Special Agent in Charge* McGuire.

He walked over, extending his hand to Ryan. "I followed the whole thing on the radio. Excellent work."

Ryan shook hands, but he didn't share McGuire's obvious triumph. McGuire introduced his passenger as Agent Walsh with Organized Crime. Walsh and Ryan exchanged nods.

"How're you feeling? A little shaken up?" McGuire asked.

"How's Melissa?" Ryan asked.

"She's headed back to the Denlinger home. Want me to get her on the phone?"

Ryan considered this but did not relish the entire FBI force listening in. "I'll talk to her later."

McGuire shrugged. "She'll be told everything—that you had no choice in being a part of the sting."

"I betrayed my wife," Ryan replied. "We never gave *her* a choice. She was terrified."

Walsh spoke for the first time. "We needed her participation. You know yourself she wouldn't have played the game willingly."

"It was a judgment call for the good of the country *and* for her own personal safety," McGuire chimed in. "Ivanov will never bother her again. Not only that, but because of you and Melissa, we caught the men on the other end of the wire transfer. The entire network is sunk. We recovered nearly half a billion dollars. Once we threaten Ivanov with extradition, he'll turn on his Russian buddies in a heartbeat."

"Just like that?" Ryan struggled to comprehend.

McGuire smiled wryly. "These boys aren't the Italian Mafia—brotherhood, honor, loyalty, all that good stuff. Believe me, at this point, Ivanov will say or do anything to avoid going back to Russia. Even betraying his friends and family."

"Any evidence of . . . compromised agents?" Ryan asked.

McGuire laughed. "Like I said before, Ivanov was bluffing. Sure, we're investigating, but keep in mind, it's almost impossible to bribe an FBI agent."

"And my parents—?"

"Safe and sound. Another one of Ivanov's bluffs."

"What about Bernie?"

McGuire's expression changed. "We picked him up this afternoon. No resistance. He was resigned to his fate. If he sings a pretty tune, I'll recommend leniency."

"Just take me home," Ryan said.

"Whatever you say, partner." McGuire patted him on the shoulder as the three of them headed back to their cars.

◆ ◆ ◆ ◆ ◆

Ryan's assigned driver, Special Agent Carlson, turned off the main highway, heading into Lord's Point. The car slowed as the road curved around toward the shoreline, then pulled into the driveway of the waterfront property. He gazed at the beautiful house and surrounding acreage. No longer did any of it belong to him.

In exchange for agreeing to testify in court, the government promised not to prosecute him for his complicity in money laundering and insider-trading crimes. Part of the deal included the forfeiture of his house and bank accounts—everything except for a few personal belongings.

All in exchange for his freedom. But freedom in itself held little appeal. Money and the possessions it afforded had long since ceased to interest him. Life without Melissa was hardly worth living.

By now she would know the truth about him, that he'd turned a blind eye to the shady dealings of his company. That he had *not* been an informant for years, as he'd told her on the phone. He'd merely made a quick deal to save his own skin. On top of everything, he had tricked her into participating in a dangerous sting.

*"No matter what happens, it's over between us."* Her words echoed in his mind, spoken in the motel parking lot in Lancaster County in the midst of his "betrayal."

Agent Carlson parked the car, and Ryan led the way into the house. Tonight he was scheduled to sleep at a city hotel, where the FBI could keep an eye on him. Tomorrow a moving van would haul away the remainder of his personal effects. Presumably, Melissa would have the same opportunity to sort out her belongings.

Where he would ultimately reside, he had no clue. The FBI was calling the shots now. They would select his next home and his new identity, until he was to be called to trial. While most informants were held in jail awaiting trial, Ryan was an exception. As the government's star witness, he was to be held under house guard. Once the trial was over, he would be given the freedom to resume a normal life again.

As usual, Daisy was waiting just inside the front door. Carlson bent down to pet the golden retriever. "Good-looking dog."

Ryan said nothing, relieved that Daisy would be shipped out to his parents.

"How long will you be?" Carlson asked.

"A few minutes." He looked around the room, seeing only distant memories. How quickly things had changed in the space of a week. He regarded the wilting lavender roses he'd purchased for his wife and considered throwing them away. Dismissing the thought, he left them on the counter.

Hurrying upstairs, he packed a large suitcase full of clothes and a smaller one for toiletry items. When he was finished, he wandered down the hall to the guest room, noting the empty space on the wall where

Mellie's painting for Denny had hung. *The Cross painting*, as Denny had so aptly termed it. The vacant wall space seemed forsaken.

He glanced at the bedside table, noticing the book *Mere Christianity*. Denny's doing. He reached for the book, deciding to pack it, as well. *I'm going to have plenty of time on my hands*, he thought, returning to the bedroom. Picking up his suitcases, he lugged them downstairs, where Agent Carlson stood as if guarding the front door.

## Chapter Thirty-four

CLIMBING THE STAIRS at Lela's for one last time, Melissa felt both emancipated and miserable all wrapped up in one confusing emotion. Her FBI escort, now waiting on the front porch, had assured her that Ivanov was behind bars. She was safe at last. At some point she would be free to live her own life. After the trial—whenever that might be.

She looked forward, with all eagerness, to flying to Colorado, where she hoped to renew her bonds with dear Mrs. Browning. Yet feelings of depression swept over her each time she thought of Ryan. Or recalled how he'd tricked her. *Betrayed* her.

"I hope I can keep in touch with you," she told Lela, paying up on the rent she owed, grateful once again for the comfort and serenity of the Mennonite cottage. Melissa knew now that the Lord had guided her steps, bringing her to the godly woman's home. "And thank you, Lela, for the Bible. I will treasure it, truly."

Lela nodded, touching her arm. "Rest assured, you're in God's safekeeping, Mellie. Remember that always."

She clasped the woman's hand. "Thank you for leading me to your God."

Lela's eyes were bright with tears. "He's *yours*, too. You are a child of the Father, to be sure."

She embraced the Plain woman quickly, then—"If for any reason you don't hear from me for a while, don't worry, all right?"

"You're in good hands. I know that."

With that, they said fond farewells, and Melissa joined the agent waiting patiently outside.

◆ ◆ ◆ ◆ ◆

They stood gawking at the old shed in the dim light of early evening, wondering what on earth they'd do with an abandoned automobile. Beyond, in the two-story bank barn, one of the cows let out a low moan, weary of the day. Crickets burst forth with their timpani at dusk, mingling their sounds with the hum of katydids and other summer insects vying for solo time.

"I daresay we're stuck with four wheels and nary a key to start it up," Thaddeus said, taking his straw hat off and scratching the back of his head.

Elizabeth clucked a little. "Now why wouldja be thinkin' thataway?" she asked. "You aren't planning to take a little drive around the farm, now, are you?"

"Well, now, I think you oughta know your husband better'n that." He pulled her close, planting a kiss on her lips.

Both laughing now, Elizabeth asked, "Why do you think Lela's guest had to up and leave so awful fast, for goodness' sake?"

"Says Lela, she had important business to be tendin' to."

"Must be mighty important." She couldn't imagine leaving behind something that must've cost a pretty penny. Not at all. "Maybe Paul Martin can teach Lela to drive it . . . someday," she added.

"Could be that he will." Thaddeus had a right nice smile on his face. "Might be just the thing to get 'em close, you know. Teachin' a lady to drive, well now, that just might be the best idea we've had in a gut long time."

"I doubt Paul needs an excuse to get close to my sister," Elizabeth replied. "He seems ready to pick up the pieces, right where he left them so long ago."

Hurrying back to the house, she checked on her cabbage chowder. *Thank you, Lord, for this beautiful day, and for the folk who cross our paths,* she prayed silently as she and Mary Jane set the table.

◆ ◆ ◆ ◆ ◆

Ryan tossed his bags onto the queen-sized bed of the motel room. Agent Carlson looked in momentarily through the open door. "If you need anything, I'm in the next room."

Ryan nodded, then scanned the sparsely furnished room. There was a TV in the far corner, a small table and two chairs near the window, a large dresser opposite the bed. His home for the night, perhaps longer. He sat on the edge of the bed and rubbed his weary eyes.

The phone rang and he reached for it cautiously. "Hello?"

It was McGuire calling to outline tomorrow's schedule. "You have a decision to make," he said. "You and the missus—are you going together or parting ways?"

Ryan didn't know the answer to that.

"She's not at the Denlinger home anymore," McGuire replied. "I'll have her call you. Let me know tomorrow what you two decide."

Ryan hung up, closed his eyes tightly, and tried to calm his still-taut nerves. Disjointed images of the day played through his mind. Ivanov's predatory eyes seemed to follow him everywhere—those little oval slits of evil, frenzied and desperate with the prospect of recovering "his" money.

Since the moment he'd seen Melissa again, Ryan had been deathly afraid that Ivanov would discover his duplicity and execute vengeance on both of them long before they reached the bank. The tension from that anxiety continued to reverberate. But most persistent was Melissa's tortured expression of disbelief. From a legal standpoint, Ryan had finally done the right thing by turning informant. The network had been crushed in one fell swoop, the money confiscated. The sting would go down as one of the biggest busts in organized crime. Yet the knowledge of it offered him scant comfort. After three years of harboring a deep dark secret, Melissa had finally trusted him implicitly. And how had he rewarded her?

With deception and betrayal.

Feelings of despondency overtook him as he grabbed his luggage, unzipping the side pocket where he'd placed the book from Denny. Intending to simply pass a few hours, he paged to the first chapter: *The Law of Human Nature*—the theme of his last religious discussion with Denny.

It was after eleven o'clock when Ryan closed the book and dropped it on the mattress next to him. The room was poorly illuminated by a single lamp on the nightstand beside the too-silent phone.

He got up and stretched his legs, walking over to the window. The beige curtains were tainted by the faint smell of cigarette smoke. Outside, the motel parking lot was half filled with cars and trucks, families on vacation, businessmen eager to get home. A small breeze through the screened window fluttered the curtains, bringing in the scent of impending autumn.

In only a few hours he had managed to read more than half of *Mere Christianity*—enough to know he was on the brink of something new. He'd expected Lewis's arguments on the subject to border on the ridiculous. Instead, the author presented flawless evidence for the truth of Christianity. The premise not only made sense but was intellectually compelling. But Ryan questioned his own judgement. After today's emotional events he was obviously vulnerable.

Ryan turned from the window, leaning against the sill. He stared at the phone before picking it up and dialing the number he knew by memory. It was just after nine o'clock in Denver, Colorado.

Two rings, then: "Hello?"

"Hey, preacher man."

Denny chuckled. "Well, howdy stranger. You finally called back."

"Sorry, Den."

"You okay, man?"

Ryan leaned back on the pillow and began to tell Denny all that had recently transpired. Denny listened, interrupting only to ask for clarification. When Ryan finished, Denny was initially silent, as if formulating his response.

"Melissa called me," Denny finally said, his tone serious. "Couple days ago. She needed . . . some advice."

Ryan considered Denny's revelation, wishing Melissa might have called *him*. "I guess I really blew it with her." Then changing the subject, he said, "I just read the book you left, most of it anyway."

"Yeah, what'd you think?"

"It's . . . actually convincing. But . . . considering everything, I'm obviously not think-ing straight tonight. I need time to think things through."

"Maybe you're thinking clearly for the first time in your life."

"C'mon, Denny, it's a cliche: *Local man loses home, money, and wife. Gets religion.* Sound suspect?"

"Maybe. But then again, that could be a good place to start. Not to sound glib, but sometimes the bad things in our lives serve as catalysts to wake us up. After all, the atheist in the foxhole turns to God because his life has suddenly been reduced to the bare essen-tials."

Ryan chuckled to himself. Same old Denny—*Preacher Man.* "Well, I wanted you to know you won't be hearing from me for a while. Not until the trial's over."

"Bummer. So who's gonna be the best man in my wedding?"

"You're getting married?"

"You don't have to act so surprised—"

"I didn't say anything," Ryan protested.

"I heard it in your *tone.*"

"You know . . . if you need someone to stand up with you, Daisy's always available. You two got along pretty well. In fact, you both shared something very deep and mean-ingful."

"Okay, this better be good. What deep and meaningful experience did I share with your dog?"

"Sausage and bacon, of course. Not to mention fried eggs."

Denny chuckled. "You're absolutely right. Greasy food *is* a deep and meaningful experience. Guaranteed to create bonds of friendship that last a lifetime. But I gotta tell you, Ryan, you don't sound like an atheist in a foxhole, anymore. You sound kinda chipper, in fact."

"Just needed a buddy-fix."

They bantered another few minutes before Ryan said good-bye, promising to visit the newlyweds when he had a chance. But his buoyed spirits sank the moment he hung up and looked about the cramped and stale-smelling motel room. Sighing, he looked back at the phone. The message light was as dim as the room. Melissa still hadn't called.

As the reality of the past few days set in again, a rush of silence seemed to inhabit the darkness of the room like a wind filling a vacuum. Accompanying the feeling of emptiness and isolation was the renewed sense of *struggle*. As if a war were being played out in his mind, tugging at the opposing sides of his reason, battling for control. Despite his apprehension concerning Melissa, he realized he had a decision to make.

*"Maybe you're thinking clearly for the first time . . ."* Denny had said.

Raking his hand through his hair, he recalled C. S. Lewis's succinct explanation of the human condition. Earlier he and Denny had discussed the nature of evil as a mere philosophical theory. But coming face to face with evil incarnate—in the form of an evil man—was a whole new ball game.

If complete and utter evil could exist in the form of a human being like Ivanov, surely goodness, on a far greater level, could also exist—in the form of God. In light of Ryan's recent experience, "depravity of man" was the only logical explanation for mankind's suffering and misfortune, a bad-to-the-bone wickedness that is beyond the reach of sheer education or human enlightenment.

The irony was that in the end, Ivanov himself was Ryan's proof of man's depravity. But a sudden realization sent cold shivers down his back, accompanied with a deeper feeling of remorse: *Ivanov—we're not so different, you and I.*

Slipping to the floor, he knelt, overwhelmed with a need for redemption unknowable to his human reasoning, longing for the forgiveness of his sin—yet beset with a lifetime of skepticism. A phrase ran through his mind—*where had he heard it?*—and he embraced it as his own: *Lord, I do believe . . . help my unbelief!*

Faltering, he prayed, a man at the end of his rope. Tears of anguish and sorrow followed. Eventually all inner resistance melted away, and he experienced something new. Something that until this moment he had only heard about but had never accepted as reality.

*Rest for his weary soul.*

◆　◆　◆　◆　◆

The morning sun flickered through the curtains as Ryan tossed the last remaining items into his overnight bag and zipped it shut. Agent Carlson was waiting in the downstairs lobby. One more meeting with McGuire.

When the phone rang, he turned, staring at it. After a solid week of waiting, there was no doubt in his mind. The caller was Melissa.

Filled with apprehension, he realized anew that his wife might never forgive him. He'd have to make peace with that someday. Either way, this was the moment of truth.

He dropped his bags on the floor and picked up the phone.

# Chapter Thirty-five

THE SUNSET SEEMED TO LINGER longer than usual as Melissa made her way barefoot over the well-known ridge to Napatree Beach. Sighing with relief, she wondered how the sun would look as it set tonight. A spectacular array of color? Or a gentle whisper of muted tones, like the still lifes she favored?

Breathing hard, she made her way to the promontory, that high area where the point reached out like a finger into the water below. Angling up to the crest, she stood there scanning the shoreline, thankful to be here. With scarcely a breeze stirring, the pre-twilight atmosphere was still. Occasional clouds dappled the line separating sky and sea. The sun had a few more fluid minutes before it dipped into the deep, flinging its molten rays wildly into a burst of breathtaking hues.

Few beachcombers were left. Three or four seemed content to roam the wet sand, scavenging for shells and other debris. One girl had a burlap satchel thrown over her shoulder, filled, no doubt, with sea treasures.

Melissa's gaze focused on the very tip of the jetty, where large rocks were stacked to create a manmade dock of sorts. Shielding her eyes from the sun as it plunged toward the ocean, she could see the figure of a man sitting there facing the horizon.

It was Ryan, precisely where they had arranged to meet, his hands folded in a contemplative fashion. She felt a pounding in her head, matching the sound of the waters beyond, as she watched him, this man, seemingly a stranger, even though it had been scarcely more than a week since her frantic escape. So much had happened since then. Events from which many married couples never recover.

She smiled to herself. But they weren't just *any* couple. After Agent McGuire's explanation of yesterday's events, Melissa had needed time to think. And to pray.

Slowly, carefully, she picked her way over the boulders, careful not to slip. Somewhere on the sandy hill behind them, FBI agents hovered near, watching like a sturdy angelic guard.

Just as she reached the end of the pier, the sun dipped past the horizon, shooting out sprays of purple and gold. Ryan turned as if on cue, hope reflected in his eyes, delight in his smile.

Three years ago she had promised to love and cherish this man. She would keep her word.

"Mellie," he whispered, gathering her into his arms.

Safe in the protection of his tender embrace, she felt the promise of a new beginning as husband and wife, under God.

# *Acknowledgments*

With sincere gratitude we wish to acknowledge our editors, Barb Lilland, Anne Severance, and Carol Johnson, as well as the editorial staff and marketing team at Bethany House Publishers. Our special thanks to Clyde and Susan Gordon who cheerfully assisted with regional research, and to Dale and Barbara Birch who proofread the manuscript. The "wonderful-gut" help we gleaned from our Plain friends and contacts made all the difference.

We treasure the ongoing prayers of our family and friends, including John Henderson who kept us in stitches throughout the writing process. Many thanks to the faithful readers who offered thoughtful words of encouragement and love.

# BEVERLY LEWIS

## LANCASTER COUNTY IS CLOAKED IN AUTUMN SPLENDOR, AND A REUNION IS IN THE AIR....

### Available October 2001

## October Song

# October Song

Awakening to darkness, Katie, in a dreamy haze, thought surely she was back in her bedroom at Hickory Hollow, that it was time to "rise 'n shine," hurry into choring clothes, get out to the barn to help with the milking. But as she lay there listening, ears attuned for her father's call up the steps, she realized she was not a girl growing up in the Lapp home. She was a young married woman, curled up next to Dan, her sleeping husband.

Morning's pale light had not seeped under the bedroom curtains, where cotton fabric gently brushed against the windowsill. Not a sound was heard, not even the first *peep-peepings* of a family of birds who'd camped out in the maple tree just yards from their window, birds who'd waited longer than usual to fly south. This being market day, a number of horse-drawn buggies would surely be passing by the house, yet the road was as still as night.

*Must be nearly dawn,* Katie thought, too weary to raise herself and peer over the blanketed mound that was her husband to see the exact time on the illuminated alarm clock.

Lying in the stillness, her drowsiness slowly lifting, she thought of Mam who'd called the other day, sharing news of a recent visit with Mary Beiler. "She misses ya something awful, Katie. We *all* do." Mam's voice betrayed a bit of sadness. "Mary's got her hands full with John's children, no question 'bout that."

"They're *her* children now, too," Katie had said, hoping her friend had fallen in love by now with the red-cheeked youngsters.

"Jah . . . but can you just imagine?" Mam hadn't said much more, prob'ly catching herself, realizing that Katie, too, had cared deeply for the Beiler brood—three boys and two girls—having nearly become their step-mamma awhile back.

"Is the youngest—Jacob—in first grade yet?" Katie had been especially fond of the bishop's mischievous blue-eyed boy.

"Jah, and such a good student he is . . . Mary tells me."

Hearing Mam talk up so 'bout Mary's stepchildren seemed ever so awkward. "That's not to say Jacob isn't *schmaert*—smart, really. Just got himself an active mind . . . awful hard to keep his attention on book learnin' when he'd prob'ly rather be outside catching a frog down by the creek, you know."

They chatted about several upcoming quiltings, though Mam wasn't the one to bring up the subject. Katie had asked about one frolic after another. Seemed there were several more 'round the corner, too, and Mam, when pressed for more information, said she would be helpin' her daughters-in-law, Annie and Gracie, put up preserves and vegetables for the long winter.

Perking up her ears at the mention of Annie Fisher, Dan's sister, Katie said, "Oh, and how *is* Annie . . . little Daniel, too?" Katie hadn't seen her oldest brother's wife and baby in ever such a long time.

Mam chuckled a bit. "Well, Daniel's growin' fast, not much of a baby anymore. He's nearly two and all mixed up on his sleep schedule. Doesn't seem much interested in napping here lately . . . puts the 'G' in go, I should say. Annie says he's been getting up in the middle of the night, just a-wailing. Must be he's cutting his second molars."

Katie could hardly believe her ears. Elam's and Annie's baby a toddler? Where had the time gone?

Mam had asked how she and Daniel were getting along, and Katie caught her up a bit on their lives, telling of one church function after another, of Dan's and her playing their guitars at small home groups, and her weekly visits to shut-ins with another friend, Darlene Frey. She told Mam that Darlene lived not far from Hickory Hollow—to the east a bit—and that they'd had such good fellowship lately. She didn't go too far with that, though. Didn't say just how close she felt to Darlene these days, them both seein' eye to eye on certain Scriptures and all.

Later in the conversation, Mam suggested Katie "drop by for a chat sometime," saying that Dat was agreeable to it, but only if the visit was kept short. Mamma's faltering manner made Katie wonder if her mother was hesitant about a face-to-face meeting. And, too, it was clear that Dan wasn't invited. Not a'tall.

Katie, of course, didn't promise anything definite, saying she didn't know how soon she could arrange a visit. Privately, she determined to talk things over with Dan first, wanting to get his opinion on the matter, whether or not he thought Katie oughta be singled out. Not that she was too timid to go alone, wasn't that. Dan just might think her parents were working on her, trying to get her "to see the light," according to the Old Ways.

Practicing hymns and gospel songs on their guitars, then leading worship at two different home groups during the past week had taken up both her time and Dan's time, so she hadn't shared Mam's phone call with him. But she would.

For now, she plumped her pillow and lay quietly. Then, gently, she reached over and laid her hand on his shoulder, waiting for dawn's light . . . and for the alarm clock. So strong was Dan, both physically

and in the faith. She could lean on him if
need be, when things troubled her. He
was her shelter in the one and only howl-
ing gale of her life, because he understood
fully the pain of shunning. Dan was under
the Bann, too, from the same bishop, the
man she'd nearly married. How strange
that her dearest friend, Mary, had become
John Beiler's young bride. Well, she was
right happy for them both. Truly, she was.

Still, she couldn't help but wonder if
Mary would go on missing her and telling
Mamma so, who in turn would relay the
information to Katie. Was it an attempt to
get to Katie, make her feel sorrowful for
leaving? To make her regret abandoning
her Amish roots for her newfound faith?

Sitting up, Katie pushed back the
covers, swinging her legs over the side of
the bed. Her feet groped about for slippers, and finding them she tiptoed across
the room. At the window, she stood silently and parted the curtains, looking
out. The dawn was as cold and gray as
any she'd witnessed lately. An enormous
cloud mass hovered over the horizon,
blocking out the sun. No wonder the
room seemed so dark upon her first awakening.

She stared down at black tree trunks,

mere etchings against a yellowing, now-dormant front lawn. In the distance, not a flicker of sunlight escaped from the gloom as the day began over wooded hills.

❖  ❖  ❖

The characters in this story were first introduced in Beverly Lewis's bestselling novel, *The Shunning*.